too blue to fly

Judith Richards

LONGSTREET PRESS
Atlanta, Georgia

Published by LONGSTREET PRESS, INC.
a subsidiary of Cox Newspapers,
a subsidiary of Cox Enterprises, Inc.
2140 Newmarket Parkway
Suite 122
Marietta, GA 30067

Printed in the United States of America

1st printing, 1997

Library of Congress Card Catalog Number: 97-71956

ISBN: 1-56352-383-3

Cover illustration by Nicholas Vial
Cover design by Neil Hollingsworth
Book design and typesetting by Laura McDonald
Electronic film prep by OGI, Forest Park, GA

Dedication

With their wit, wisdom and indomitable spirit, these women enriched my life: the Totten sisters Joyce, Holly, and Claire; my wonderful friend Cecilia Pulido Abadia; and last but never least, my mom Wilma Anderson Richards.

Acknowledgments

In the quest for accuracy, an author calls on many people. I am especially grateful to Ernie Youens for his knowledge of antique cars. Thanks also to Elaine Engst, Jim Tyler, and Gould Coleman archivists at Cornell University. Dr. Bill Williams, meteorologist, helped me make it rain—or not—as it really happened. And we appreciate the Fairhope Public Library staff, Betty Suddeth, Jane Barton, Linda Champion, Susan Diemert, Patty Gipson, and Marie Schreiner, for years of invaluable assistance with every book. Friends who have taken time from their own work to help us: Hennie and Bozie Dietze, Annette and Ben Meginniss, Don Andrews, Bobbie and Monroe Thompson, Larry Allums, and the staff of the Page & Palette book store, Betty Jo Wolff, Gwinelle Allums and crew. And, of course, my editor, Chuck Perry who knows how to make an author feel important. Needless to say, many thanks to Linda Cline and my husband, C. Terry Cline, Jr., and our in-family readers, Marc Cline, Blaise Cline Pecorino, Cabeth Cline Husbands, and Charles Kriel.

Hear that lonesome whippoorwill,
He sounds too blue to fly.

Hank Williams

too blue to fly

chapter one

Wally had always known who he was and where he belonged. In the spring of 1947, he was a fifth grade student at the Atlanta Montessori School. He was eleven years old, the son of Kathryn McManus, and his place was with her.

Then everything changed.

When Mama discovered her illness, she told Wally in the same quiet way she always revealed bad news. The cancer was ovarian, she said, and it had spread throughout her body. With her usual straightforward bluntness, she said there was no chance she would recover and they hadn't much time. What would he most like to do in the weeks they had left?

"You're going to die, Mama?"

"Yes, I'm dying."

He remembered the way the air smelled, too rich to breathe, and how it burned his nostrils. She had taken him to the old quarry near Stone Mountain for a picnic. It was one of their favorite places. "Who will look after me, Mama?"

"I wrote your father and told him you'll be coming."

"I don't even know him. Does he want me?"

"Anthony is a man who rarely knows what he wants until he has lost it. But in you he'll see himself, Wally, so yes, he'll want you."

Sunlight reflected on the dead green lake of the rock quarry, and birds flitted to and from their nests in the granite walls. Crows beckoned from afar. Everything lovely had turned ugly. "My father never came to visit me," Wally said.

"We've never been to see him, Wally."

"Mama, please, I don't want you to die."

"And I don't want to, Wally, but it's going to happen. Now then, how shall we spend our time together?"

At first he punished her for being ill. He pulled away from hugs and turned aside kisses. He sulked and pouted and poisoned the moment as though dying were a selfish choice she'd made. She seemed to understand. "When you think back on this later," she'd said, "don't feel guilty. I acted the same way with God."

She took him out of school and cashed in her war bonds. She wanted to go back to towns where she'd lived and live her life again, she said. "It will be like playing a movie backwards. We'll pretend we don't know the ending and visit all the places that ever meant anything to me."

Over the next two months they searched for landmarks, most of which were gone: the restaurant overlooking the Hudson River where Anthony Edward McManus proposed marriage, the cold-water flat where they lived in Greenwich Village. None of the visits were happy. Mama spoke of marital disputes, "like sparks of flint—sharp, quick, and gone—but each spark left smoldering resentment."

During the trip Wally changed because she changed. Slow death stole her life in pieces. First it took Mama's weight, the soft places where she held Wally's head when he needed cuddling. Then impending death extinguished the twinkle in her eyes and left them deeply set above hollow cheeks. It hurt her to be hugged, so he was limited to holding her hand.

They went back to Atlanta and she bought him a one-way bus ticket to Belle Glade, Florida. "Use this when you have to," she said, and tucked it into one of the bags packed for his trip. Every day thereafter she grew weaker.

"Are you going to be a big boy about this?" his mother had asked.

"Yes, Mama."

"Going to live with your father?"

"Yes, Mama."

"Good," she'd sighed. "He's expecting you."

It was their last conversation. She died that night.

Wally was jarred back to the moment by the bus driver's announcement, "Belle Glade!"

The noonday sun was so bright that Wally peered from beneath cupped hands. The hot concrete sidewalk burned his feet through the soles of his shoes. Every inhalation was as though from an oven. Unlike Atlanta, south Florida humidity soaked his clothes and plastered sandy hair to his forehead. Sweat traced his spine and crawled down the backs of his legs.

The bus driver put Wally's luggage on the ground. "Three bags, right?"

"Yessir."

Air brakes sighed, the diesel engine rumbled, exhaust fumes enveloped Wally and the bus pulled away.

The street was deserted. Stores were closed. Mama had warned him that Anthony was seldom on time. He thought of his father as "Anthony" because that's how she spoke of him. "Anthony was late to our wedding," she'd said. *Undisciplined,* she'd said.

Wally dragged his bags toward the shade of a palm tree but halted abruptly when he realized the shadow was filled with thousands of droning bees. The insects swirled around a droop of dates hanging from the palm, and below them sat a shirtless and barefoot black boy on a wooden bench. Slowly, the boy reached up to pluck a date and bees dripped from the swarm like living liquid, down his arm and off his elbow.

"For a nickel," he said, "I'll weave a spell so they won't sting you."

"I don't have a nickel."

"Yes you do." Again, slowly, he shoved his hand into the mass of bees and plucked another date.

"If you eat a green one," he said, "it makes your tongue curl. For a nickel I'll get you some ripe ones."

"No, thank you. I won't be staying long."

The black boy surveyed the empty street in one direction, then the other. "I don't see nobody rushing to fetch you. Give me a dime and I'll buy us an orange soda."

"I'm going soon," Wally said.

"Where you going, white boy?"

"To live with my father."

"Your father a white man?"

"Of course he's white."

"You say 'of course' like I'm stupid to wonder," the black boy said. "Look at me. You wonder if my daddy is black?"

He was the color of dark honey, his body powdered with dust made gray by the tone of his complexion. His eyes were pale green.

"Is your daddy a tall white man, or a short one?" he asked.

"I'm not sure," Wally said.

"For a nickel, I'll help you watch for him."

"I'm not giving you a nickel," Wally replied evenly.

"I ain't asking you *give* me anything. I'm willing to earn it. You being a city boy from Atlanta, you going to need somebody to get you from here to someplace without getting gator ate. I'm willing, but I ain't begging."

"How did you know I'm from Atlanta?"

"By the tags on your bags. Besides, I was sent to get you. I'm your brother, Jeremiah."

"My brother! You—you don't look like me."

"My mama don't look like your mama," Jeremiah said, "but your daddy is my daddy. I know all about you. You're here because your mama died and you got no place else to go. My mama said you'd be sitting on the curb, knees together, hands in your lap like a whipped sissy."

"She doesn't know me. Why would she say that?"

"Guessing what you'd be, most likely. Shiny shoes and iron pants."

"Iron pants?"

"Starch and iron. You're what I expected too. Won't even share a nickel with your own brother."

"I don't believe you're my brother."

The boy peered at Wally with eyes the green of new grass. "You ever see a colored boy with eyes like mine? Or hair so silky it drives womens crazy? I'm your brother all right, and you can praise God I am, too. Else you'd be standing here day after tomorrow waiting for somebody who ain't coming. Give me a quarter and I'll help tote the bags."

Defeated, Wally dug change from his pocket and relinquished twenty-five cents. Jeremiah was taller, more muscular, at least a year older than Wally.

"My mama sent me to fetch you, knowing Mr. McManus wouldn't do what he ought to."

"Where is he?" Wally asked.

"Getting some libation. That's what he calls anything he doesn't chew. On the Sabbath in Belle Glade, the only place to get a drink is at a shot house in colored town. I'll carry the little bags, you bring the big one."

"Does Anthony say you're my brother?"

"Is that what you call him, 'Anthony?' He gives money to my mama, and she tends his manly needs. You know what I mean?"

Before Wally could summon an answer, Jeremiah said, "She cooks the meals and sleeps with him. Around the house you'd think he was her husband. But no, Mr. McManus don't admit nothing."

Wally followed him down an alley. Ebony men threw dice at a wall. Women in colorful skirts and low-cut blouses loitered nearby. When they saw Jeremiah, the women hooted.

"What you got with you, Jeremiah? Look like a puppy to me."

The smell of food cooking tantalized Wally. He hadn't eaten since his mother's funeral.

"Say what he be, Jeremiah?"

"Ignore them niggers," Jeremiah said loudly. "They won't touch us. The Klan would skin them alive and burn this place to the ground."

His threat didn't intimidate them. A woman stepped forward to stroke Wally's head and tweak his earlobe. "Got no color, like the belly of a suckling pig," she said.

"Pay no mind," Jeremiah said. "They ain't nothing to be scared of."

Wally fought an urge to hurl aside his luggage and flee. Run! But where would he go? Back to Atlanta? Mama wasn't there.

She was buried under a mound of red clay. Suppressed anger erupted and Wally knocked aside the colored woman's hand. Why hadn't Anthony come to the funeral? Damn him for leaving Mama to die alone. Damn him for letting years pass without a visit. And now, trembling with rage, Wally was going to meet him at last. Jeremiah stepped into a doorway so dark it swallowed him. The interior pulsed with music that throbbed in Wally's bones.

Jeremiah reappeared. "You coming or not?"

"How do I know he's in there?"

"You look and see, that's how. Come on."

After bright sunlight, Wally was blinded. He stumbled into tables and chairs. The smell of rancid beer and musky bodies was a stench.

A man on a bar stool grabbed Jeremiah by the arm. "What you doing with that white boy, Jeremiah?"

"Looking for his daddy."

"I don't want no white children in here. Get his daddy and go."

"We're going."

At the very back, in a wooden booth with high walls that made it private, was Anthony Edward McManus. A flickering candle stuck in a whiskey bottle provided the only light. From an overturned bottle, beer flowed across the table and trickled off the opposite side. A dozen times Wally had rehearsed what he'd say, but his preparation was useless. Anthony lay with his head in spilled beer, eyes open but unseeing.

"Is he dead?" Wally asked.

"He's not dead, he's drunk. Didn't your mama tell you he's a drunk?"

Maybe she didn't know. Maybe she hoped Anthony would change with a son coming—or, she forgot. More likely, she hadn't wanted to alarm Wally. Had Wally known, it would not have changed a thing. She must have hoped for the best and expected Wally to cope with the worst.

The thunderous music created ripples in puddles of spilled beer. Wally watched Jeremiah shake the man, yelling, "Mr. McManus! Wake up, Mr. McManus. It's time to go home!"

Anthony's eyes closed slowly and opened again.

"I got Precious with me, Mr. McManus!"

Before his mother died, when Wally realized there was no way out of coming here, he'd made it a point to read Anthony's books. He wanted a topic they'd have in common. He'd been struck by the simplicity of writing and wisdom of the author. Wally had told his mother, "He knows so much about people."

"Everybody but himself," she'd replied.

Now here was his father, face down in a colored town bar where illegal drinks were sold one shot at a time, and beer was dispensed at double the regular price on Sunday. Here was Anthony, too drunk to acknowledge the arrival of his latest obligation—his son, the sissy white boy—"Precious," Jeremiah had called him.

chapter
two

Wally watched as two black men and the bartender dragged his father out a rear door past smelly garbage cans and the men shooting dice. They dumped him into the rumble seat of a beige 1939 Ford coupe. One of his legs stuck up in the air, sockless, wearing a brown and white dress shoe. The crapshooters whooped.

"Who's going to drive?" Wally questioned.

"I am," Jeremiah said.

"Are you old enough to drive?"

"I do, so I reckon I am."

"How far are we going?"

"Three miles."

Alarmed, Wally said, "Do you have a driver's license?"

"You want to walk or ride? Get in."

Jeremiah admitted he knew only two of the four gears. He had to perch on the edge of the seat to see over the steering wheel. He couldn't use the accelerator and the clutch at the same time, so he set the speed of the motor by adjusting the throttle. The motor roared and the car shuddered. When Jeremiah took his foot off the clutch, the Ford jumped forward.

The pace was alternately too fast or too slow, but in all cases it was the same gear, through colored town, across a rickety wooden bridge, horn blaring to warn aside pedestrians and other motorists. Jeremiah turned corners so recklessly the tires squalled. He leaned forward with teeth exposed in a huge grin.

They passed between packing houses where men and women sorted vegetables. Hampers were being loaded into boxcars. Despite an approaching train, Jeremiah went toward the railroad tracks no faster or slower than before. The oncoming engine screamed alarm. . . . Wally heard Jeremiah laugh as the train fell away behind them.

There seemed to be a canal beside every road in the Everglades, and this road was no exception. Through cattails and tall reeds, Wally saw alligators lounging on a far bank.

"There's a dike around Lake Okeechobee," Jeremiah said.

"What about it?"

"We have to get up speed to make the grade." Jeremiah pulled out the throttle and depressed the brake. The motor struggled to run free while the brakes held the car in check.

Ahead loomed the dike, a steep shell mountain rising out of saw grass like an earthen barrier. Jeremiah snatched his foot off the brake and the car lunged, pinning Wally to the seat.

For a moment, all he saw was blue sky as they shot upward. Jeremiah blew the horn in a long final warning to anyone on the far side. The car topped the dike and Wally's stomach lurched into his throat as they plunged toward a one-lane bridge. Fishermen clambered up steel latticework of the span. Children dived into murky waters below. The car sailed past a bait store and a sign that said "Chosen." When they hit the dirt road beyond, the chassis bounced and they raced along a weed-choked lane.

"Exciting, ain't it?" Jeremiah adjusted the throttle and the motor eased.

Thistles squealed against fenders and bramble raked the running boards. Twin plumes of silt furled behind them. To the left, an unpainted shack sagged amid disabled cars. Chickens ran loose in the yard. Dogs rose up from beneath a collapsing stoop and rushed toward the road. Three men were lifting the motor from a car on blocks.

"Those are the Festers," Jeremiah advised. "Don't mess with them."

Two of the men were barefooted. A third wore overalls but no shirt. When he saw the car, he turned and spit.

"It's folks like the Festers makes us high society," Jeremiah said.

Wally looked back as a cloud of dust settled over the Festers.

In nearby trees, waterfowl were feathery blossoms of coral, blue, and white. Through the trees, Wally saw Lake Okeechobee and more birds on the water. They walked in it and floated on it and dived at it. They skimmed the surface, while overhead even more birds soared in flocks of thousands.

Jeremiah turned off the motor and coasted into a yard. "Here we are," he announced. "This is home."

The house was built on stilts above the highest ground in swampy terrain. Toward the rear a thicket of bamboo, with stems thicker than Wally's waist, rose taller than the roof. The front yard was shaded by a massive water oak, and Spanish moss draped the tree like tattered sleeves of a witch's frock. A chemical odor in the hot air reminded Wally of a salve his mother rubbed on his chest when he was congested.

"What is that smell?" he asked.

"Camphor trees." Jeremiah got out and slammed the door. "If it wasn't for camphor trees we'd be feeding mosquitoes every second. Get your bags and let's go inside."

"What about Anthony?"

"He'll wake up directly. Come on."

With that, Jeremiah banged one side of the coupe, hollering, "Mr. McManus! Me and Precious going in the house."

The interior was dark and cool. Jeremiah got two bottles of Nehi orange soda from an icebox, and using his teeth as an opener, snapped off the metal caps.

He gave one bottle to Wally and then sat at the table with his legs spraddled. "This is it," he said. "What did you expect?"

"I didn't expect anything."

"And that's what you get. For lights we use kerosene lamps. We drink rainwater that collects in a tank out back. Hot water comes from sun shining on pipes spread on the tin roof. Sometimes it comes out of the spigot scalding, but if hot water is important to you, it's best to bathe 'fore sundown."

The furniture was simple, an unpainted wood table and cupboard, ladderback chairs with caned bottoms. There were cracks in the floor through which Wally could see the ground ten feet below.

"My mama baby-sits an old woman in Belle Glade on Sundays," Jeremiah said. "That's why she's not here. Okay, these are the rules: It's all right to swim on the lake side, but not in the canals. You get ear infections in canal water, and if you swallow it you'll live in a toilet for a week or two. Before you dress in the mornings, shake out your pants and shoes to be sure there ain't no scorpions in them. It won't be long before you give up that shirt."

"I have to wear a shirt. I sunburn."

"Don't those freckles ever run together and make tan?"

"No."

"Okay." Jeremiah looked around the room as if for a cue. "What else?"

Wally followed his gaze. The windows were bare of screens. No curtains. Full-length shutters opened by pushing out the bottom.

"Two things don't ever do," Jeremiah cautioned. "One, don't leave the icebox open because ice is one thing Mama gets crazy about. If you make the ice melt, you're the one who walks to fetch some more. That's a rule."

He sucked on his orange drink and continued. "Second thing never do is mess with the Festers. They poach game out of season and run moonshine from Kramer's Island. Ike Fester will cut your throat just to hear you gurgle. They're murdering, lying, thieving, no-good white trash. That's what Mama says."

"Where should I put my bags?"

"Same room with me whether I like it or not. The bed by the window is mine. Another rule: don't go talking in town about what you see or hear. When the moon is full and the sap is rising, I come and go. Chasing womens."

"Aw, you lie."

"I bet you never kissed a girl," Jeremiah said.

Wally placed his luggage between two iron bedsteads. He could hear a breeze rustling bamboo beyond a wide porch that girdled the house.

"Since you don't know, I'll tell you now," Jeremiah continued. "Womens can't keep their hands off me."

Wally didn't believe it, and he didn't want to hear it.

"The last woman I went with had hair like spun silk and it ran up her belly to her navel," Jeremiah recounted. "When she unhooked her bra, it sounded like two water-filled balloons falling into a wet tub. I could smell her breath and it made me think of cinnamon tea."

Wally recognized the lines from an Anthony McManus novel. He picked up the quote, "'Her hair was the scent of gardenias in bloom. Freckles sprinkled across her nose as though God had flicked a brush in her face.'"

"Where did you hear that?" Jeremiah said.

"It's from one of Anthony's books."

"Where'd you see his books?"

"At the Atlanta library."

"His books are in libraries?"

A car door slammed and Jeremiah peeked out the window. "It's my mama," he said.

Looking at the woman from the bedroom window, Wally was reminded of a description from one of his father's novels:

She was the best of both races, with finely sculpted European features wrapped in flesh the hue of butternut. Her eyes were black as wet coal, and so too her hair. She was blessed with a grace of movement as innate as that of a deer.

Jeremiah spoke as though reading Wally's mind. "Yeah, she's pretty. Everybody says that."

Jeremiah's mother stepped away from a black hearse that had delivered her home. It backed out and departed in the direction of Belle Glade. She turned to confront the single leg jutting from the rumble seat. She glanced at the house, hiked her skirt, and climbed into the car with Wally's father. His drunken protests were soon tempered by feminine reassurances.

"Jeremiah!" she called.

Unseen, Wally stepped back from the shuttered window as if he'd been caught spying. "Jeremiah!" she hollered. "Come help me!"

"Whether I like it or not," Jeremiah muttered. He stepped out the window into view. "Precious is here," he said. "You want him, too?"

"Yes. Come help me."

Somehow they wrestled the man upright, got him out and on his feet, then supported him up steps, across the porch, through the house to a bedroom where they let him fall onto a mattress.

"Pull off his shoes, Jeremiah."

Wally stood by watching as they undressed his father, peeling away clothes to reveal skin the pallor of Kathryn's after her heart stopped beating.

"I'm Hattie Willoughby, Wally. I'm Jeremiah's mother."

Hattie ran a tub of water and they eased Anthony into it. "I'm sorry you had to see this the first day," she said. "But maybe it's best to get it out in the open."

She knelt at Anthony's side to bathe him. "Go in the other room," she said. "Shut the door, Jeremiah."

At the kitchen table waiting, Wally realized he was sitting as Hattie had predicted, hands in lap, knees together. He spread his legs and hung one arm over the back of his chair. Jeremiah ate a slice of loaf bread, watching him.

In the next room, Hattie argued. "You have to face this sooner or later, Anthony. It might as well be sooner."

Nothing seemed real. Not the shadows and sunlight making zebra stripes across the floor, nor the peep of birds or the whir of insects. Odors wafting through the windows were a mixture of fragrance and decay.

"Why are you staring at me?" Jeremiah snapped.

Nothing felt comfortable to Wally. These people were not his family. He felt like an intruder.

The bedroom door opened and Hattie helped Anthony Edward McManus to a chair at the kitchen table. His eyes were bloodied by bursted veins. He avoided Wally's gaze, peering out a window toward the waters of Lake Okeechobee in the distance. His wet hair had been carefully combed, but as it dried it rose at odd angles. His hands quivered. "I suppose we'll get through this," he said.

A tic tugged one side of his mouth, and Anthony said, "I'm sorry about your mother, Wally." He cleared his throat and turned to Hattie.

She studied Wally's face, his ears, chin and forehead. "He has your bones, Anthony. I see you in him. I could've picked him in a crowd of a thousand."

"Same skin," Jeremiah added. "He'll sunburn by candlelight."

Then with effort, Anthony tried to smile at Wally, but his cheek twitched and the smile faded. "We'll be all right," he said. "We'll be fine."

As if to dismiss them all from torture, Hattie said, "Make space for his clothes, Jeremiah," and Jeremiah took Wally into the bedroom. He allocated one half of a chifforobe and helped Wally make his bed with clean sheets. During this, Wally heard Hattie demand, "Where're you going, Anthony?"

"Back to town for a while."

"No, you aren't, Anthony. You've had enough for one day."

"Enough of what, Hattie?"

"You know what, so stay put. I'm not entertaining Precious while you embalm your innards."

Jeremiah acted as though nothing were happening. "You can have the bottom drawer in the dresser," he said. "It sticks and I never use it anyway. Or you can leave some of your stuff in a suitcase under the bed. How much money do you have?"

Wally was listening to Hattie in the next room. "You wanted catfish and hushpuppies; that's what I'm cooking. You aren't going anywhere."

"The reason I ask," Jeremiah continued, "for you and me to be partners, we have to know where we stand on things."

"Partners in what?"

"Could be anything," Jeremiah suggested. "Buying a good gig and head lamp, maybe. You wouldn't know a real deal if it fell on you. I'd handle it for you, so you don't get cheated."

"I won't get cheated. I don't want a gig and head lamp."

"How you going to keep yourself in money? Gigging frogs makes fifty cents a pound dressed out."

"I haven't seen much to spend it on."

"See, that's what I mean. You think Belle Glade is what you saw today and nothing more. I know every juke joint and dance hall from Pahokee to Clewiston. And the womens! You never knew womens like I know. Or we could go to West Palm Beach where ritzy womens go. Rich womens don't have a scar on them. A doctor takes out her appendix, he sews her up so neat a scar looks like a natural wrinkle. If we go to West Palm, I'll have to pretend I'm Spanish, but I could pass, especially with money."

"I'm not interested, Jeremiah."

"This is just like white folks," Jeremiah said. "I tend me and you tend you, that's what they say. But let a white man get up to his armpit in quicksand and listen to him plead. Or snake bit and needs somebody to suck poison, see how he talks. When he's got a row to hoe and needs a strong back, listen how he talks about partners—you and me, he says. I want to know what good is money in a sock?"

"I told you before, I'm not giving you money, Jeremiah."

"I ain't asking you *give* me something, then or now."

"Fine. If you've earned it, I'll pay."

"So you do have money?"

Through the bedroom window Wally saw his father at the Ford coupe. Hattie sat on the running board with Anthony, her arm around his shoulder. Anthony was weeping. Out on the lake, long-legged cranes stalked minnows in the fiery reflections of a setting sun. Wally had read about the semi-tropical climate of south Florida and the rhythms of wildlife. Naturalists described the glades as "Eden aplenty," a place of great beauty.

Maybe so. If Wally were here with his mother and she enjoyed it, perhaps he'd see the grandeur of flora and fauna. But at this moment he could see only the worst. His father sobbing, the oppressive heat and drenching humidity. He despised the stench of swampland muck and the screech of teeming fowl fighting for every scrap of food.

Wally wished he would wake up tomorrow and find this had been a terrible nightmare. He wished he could feel his mother's arms again.

"I'll tell you what," Jeremiah intruded. "I'll sell one top drawer for half a dollar. What do you say?"

Wally awoke to the toot of a car horn. For a moment he expected to hear his mother's voice. "A great day!" she always said. The car horn blew again and Hattie yelled, "I'm coming."

Sickly, Wally realized where he was, opening his eyes to unfamiliar surroundings. Through the shuttered window he saw Hattie get into a long black hearse and the vehicle depart in swirling fog.

Jeremiah was gone, his bed smoothed and covers folded. Wally made his own bed then shook his trousers vigorously. No scorpions. He dressed in the clothes he wore yesterday and went into the kitchen.

Anthony stood at the wood-burning cookstove, pouring coffee in a cup that jiggled in a saucer. Before Wally could speak, he said, "When I'm thinking, I'm working, and when I'm working, I can't talk. It disturbs my thoughts."

"Yessir."

"We fend for ourselves around here."

"Yessir." Wally's stomach growled. He peeked in the icebox. No eggs, no milk. He searched a cupboard. No bread. He was so hungry his stomach hurt.

"What are you looking for, Wally?"

"Breakfast."

"Eat anything you want."

"What is there?"

Anthony clamped his cup to stop the chatter. "Now see," he said, "I've lost my train of thought. It may take an hour to immerse myself in the scene again."

His father turned abruptly and went into a room furnished as an office. He rolled paper into a typewriter and with slow one-finger pecks struck the keys ten times and sat back.

In the oven Wally found one fried catfish wrapped in a brown paper sack. There were two hushpuppies in the same package. From the kitchen table he could see Anthony's "office," and still as stone his father sat staring at his typewriter.

Wally ate the fish. Still hungry he went out onto the front porch and sat in a swing. Because the chains creaked, he didn't sway. The morning sun painted tops of trees. Dirt daubers added to adobe dwellings between rafters.

About midday when every object stood in its own shadow, he heard his father snatch paper from the typewriter. A moment later, without a word, Anthony walked out, down the steps and across the yard. Hands clasped behind his back, he strode away west down the narrow lane.

Now what?

Wally ransacked the kitchen for food. There was a chunk of hoop cheese which he devoured. He found a package of soggy saltine crackers and ate them too. He got an orange drink from the icebox and returned to sit on the porch waiting—for what?

He spoke aloud to his mother, trying to put the best face on things so she wouldn't worry. He wondered if dead people worried.

He told her he was all right, but surely she knew better. He said he hoped she was all right, and how much he missed her, and how he wished he could go home to Atlanta.

Later, he went out to the Ford coupe and pretended to drive it, sitting as Jeremiah had on the edge of the seat behind the steering wheel. His mother had never had a car, so Wally had never been in a driver's seat before.

Minutes passed with agonizing slowness. Afternoon shadows stretched away east. Up on stilts, the house cast a shadow that resembled a giant spider poised to leap.

It was probably the most boring day of his entire life. Gnats buzzed, sweat seeped, and he was still hungry. He told Mama he hoped she was there.

Was he talking to himself? Did a spirit abandon the world and fly away? Was death the end of everything? He went back to lie on his bed, listening to the sheet metal roof crackle as the shady side contracted. He returned to the front porch swing and swung high as it would go, falling on his side to let momentum slowly die.

He wished he were dead.

When the setting sun touched the rim of the lake, and doves began to chortle, the Fester hounds announced arrival of the black hearse. Hattie emerged with a sack of groceries and a large block of ice wrapped in a burlap bag.

"Anthony's gone," Wally said.

"He'll be back."

A few moments later, Anthony mounted the steps, and shortly thereafter Jeremiah came in.

Nobody said anything to anybody. Hattie didn't inquire about Anthony's writing. Anthony didn't question Jeremiah's absence. None of them seemed interested in Wally's day.

They had a set routine and Wally wasn't a part of it. Anthony built a fire in the cookstove; Jeremiah lit kerosene lanterns; Hattie pan-fried bread and scrambled eggs. When Wally asked if he could help, Hattie shook her head.

Sitting at the table, nobody offered to pass anything and Wally had to ask for salt.

Jeremiah shoved it toward him.

Wally's mother would have been horrified to see Jeremiah chew with his mouth open, smacking his lips rudely. Kathryn McManus would not have permitted such behavior. She would have been eager to hear about Wally's day, hanging on every word he spoke.

The next day, same thing, except Hattie didn't bring home ice.

And the next.

And the next.

Every morning Anthony took his chattering cup of coffee and went into his office. Every day he rolled paper into the platen and hit the keys ten times. Then he sat back and stared until noon when he snatched it out and threw it away.

Wally retrieved a sheet from the wastebasket and smoothed it. At the top center it said CHAPTER ONE.

The trash can was filled with pages that said CHAPTER ONE.

Wally trailed his father as Anthony strolled with hands behind him, head hung. Out of knee-high grass insects rose in swirling funnels, but Anthony ignored them. Finally he turned off the lane and went to a spit of land jutting into the lake. His arrival sent thousands of birds to wing. He sat on a log, elbows on his knees, staring across the lake as the startled fowl slowly settled around him.

One afternoon a storm came across the lake, rain falling from a churning dark cloud. Wally watched his father take a soaking without moving. When the cloud passed, Anthony sat there drying, steam rising from his sodden back.

And every day, Jeremiah was gone at daybreak. Hattie had departed in a dead man's wagon. The hours seemed an eternity and there was nothing to anticipate.

One evening after they went to bed, Wally asked, "Where do you go, Jeremiah?"

"For a dime I'll tell you."

A lifetime of this was so depressing to contemplate, Wally barely resisted weeping.

Nobody marked the limits of Wally's confinement, but he was confined nevertheless. Trapped by the lake spreading forty miles north and swamps encircling the south. But most of all he was imprisoned by snarling black-and-tan hounds which belonged to the Festers. When Wally walked in that direction the hounds bounded onto the road, lips curled and legs spread, daring him to come nearer. And yet, somehow, Jeremiah walked by every morning without a sound from the dogs.

"How do you get past the Fester dogs, Jeremiah?"

"Give me fifty cents and I'll weave you a spell."

"Jeremiah, do you ever do anything for free?"

"Do you ever pay for what you want?"

Determined to discover Jeremiah's secret route, the next morning Wally was fully clothed and pretending sleep. Jeremiah shook his trousers briskly, slipped out the shuttered window, and jumped off the porch. Wally was a few seconds behind him.

The moon was like a cold white sun, and under lunar glow the ground fog was a silvery blanket up to Wally's waist. Not a frog peeped, no bird cried. He watched Jeremiah walk straight down the road with no attempt to hide. When he reached the Fester house one hound gave a soft *woof*, and that was it.

Wally matched Jeremiah's pace, glancing at the Fester shack in passing. Low growls ascended to snarling menace and he stopped. Then two massive heads came bounding through the fog.

"Jeremiah!" he screamed.

Jeremiah wheeled and shouted. "Go home. Run!"

He did, faster than he'd ever run before, back to the house with the hounds in pursuit. Up the steps and into the window, back in bed, Wally's legs quavered. Frightened and angry, he reconsidered the wisdom of buying a spell. Obviously Jeremiah had *something*. The animals hardly noticed him.

But Jeremiah's attempt at extortion made Wally furious. There had to be another way.

Minnie Lou Jackson was the tallest woman Wally had ever seen. She was so black she had no features except in bright light. "I be Minnie Lou Jackson," she introduced herself. "I comes to do the house."

Every week she would come, walking past the Fester's place with a large bundle of clean clothes balanced atop her head. The hounds ran after her, snapping dangerously close to her legs, but Minnie Lou walked in even strides, her head high as though unconcerned.

When she reached Anthony's house, Minnie Lou filled her lower lip with snuff and set about housekeeping. She swept floors, sending dust sifting through to the ground below. She burned garbage, washed dishes, scrubbed the bathtub and lavatory.

Starved for conversation, Wally followed her from room to room.

"What kind of bug is this, Minnie Lou?"

"Look like he sting, don't touch him."

"See the bird up there, Minnie Lou? What is that?"

"Don't know, but it sure can fly."

It was like talking into a dark closet. Wally's voice was absorbed. Minnie Lou's comment, negative or positive, was "Ummm-mmm-mmm." If something was better than she expected, or not to her liking, she said, "Ummm-mmm-mmm."

Upon her third arrival, Wally asked, "Minnie Lou, may I walk back to town with you?"

"Mind them dogs."

"Yes ma'am."

"Got jaws like gators."

"I'll walk close to you," he promised.

"I feels the hot breath from 'em," she said. "Slinging they slobber, snapping and gnashing."

Wally wasn't sure he had the courage, but he was bored to the point of pain and ached for the taste of a chocolate candy bar, a bowl of ice cream. He longed for the smell of automobile exhaust fumes and the hubbub of humanity. If Minnie Lou could do it on sheer guts, so could he.

"We got as much right to the road as any dog do." She tied a bundle of dirty laundry to take home with her. "Festers don't own that road and neither do them dogs." She balanced the bundle on her head, took a dip of snuff and descended the steps with Wally at her side. "And Precious—"

"Yes ma'am?"

"Don't run."

Wally wanted to hold her hand, but Minnie Lou clutched her skirt, arms rigid at her sides, chin lifted, eyes ahead. The hounds came racing toward them snarling, slavering, while the Fester men hooted that ugliest of slurs, "Nigger!"

"Ummm-mmm-mmm," Minnie Lou said.

To Wally the dogs were the size of tigers, their fangs long as his finger, and indeed, he felt the hot breath from them.

"Ummm-mmm-mmm," Minnie Lou said.

It seemed forever before they reached the far bend in the road where the dogs dropped back, marked their boundary, and returned home in a stiff-legged trot.

"Oh, wow," Wally shivered, "that was scary!"

"Ummm-mmm-mmm," Minnie Lou said.

When they arrived at the outskirts of Belle Glade, Minnie Lou turned off on a narrow footbridge crossing a canal. Wally followed and she halted. "Where you going, Precious?"

"Town."

"The next bridge, that's the way to town."

"Can't I get there this way?"

"Do like I say. Go to the next bridge."

"'Bye, Minnie Lou."

"'Bye you self."

The first thing he did was buy a banana split with extra cherries. He ate it so fast it gave him a stomachache. Then he went to the five-and-dime store where a woman was popping corn. He bought a tall sack, greasy, salty and delicious. Then he wandered around town until he found the library. He had to sit on the steps until he finished the popcorn because a sign forbade "food, drink, or loitering."

When he entered the hushed room, the aroma of ink and paper was comforting, a reminder of his mother. They'd spent many hours in the Atlanta Public Library.

The Belle Glade librarian was an unrouged woman with auburn hair pulled to a severe bun at the back of her head. When she saw Wally, she said, "We're closing, little boy. You'll have to come back tomorrow. We're open from eight to noon on Saturdays, ten to six weekdays.

"I won't be able to come tomorrow," Wally said. "Could I check out a book on birds?"

"Not today. Bring your library card tomorrow."

Out on the street again, Wally noticed it would soon be dark. The prospect of confronting the hounds at night was terrifying. Wally ran toward Chosen clutching change in his pocket to keep it from bouncing out. He wished he had paid Jeremiah.

At the dike, exhausted and winded, Wally had to crawl up the embankment. The last of the sun sank into Lake Okeechobee. It would be completely dark when he faced the dogs.

"Uh-huh, look at you," Jeremiah's voice came down from the bridge trellis. "Everybody's moaning, 'Where's Precious?' Maybe ate by gators! I knew you went to town with Minnie Lou."

Wally sank to all fours, gasping for breath.

"Coming on night," Jeremiah said. "The Fester dogs licking their chops. I figured you'd be ready to buy a spell."

He jumped down and put a hand on Wally's shoulder. "If you'd loosen up a buck or two, we could have fun. What good's a dollar when you don't spend it? Give me a dollar and I'll get you past the hounds."

"You said fifty cents, Jeremiah."

"That was before. This is now. But all right, since you're my brother, put fifty cents in my hand and I'll spell you."

After buying a banana split and popcorn, Wally had forty-seven cents. He offered it and Jeremiah said, "You owe me three cents, plus a nickel interest. Agreed?"

Wally nodded and Jeremiah said, "Say 'agreed.'"

"I agree."

Jeremiah pulled a long scarf from his pocket. "When the dogs come at you, wave this and they'll bite it. Let them have it."

"How do I know they'll stop?"

"If they don't stop, you can forget the three cents."

When the dogs bounded up Jeremiah said, "Dangle the rag, Precious." The hounds took it. For a moment they fought over it, then both dogs snorted. They rubbed their noses along the ground and pawed their faces.

"Get the rag and bring it with you, Precious," Jeremiah said. "We might need it again sometime."

"What's in it, Jeremiah?"

"A conjure man shouldn't tell his spells," Jeremiah said. "But since you're my brother—I soaked it in 'possum blood, rolled it in stinging nettle and red pepper. One sniff sets their noses on fire."

Jeremiah draped an arm around Wally's shoulder and gave a gentle hug. "Remember," he said, "you owe me three cents, plus a nickel interest."

chapter four

Days were long and lonely, but evenings were worse. Wally's bed shared a common wall with his father's room so every night he heard Anthony and Hattie talking. Outside, katydids fiddled, cicadas whined, and frogs of every voice burped, tweeted and grumped. Even so, he heard his father: "I don't know what to say, Hattie."

"Therefore you say nothing," she said.

The argument had become a nightly event. "You don't know what to say to *him*," Hattie accused, "so you say nothing to anybody. You've pulled back from Precious and shut out me and Jeremiah, too."

"I'm working. You know how it is when I'm working."

"You work less with Precious here than you did before he came. What happened to the short story you were writing?"

"It didn't work out."

"It was good."

"It began good, it ended badly."

"Anthony, pretending he isn't here won't make that boy go away. If you want him gone, you'll have to send him someplace."

Wally pressed nearer the wall. After a long pause, Anthony said, "Send him where?"

"A school someplace. One of those military schools, maybe."

Insects shrilled. Wally heard their bedsprings squeak. Anthony said, "You think I should send him to a boarding school?"

"You aren't going to do what I think you ought to, Anthony, so yes, send him to a school."

"Tell me what you think I ought to."

"You ought to spend time with that child."

"We're together all day."

"Him making do the best he can. Jeremiah said he just now went to town by himself."

"What did he do?"

"Bought ice cream. Went to the library."

Wally twisted to peer at Jeremiah's bed. Asleep.

"We can't go on this way," Hattie said. "You got to do this for yourself, Anthony."

"Do what? Be specific!"

"Talk to him!"

"I said I don't know what to say."

"Then look him in the eye and listen. Truth be known, I don't care what you do with Precious. I do care what you're doing to you and me."

"I never wanted to be a father. I'm no good at it. Kathryn was the one who wanted a child. I'm not a nest builder, Hattie."

"Then send him away."

"I hate the paternal role. Cooking marshmallows over a campfire, that's not me. Fathers should dispense fatherly advice, teach their sons how to be a man. That's not me, Hattie."

"Send him to a school."

"I should. I really should. And I would, but every time I think about Kathryn, I get depressed. *This one thing*, I can hear her saying. *This one thing, Anthony! Can't you do this one thing?*"

"Do something, Anthony," Hattie said. "But don't keep doing this to me."

"I wish I were a better man."

"Don't start that!"

"I've disappointed every person in my life. My father—"

"Anthony—"

"All I ever wanted to do was write. I think I told you—"

"You told me, and I don't want to hear it again."

"I wanted to write. Nothing else appealed to me."

"And you did, and it was good," Hattie mocked, "but something went wrong."

"Something went wrong," he said. "My books did well. Other authors admired me. Did I ever tell you about walking the Champs Elysees with Ernest Hemingway and Scott Fitzgerald?"

"You told me."

"Bending elbows with the mightiest authors of our lifetime. I was euphoric. But Kathryn wanted a child. She knew that was not for me. She knew it!"

"Do what you want, Anthony. Do what you must, but do something."

Out of an expanding silence, rhythmic bumping of their headboard signaled an end to the dispute for now.

Lately, Wally had been replaying conversations he didn't know he remembered. Into his mind came moments unbidden, like the last time he and his mother rode an Atlanta bus from downtown out to Decatur. She wanted to see the dogwoods in bloom. Frail and drawn, she smiled faintly as the electrically driven bus followed Ponce de Leon toward the suburbs.

"What would you have thought had I gotten married again, Wally?"

Surprised by the question, he said, "Are you thinking about it?"

Because she was dying, she laughed at that.

"If a husband made you happy, I'd be happy," Wally said, and she took his hand and squeezed it.

"Do you wish you'd married again?" he asked.

"I wondered if *you* wished I had."

"I have you, Mama. You're enough." And he realized that was truly her question.

"I don't need a daddy," Wally had said.

Especially a man who hated the role of father. Wally had no wish to roast marshmallows over a campfire. He wanted nothing from Anthony but a roof and food. He barely had that. Now they wanted to send him to a military school.

In Atlanta, their apartment was not far from Longstreet Military Academy. Toward the end of his mother's illness, Wally had sat on the balcony watching cadets with GI haircuts march to and from classes. He'd heard them count cadence, playing soldier. He had observed them bullied by authority and quick to bully their underlings. He found nothing to admire in the military.

Mama didn't like the army either. She'd once read aloud Tennyson's "The Charge of the Light Brigade" to make a point:

Theirs not to make reply, Theirs not to reason why,
Theirs but to do or die.

"What a waste," she'd said of the doomed brigade. "I hope you never want to make the military a career, Wally."

Mama would not have sent him to a boarding school, putting him at the mercy of rigid military discipline. And although Wally didn't like Belle Glade, he would hate an academy even more.

But what could he do? Run away?

He'd have to steal food and travel under cover of night, hop on trains and sleep below railroad trestles, always moving to evade the law and reform school. He imagined his mother's distress as he escalated from small offenses and petty misdemeanors to armed robbery and, finally, deadly assault. He'd end up in a jail cell wondering how it came to be. And what would Mama think?

The thought made him yelp.

In the next room the creaking of springs ceased. His father called, "Are you all right, Wally?"

"Yessir."

"Well. Good night then."

The next evening at supper, Anthony said, "I want to talk to you boys."

Wally saw Jeremiah get wary.

"Part of being a family means doing things together," Anthony said.

They ate in silence a moment and then Jeremiah said, "So?"

"So I want you boys to spend more time together."

"Doing what?"

"Whatever it is you do, Jeremiah."

"Anthony," Hattie said, "this is not what I meant."

"But this is essential, Hattie," Anthony said. "My actions alone will not make or break this family. It takes all of us working together to become a family. Jeremiah, I expect you to spend your days with Wally."

"Wading in the lake? Looking for tadpoles? Doing what?"

"Doing whatever it is you do."

"And how much I get paid for this?" Jeremiah demanded.

"You'll receive the same thing I get for putting a bed under your butt and food in your mouth. You'll do it because we are a family, Jeremiah."

"What can I do with Precious hanging onto me? That's all I need, going through colored town with a white shadow."

"Take him with you or stay home," Anthony said.

"And this makes us a family?" Jeremiah wailed.

"It's a step in the right direction."

"And what's Precious supposed to do?" Jeremiah said. "All this is on me alone, or is he going to do something in return? He don't share nothing with nobody. He takes but he never gives."

"Share with Jeremiah," Anthony directed Wally.

"And you think saying that makes it so?" Jeremiah cried. "He's got the first penny he ever found, says he don't have a penny when he does. Am I supposed to pay his way to everything? I need some kind of allowance for this job. Or you want me to spend my own money supporting Precious?"

"I want you boys to share and share alike."

"That's more like it," Jeremiah said.

"I'm not speaking solely of money," Anthony said. "I'm speaking of the bonding of brotherhood."

"What if we get off someplace and a gang jumps on Precious?"

"If that happens, Jeremiah," Anthony said, coldly, "you'd better come home with bruises to match. I expect you to stand together."

Hattie took her plate to the sink, then went out on the porch. Anthony pushed back his chair. "I've said what I have to say on this matter," he declared. "One for all and all for one, that's what I want to see."

When the adults were outside on the porch, Jeremiah hung an elbow on the table and poked his food with a fork. "You going to share with me?" he asked.

"If you mean pay for company, I will not."

"Okay," Jeremiah said ominously. "You'll be with me for free, so you'll do what I say."

From the porch came voices too subdued to understand, but tempo and tone suggested anger. A moment later, the car door slammed, the motor started, and Anthony drove off in the night.

"Now he's going to get drunk for a week," Jeremiah sneered, "and I'll have to go and fetch him. I hate doing that."

But a few minutes later the car returned, the door slammed, and Anthony mounted the steps again. He burst into the room, his eyes flashing.

"You do as I say, Jeremiah, understand me?"

"I understand you."

"Then do it."

"I never said I wouldn't."

Anthony stamped into the bedroom and a minute later Hattie followed.

"Okay," Jeremiah said. "I'll do it, like it or not."

"I haven't said I wanted to go with you," Wally noted.

Jeremiah leaned close. "I'm not messing up my mama's life because of you. You'll go with me starting tomorrow morning. I leave early, so get some sleep."

Hattie returned to the kitchen wearing a robe. She started to gather dishes and Wally said, "I'll do that."

"Have you washed dishes before?"

"For my mother."

Hattie's eyes darted as if searching for something. "Washing dishes would be nice," she said. "I appreciate it."

So Wally did, and he dried them and put them away. By the time he went to bed, Jeremiah was asleep, or pretending to be.

When Jeremiah woke him, Wally was dreaming about his mother. He savored dreams about her because it was like she'd returned to visit.

"Get up, Precious. Let's go, let's go," Jeremiah commanded.

Two hours before dawn and the fog was pale as snow in

moonlight. They trotted past the Fester's house without so much as a woof from the hounds. Before Wally could ask, Jeremiah said, "Probably took the dogs with them. Gone to Kramer's Island to make shine."

Jeremiah could run as though he had unlimited wind and inexhaustible reserves. By the time they reached the bridge, Wally was wheezing. Jeremiah slowed to a fast walk until the ache in Wally's sides had eased. Then he began to lope anew.

It was a wonder, Wally said, they didn't step on snakes lounging on warm pavement. Jeremiah said it was the pounding of their feet that warned reptiles away, since snakes have no ears but can detect vibrations. Talking as he ran, Jeremiah said water moccasins were so sluggish they wouldn't move without a prod, and they were too lazy to bite unless stepped upon.

And on they ran, past packing houses brightly lit for all-night work. They scooted under railroad cars, across tracks, and through colored town. The houses were tightly clustered, yards fenced, gates closed. Having passed the residential area, they ran between three-story tenement houses where people sat on open balconies to escape the heat inside.

There was a smell to the tenements, of peppery spices, pomade, and scorched cloth from take-home ironing. Jeremiah slowed to a walk and held Wally's forearm, leading the way through a crowd of hundreds of men and women standing in the street. They'd built fires in metal oil cans to ward off mosquitoes. Flames painted ebony faces with ocher lights, their teeth and eyes shining in the predawn darkness. White men on trucks tried to entice them by calling out the wages they'd pay for field hands that day. Like auctioneers they bartered for stoop labor. Ten cents a hamper for string beans. Thirty cents an hour for cutting cane.

Jeremiah led the way down a narrow alley to the rear of a grocery store. Yellow light flowed from an open door. Inside, at a long table, women worked a production line making sandwiches. One laid out slices of bread, another applied mustard, another put on meat and closed the sandwich while a fourth woman cut the product diagonally and wrapped each half in waxed paper. It was she who spoke.

"You're late, Jeremiah."

"I had to bring my brother."

"Your brother!" Wally squirmed under her scrutiny. "That boy is white as a peeled egg, Jeremiah."

"But he's my brother. His mama died and he came to live with us."

"You're lying, Jeremiah."

"Our daddy said I had to bring him with me or stay home," Jeremiah explained.

The woman stared at Wally as she worked. He fought a tremor in his legs. "I don't need trouble with white folks, Jeremiah."

"Won't be any," Jeremiah said. "Besides, I can handle twice as many baskets with him helping."

Jeremiah handed Wally two woven wicker baskets filled with sandwiches. "I'll do the selling," he said, "you tote and stay close."

The containers were so large and heavy, Wally had to walk with elbows bent to keep the baskets from bumping ground. The moment they reached the crowded street, Jeremiah advertised their wares in a clear voice that stole attention from white men bidding for labor.

"Yo now!" Jeremiah yelled. "Spam, ham and bologna ma'am! Ten cents, one dime, made today, take it away—Spam, ham and bologna, ma'am!"

Within minutes the baskets were empty and they had to run back for more. The farmers had begun to load workers. Wally ran behind Jeremiah alongside the trucks. "Peanut butter-banana sandwiches—one dime, ten cents, liver loaf or ham!"

The last truck soon pulled away, the human cargo singing, some swaying, as they left for distant fields.

While Jeremiah settled accounts with the owner of the grocery store, Wally sat on a high wooden stool beside a walk-in cooler. His legs ached from unaccustomed activity, and when he put his foot on the floor he couldn't stop a jiggling that immediately set in.

Without looking at Wally, the woman said to Jeremiah, "What's his name?"

"We call him Precious."

"And his mama be dead?"

"Yes."

"Well, y'all did good," she said, and she gave Jeremiah four dollars and eleven cents for 411 sandwiches sold.

When they emerged from the store into the alley, the sky had turned milky blue with first light of day. Out of the tenement houses came the wail of children. There was laughter too, and a garble of radios. From dozens of kitchens rose a smell of frying meat. Wally had eaten so many sandwiches he wasn't hungry. He and Jeremiah had been offered any that had become smashed in the bottom of the baskets.

"Where're we going?" Wally asked.

"How come you want to know everything before it gets here? Just watch and maybe you'll learn something."

They walked through the same bar where Wally first saw Anthony. Customers drank their breakfasts. Out back in the alley, men pitched dimes at a wall. A coin nearest the wall won all the other coins.

"Who's that with you, Jeremiah?" somebody asked.

"My brother. Whose pitch?"

"Yours if you've got a dime. What you mean, your brother? That boy wouldn't brown in an oven."

"I'm not his brother," Wally said.

They turned to stare at him. "You ashamed of it?"

"I'm not ashamed and have no cause to be. He's not my brother."

"Who knows but your daddy?"

"My mama knows," Wally said. Jeremiah pitched a dime and it bounced off the wall. He lost.

"White folks talk about a nigger in the woodpile," a man said. "Seems to me black babies get lighter and their daddies sure ain't coal-dusted crows. Pitch again, Jeremiah."

Jeremiah lost every cent.

Wally had never asked why his mother's marriage failed. When she spoke of their years in Paris, there had been mention of all-night parties with other writers. But she never accused Anthony of being unfaithful. An unfaithful, cheating drunk.

Wally despised his father for the pain he must have caused Mama when she discovered his infidelity and a pregnant lover. Surely that was why she'd left him.

And now that he knew, Wally was even more resentful of the isolation he felt, and the lack of electricity and plentiful food. That was one reason he'd decided to go with Jeremiah every morning. At least, they could eat all the sandwiches they wanted. And they made money.

"I'm cutting you in for a share," Jeremiah had said. But when he lost his own money gambling he turned to Wally.

Jeremiah pitched dimes in an alley, played pool in a beer joint, and gambled at poker in the rear of a colored barbershop. His opponents were grown men who sat in a cloud of cigarette smoke and drank liquor as they played.

"That white boy going to sit in for a few hands, Jeremiah?"

"He doesn't know how. I'll see your quarter and raise a quarter."

One player nudged another beneath the table and they traded winks. "We'll be glad to teach that white boy how to play," the man said, and everybody chuckled.

"He's got no money after paying his Klan dues," Jeremiah said. "I call. What you got?"

It didn't take long. Jeremiah lost. He pulled Wally aside. "Loan me three dollars."

"They're cheating, Jeremiah."

"Watch your mouth. Talk like that will get your legs broke. I'm having bad luck, that's all."

"I saw them signal one another, Jeremiah."

One of the gamblers winked at Wally. "That white boy loves you, Jeremiah, any fool can see it."

"Okay," Jeremiah said, "loan me two dollars."

"Nobody wins as many times as they do," Wally reasoned. "They're cheating you."

"Yessiree, that white boy would do anything to help you, Jeremiah."

"Cheating how?" Jeremiah asked.

"I don't know, but they're working together to beat you."

"You don't know nothing from nothing," Jeremiah said. "I find a way to make you money and this is the thanks I get. How many dollars you got right this minute?"

"Take the money, Jeremiah."

"Like you're doing me a big favor. Okay, I'll take it. I'll borrow—how much is this?"

"Three dollars."

"Until tomorrow," he said.

But Jeremiah didn't repay even when he was winning. Shooting dice at a packing house, his hands were full of dollar bills, his pockets stuffed with money. It was payday and workers crowded around to see "the kid roll bones."

"Seven come eleven, the Devil's going to heaven—"

Surrounded by mounds of burlap sacks, people sat on the rafters to see Jeremiah rake in the cash. Again and again he scooped up the pot and men wailed and cursed and came back for more.

Then suddenly it was over. Jeremiah had lost it all.

He blamed Wally for breaking his concentration or for some other imagined wrong. He said Wally was a jinx, that bad luck rode his shoulder.

Anything Wally earned Jeremiah took away, so what was the point? The next morning, Jeremiah shook him. "Wake up, Precious. Time to go."

"I'm staying home, Jeremiah."

"You can't. They're making more sandwiches than I can sell by myself. Now get up and let's go."

"I'll go, but I'm not staying with you," Wally said. "I'm tired of you taking my money."

Thereafter when the last sandwich was sold, Wally retreated to the library to wait out the day.

The librarian watched him suspiciously. "You've been in here quite often," she said. "Are you a visitor to Belle Glade?"

"I came here at the beginning of summer."

"From where?"

"Atlanta."

"Then you have not attended school in Belle Glade?"

"No ma'am."

"Oh dear," she said, as if disappointed. "Our books are for members in good standing, or for students of Belle Glade schools. I don't believe you are a member."

"I'm willing to join."

"Being willing is not enough," she said. "Members must be accepted. Who is the colored boy who waits for you outside?"

Losing library privileges would be like losing a friend. Wally said, "My father is a writer. You have some of his books here."

"Oh? And who is he?"

"Anthony Edward McManus."

Her eyes hardened and she said, "Oh, yes. McManus. And the Negro boy lives with you?"

She reached past Wally and took the book he was reading. She closed it and held it to her chest. "Until you've paid dues, or until you are a full-time student in a Belle Glade school, and until your membership has been accepted, I'm afraid you'll have to find somewhere else to while away your time. You saw the sign, 'No loitering.'"

"I'm not loitering. I'm reading."

"And none of your sass, young man. Go along now."

Stung, Wally went out into searing noonday sun. Heat rose from the tops of cars. Across the street at the courthouse, Jeremiah was trying to sell shoeshines with a kit he'd borrowed from the colored barbershop. When Jeremiah saw Wally, he came over, dropped his hod and sat on the library steps. "You can't sell shoeshines when it's so hot wax melts in the can," Jeremiah said. "Why are you out here?"

"The librarian made me leave because I'm not a member."

Jeremiah rose and stared through the glass front doors. "I bet you told her Mr. McManus is your father."

"She asked."

"Yeah. Well. You'll be spending a lot of time sitting on the street. Might as well get used to it. There isn't but one white man in Belle Glade living with a colored woman, and everybody knows who he is."

Wally turned to look back at the librarian. She was watching them from her desk.

"This is why I want to go to Paris," Jeremiah said. "Mama says French people treat coloreds same as whites. She says the most popular singer in France was a colored woman named Josephine Baker. Soon as I make a mark, that's where I'm going. Grow me a little mustache, buy some patent leather shoes and a diamond stickpin. Get a woman that moves like greased possums in a silk sack—"

The librarian came to the door. "Boys, you can't sit here. You'll have to find somewhere else to loiter."

"I'm not loitering!" Wally shouted.

After she left, he stood up. "I don't feel good."

"Probably the heat," Jeremiah said. "Does it get this hot in Atlanta?"

Wally's head was swimming. "I think I'll go home."

"You can't do that. I told Mr. McManus I wouldn't let you go home until dinnertime. Listen, you want some ice cream? I know a place where we can get it free, and all you want."

"Where is that?"

"My granddaddy's place. Let's drop off this shoeshine kit at the barbershop and we'll go. Granddaddy's got refrigerated air like a movie house. Maybe we'll see dead people. I can show you how to embalm somebody if you want to know."

"I don't want to know!"

"Okay, we'll have ice cream. Cool off in refrigerated air."

Wally allowed himself to be pulled from one shady place to the next. His feet had toughened since he started going without shoes, but he still couldn't cross melted asphalt. At each intersection Jeremiah gave him a piggyback ride to the far corner.

"Have you ever laid down in a coffin?" Jeremiah asked. "There's enough room for a body, but if you wanted to roll over it'd be a tight squeeze."

The afternoon was so hot residents of colored town had withdrawn to darkened doorways where they waved cardboard fans or horsetail switches to move the air and chase away flies.

Now and then somebody called out. "Who's your tag-along, Jeremiah?"

"He's my brother."

"Your brother? He ain't the right flavor to be your brother."

"Used to be chocolate," Jeremiah replied, "but Daddy vanillanated him."

"Come over here and tell us another lie, Jeremiah."

"Haven't got time. We're going to the funeral parlor to bury an elephant."

Back to Wally, Jeremiah said, "It's sort of spooky what undertakers do to bodies. They flush out the juices—I'll show you."

A sign in front of Three Palms Funeral Home advertised, PICK UP AND DELIVERY. DON'T WAIT, PLAN NOW.

Off to one side of the building was the Eternal Peace Columbarium, and on the other side stood the Willoughby Monument and Quality Casket Company offering marble statuary to fit any budget. "Granddaddy doesn't like me to call them tombstones," Jeremiah said, "but that's what they are."

Two large Packard sedans were parked under a breezeway, each with a brass fixture on the bumper which said *Funeral*.

Jeremiah stepped through a side door but stopped immediately. His grandfather, Harold Hubert Willoughby, was consoling a customer. He'd seen Jeremiah and held up a hand. It was the raised hand that stopped Jeremiah. Refrigerated air dried Wally's perspiration.

"My Rachel looks better dead than she did alive," the elderly customer said to Mr. Willoughby. "You made her look natural, Mr. Willoughby."

"Thank you, Mister John. Everybody will miss Sister Rachel."

"I'll be like one leg off a milking stool without her," the bereaved man said. "Won't a day go by but what I have to catch my balance."

Jeremiah's grandfather was a tall, straight man with wide shoulders. His hair was uniformly curly, going gray at the temples, a color his suit and tie matched perfectly.

"I want to spend some time with my Rachel before everybody gets here," the grieving man said.

"That's fine, Mister John. Go right on in."

Wally smelled gladioluses and got queasy. There'd been a lot of gladioluses at his mother's funeral.

The uplifted hand motioned Jeremiah nearer, and Mr. Willoughby said, "Jeremiah, how many times do I have to tell you not to come in here looking like a half naked savage? Who is this?"

"He's Wally."

In a sanctuary, beside an open coffin, the elderly man bent to kiss a corpse. Wally's stomach churned. The smell of flowers, soft strains of organ music, the way Mr. Willoughby spoke in hushed tones—awful memories assailed Wally.

"This is no place to play, boys," Mr. Willoughby said. "It shows no respect for the deceased."

"We came to see Mama," Jeremiah said.

"Hattie is upstairs with your grandmother. Don't be making happy sounds during the funeral. And Jeremiah—"

"Yessir."

"Stay out of the Memorial Garden fountain. Don't let me catch you swiping pennies from the reflecting pool."

"Yessir."

Wally followed Jeremiah down the long corridor, past three women sitting at desks in an office. "That's where Mama usually works," Jeremiah said. "Except when she has to sit with Grandmama, which is all she does on Sundays, whether she likes it or not."

They climbed a flight of stairs and entered a living room, where a couch and chairs had been pushed against a wall making space for a hospital bed. Cranked to an upright position, a withered woman slowly opened her eyes. When she saw Jeremiah, she croaked, "Good God, it's that boy. Hattie! Hattie!"

Jeremiah's grandmother was white as any white person Wally had ever seen. Even the little pigment she had was being taken by illness. Her eyes were sunken chocolate buttons.

"Hattie!" she called, and coughed. "Where is that girl? Hattie, come here!"

"I'll find her, Grandmama."

Abandoned, Wally watched the woman's tongue protrude as she coughed, gurgled, and coughed again.

"May I do something?" Wally offered.

"What could you do for me, boy?"

"Some water, maybe."

"Hattie! There's a white boy in my house!"

Hattie came running, wearing an apron and one oven mitt. Her head was bound in a red and white bandanna. "It's all right, Mama," she soothed. "This is Wally."

"Wally? That's him? God Almighty, is there no rest for me?"

"Wally," Hattie said, "this is my mother, Mary Bethune Willoughby. He came to meet you, Mama."

"I'm not receiving."

"We wanted ice cream," Jeremiah said.

"They want ice cream, Mama." Hattie straightened the bed sheets. "Go in the kitchen, boys. You know where it is, Jeremiah."

They owned the largest freezer Wally had seen outside a restaurant or grocery store. "This is where Granddaddy keeps dry ice," Jeremiah said, his breath a frosty plume. "Sometimes he has to ship a body someplace and dry ice keeps it fresh."

Wally's stomach knotted.

In five-gallon containers were chocolate, strawberry, vanilla, and various sherbets. "Ice cream is about all Grandmama will eat," Jeremiah spoke as he scooped. "It makes her throat feel better."

"Jeremiah, I don't want any ice cream."

"I'll eat what you don't," Jeremiah said. "We only get one bowl, but it can be the size of a bucket, so take it."

They sat on the screened back porch looking down on driveways and a fountain that created misty rainbows in hot afternoon air. Pools of water reflected blue skies and white clouds. At one end, a sculpted marble woman posed with a jug on her shoulder from which water poured into the pond.

Jeremiah sat in a swing kicking one foot to maintain momentum. "They don't like me here," he admitted. "I got sent here because of the war in France. The minute she saw me, Grandmama had a conniption. They hate Mr. McManus. Bad enough he's white, but he's a drunk too. Granddaddy calls him a 'Caucasian son of a bitch.' I gave you four flavors, eat it."

"I'm not hungry."

"It's the heat. Eat ice cream and you'll feel better. I got sherbet. You want to trade?"

"No, thanks."

Mourners arrived for the funeral; cars washed and waxed, the women wearing hats with veils, the men in sharply creased trousers, white shirts and black ties. Their feet crunched on bleached seashells in the curved driveway. Wally heard somebody crying.

He recalled the sour taste of grief, the ache of trying to be grown up when he hadn't felt grown up at all. For a horrible moment he thought he might cry right in front of Jeremiah.

"They don't like my mama either," Jeremiah said. "She gets insulted here, and when Mr. McManus drinks she gets insulted at home. Mama says it don't mean anything, but I get mad enough to kill somebody. Sometimes I dream about how I'd like to torture anybody who hurts Mama. You ever have dreams like that about your mama?"

Watching mourners move inside, Wally wondered if they'd do like people at his mother's funeral. Her body was so thin that nobody recognized her, but people complimented her makeup, a thick mask that only accentuated her look of death. Women had kissed Wally and men spoke in doleful low voices. Suddenly somebody had laughed. The sound was shocking. Wally had lost the most important person in his life and somebody laughed! How could there be joy in life for anyone?

"There's no point staying mad with people who insult Mama," Jeremiah continued. "She says don't fret the little stuff."

What Wally said then caught him by surprise. He had no intention of sharing a thought about his mother. But words fell out of his mouth, quoting what Mama had said when Wally felt so enraged by her impending death. "Growing up is what we do when we realize some things cannot be changed."

"In that case," Jeremiah said, "I ought to be a hundred and two. I sure can't change anything. Come on, I'll show you how they pump out the juices."

Wally resisted seeing the embalming room, but Jeremiah said, "We have to leave this way."

The floor and walls were ceramic tile. An enamel table stood over a drain in the center of the room. From the ceiling hung a hose used to rinse the area, and a flexible apparatus for cutting and grinding, Jeremiah said. "It's like a drill in a dentist's office. I'd show you, but Granddaddy might hear us. Over here is the pump. They use this to flush out blood and stuff."

The room was even colder than the freezer upstairs.

"Look at the size of this needle," Jeremiah said as he lifted one from a tray. "How would you like a shot with this thing?"

Wally instantly felt nauseous, thinking of anybody cutting his mother, replacing her blood with embalming fluids.

"When there's an accident or murder," Jeremiah persisted, "Granddaddy does autopsies." His voice echoed in the barren room. "Sometimes he takes out a brain or the liver and sends it to a laboratory to be studied. In case there's been poisoning, or a stroke maybe."

Jeremiah opened a square door set into a tiled wall and pulled out a long porcelain shelf with a body on it. Wally groped for support.

Jeremiah peeled back a green sheet. A woman. She seemed

asleep. Not at all like Wally's mother whose skin was so taut it revealed the shape of her skull, this woman looked as though she might take a breath and open her eyes.

Jeremiah lifted the sheet for an intimate peek and laughed. "Want to see?"

Wally pitched headlong to the floor.

He awoke to an angry voice. Hattie held something to Wally's nose and he snorted. "You're all right," Hattie said. He felt a pillow under his head.

Mr. Willoughby restrained Jeremiah by one arm, shaking him. "You got no sense at all, boy. This child just lost his mama and you bring him in here to see those things? What's the matter with you?"

Jeremiah was completely without expression, but he said, "I'm sorry, Granddaddy."

"I want you out of here and don't come back, Jeremiah. Don't come back unless you are invited, understand me?"

Mr. Willoughby turned to Hattie kneeling beside Wally. "This child brings nothing but trouble, Hattie. I won't tolerate it. He is forbidden to set foot in this building without my permission."

"Yes, Papa."

Hattie helped Wally sit up. His head throbbed, his feet tingled.

"Last month," Mr. Willoughby recounted, "Jeremiah put Oxydol in the fountain and it took a week to get rid of the suds. Time before that, he brought baby ducks that ate every goldfish in my reflecting pool. I've caught him pilfering coins from the pond, and you, Hattie, living with that no-good drunk!"

"I'm sorry, Papa." Hattie looked like she would cry.

"If word of this gets out it would ruin my business," Mr. Willoughby stormed. "Two boys looking at a dead woman's naked body! It's a desecration, Hattie. Jeremiah shows no respect."

Once again Mr. Willoughby shook Jeremiah and Jeremiah yelped, "Oww, Granddaddy!"

"Because you're my daughter, Hattie, I've allowed this hellion to come and go. You asked for work and I gave you a job. A job a lot of folks would like to have. I'm so furious I could—"

Wally crawled toward the exit. He wanted air, sunshine. His ears rang and he was ill. The fall had raised a bump on his head.

"We sent you to college and paid your way to Europe," Mr. Willoughby raged. "Gave you opportunities few people are privilege to and what do you do, Hattie? Send home a drunken bum's baby! Then show up in Belle Glade to live with him. What possesses you, woman? Have you no shame? Look what is happening to Jeremiah, prowling town, gambling, running with trash. He's getting no guidance from you or that Caucasian no-good bastard."

"I'll try to do better, Papa."

"Do better how? The only better would be to throw that man out! Send Jeremiah to a decent school. A Negro without education is doomed to hard labor. Your mother and I worked to give you every advantage—"

Wally was out the door when Jeremiah bolted past him, across the lawn, dodging mourners and the hearse into which they were loading a casket. Jeremiah hit the road, his bare feet making puffs of dust as he ran.

At the footbridge under the railroad trestle, Wally met Minnie Lou coming his way. "What you doing in colored town, Precious?"

Wally wanted to move around her but the bridge was too narrow.

"Somebody messing with you, Precious? Where is Jeremiah?"

"He's gone home. Could I get by, please?"

She lifted Wally, turned, and put him down on the other side of her. "How'd you get that goose egg? Stop by the icehouse and get a penny's worth. You got a penny?"

"Yes ma'am."

"Hold ice to that bump and it'll go down."

But Wally did not go to the icehouse. Dreadful images tormented him. He imagined his mother on a cold table while strange men examined her nude body, making snide remarks. Damn them! Damn Jeremiah for showing what they do.

Hot soil seared the soles of his feet, but Wally wanted to savor the pain. He slapped himself in the face to increase his suffering. If he'd had a knife he would've cut himself.

He despised this place with white sunshine and blinding blue skies. He loathed the stench of decaying hyacinths and the constant hum of insects. He hated his father for subjecting him to it.

When he reached the top of the dike he looked out over the high bridge and the tannin-stained dark waters flowing beneath it. He was too weak to swim, too angry to reason. He could throw himself off the span and plunge to eternity. To join his mother—

But he stumbled past fishermen on the bridge, past gasping catfish in buckets of warm water. His clothes were wet with perspiration, and he felt his face burn in the sun. He passed the Fester house without fear. The dogs were gone. Anthony's car was gone too.

Wally went inside, gathered bread, cheese, and two bananas which he put in a paper sack.

Before his mother became too weak to sit up, she'd sewn money into Wally's only jacket. Tens and twenties were hidden in the lining of the coat. "Don't ever tell anyone you have this cash, Wally," she'd warned him. "Not your father or your most trusted friend. Money means freedom if you need it."

He heard a car door slam and looked out to see Anthony lift a block of ice from the rumble seat. Wally slipped out the bedroom window, timed his jump to avoid his father, and then ran—but not toward Belle Glade, for surely Jeremiah or Hattie would see him. He ran west, out the lane and past the spit of land where Anthony strolled every afternoon. Beyond the farthest point Wally had ever hiked, he trudged through the swampy bog. Clouds of gnats and swarms of mosquitoes beset him. He smeared mud on his arms and legs to stop the bites, and hugged the jacket that held all his money.

Wally didn't know how much money he had. He didn't think Mama knew for sure but she'd kept adding to it as she became more and more ill.

The setting sun turned the lake to a bloody glow. Fish leapt. Night birds swooped for flying insects. He had to find a place to stay. Don't sleep on the ground, he'd been warned.

That's when he saw a woman far ahead in a distant bend of the shoreline. "Come on," her gesture urged. "This way—"

chapter
SIX

Daggers of cattails rose from the shoreline, and Lake Okeechobee was smooth as a mirror and black as lacquer. Wally waded away from water grasses lest he encounter snakes hidden in the shallows. Up ahead, the woman watched and waited.

She was too distant to be seen clearly, the sun setting behind her. But her hair was the color of moonlight on summer smoke and it fell in a long braid over her shoulder. She walked up a slight incline and peered back at him.

She wore clothing alien to the glades, a blouse with long full sleeves and riding trousers Wally's mother had called "jodhpurs." Mama bought a pair once when they were thinking about learning to ride horses. The idea was short-lived. They became so saddle sore the first day, they never wanted to sit on a horse again.

Wally sloshed on, closing the distance between them. He clutched his money coat and the sack of food and began having misgivings about coming out here. He anticipated what the woman stranger might say. Perhaps she'd tell him how foolish it was to enter the swamps without a safe destination in mind. She'd remind him not to lie down in the bogs. And maybe she'd escort him back home again as adults tended to do.

Apparently satisfied that he was coming, she moved over the crest of a low dune and disappeared from sight. *Leading the way*, Wally thought.

The sun had never seemed larger, gently settling onto the lake, casting a fiery reflection toward Wally. He placed his money coat and food on a log and washed away the mud he'd smeared on his arms and legs. Then he went toward the last place he'd seen the woman waiting.

Beyond the dune, there she was, standing on the porch of a shack. Built of unpainted cypress, planks had warped and curled. The roof was rusting sheet metal which had pulled loose and jutted at odd angles. The snags and jags of timber and tin made Wally think of a ruffled creature with matted hair. The windows were gaping holes, like woeful dark eyes returning his gaze. There were no doors, and the house was divided from front to back by a wide breezeway.

Beyond the building spread a vast field of saw grass punctuated here and there by scrub pine trees, the kind with short needles and stubby cones deformed by bad soil. Here and there on higher ground grew thickets of palmetto. Wally heard a dog barking in the distance but saw no other houses. When the barking stopped, the silence was complete. Not a breeze whispered. No flocks of birds jabbered here. In the distance to the west and north tongues of lightning licked the lake and the horizon pulsed with shifting electrical currents.

The woman turned and went inside.

The hungry hum of mosquitoes rose around Wally. In ebbing light of the setting sun, the weathered gray shack bled red. Wally climbed to the porch over missing steps and he rapped on the jamb. "Hello?"

He stepped inside and knocked again. "Anybody home?"

No furniture. Part of the ceiling was falling in.

Toward the rear at the last doorway he stopped. To his right was a room filled with metal oil drums, some tightly capped with steel bands to secure the lids. Empty sugar sacks littered the floor, and in one corner lay a pile of burlap bags with printed notice of "hulled corn, tender white."

In a room across the hall, wood had been cut as if for heat, but there was no fireplace. Boxes were stacked against a wall, filled with canning jars in one-quart sizes. Other crates held gallon jugs.

A tingle rippled up his spine and spilled down his arms. A mosquito buzzed near and Wally waved it away.

"Ma'am? Are you here?"

If so, she wasn't talking. Wally still didn't have permission to stay and until he did he was trespassing.

Then he heard voices and looked toward the lake. Topping the dune, headed this way, unmistakable in their overalls—he recognized the Fester boys and their father. Wally remembered Jeremiah saying they made whiskey at Kramer's Island. They would not be happy to discover him here.

One of the men whistled, and to Wally's horror, their hounds loped into view, snuffling the ground.

There was no escape out the back way. He couldn't get through the saw grass and palmetto without scaring up snakes, and surely the Festers would see him. The only way to go was up.

Wally climbed on top of a metal barrel, threw his coat and sack of food into the crawl space above, then hoisted himself between rafters. Decaying wood fell on the barrel below. He heard the Festers on the porch and the hounds coming down the hall.

"How much sugar you want us to take, Pa?"

"Bring a barrel."

With a soft *wuff*, a hound looked up. Wally pulled back from the opening. He heard one of the boys say, "Get out of my way, dog!"

The hound *wuffed* again and Wally held his breath.

"I said, git! You dumb dog."

They tramped out the front, the Fester boys carrying a barrel between them. Wally pushed up a loose sheet of roofing and watched them load the barrel into a flat-bottom boat. They poled away from shore.

Wally shuddered so hard the sheet metal rattled. He climbed down, ready to run, but across the lake lightning tiptoed toward him, and the low rumble of thunder warned of a storm to come.

He took some of the empty burlap sacks and climbed into the attic again, feeling his way to a corner. He spread the bags between rafters to make a pallet near a slope of the roof. By pushing up the metal he could see the lake.

Thunder grumbled, and through his opening he spied the Fester lanterns wigwagging through pines and palmettos.

Wally ate his bananas, then cheese and bread, listening to the approaching storm. He wondered if anybody at home would notice he was gone.

And the woman down by the lake. Where was she?

"Ma'am?" Wally called softly. "Can you hear me?" But she did not reply.

The rain came in a torrent. Wally lifted the flap of loose roofing and by the flash of lightning he saw the lake churning.

The Festers soon returned, thoroughly soaked, yelling vulgarities at the weather and one another. They chained their hounds on the porch and took off every stitch of clothing which they hung on barrels to dry. Through cracks in the ceiling, Wally saw the Fester boys naked and hairy. He thought of them as "boys" but they were grown men.

Ike Fester said, "We got fatback, cold chicken, and biscuits for supper—would you lookit this? Your ma sent wings again. Feed them to the dogs."

Lightning crackled and the sheet metal roof snapped in the wind. On the porch the hounds cowered and whined, ignored by their masters.

When the storm eased, the Festers put on their clothes, took the dogs, and poled their boat to a nearby point that they seemed to favor. Wally watched the wink of lanterns between trees. Safe again, at last he fell asleep.

He awoke at dawn, listened for voices, and hearing nothing, cautiously crawled across the rafters to ease himself down. He went to the lake and looked for the Festers, but they were gone.

He ate their leftover fatback and crumbs of biscuits in the bag. He found a gallon jug of what looked like water, except that it wasn't water. It smelled like weak kerosene. Wally tilted the jug and touched the liquid with the tip of his tongue. Whiskey! He sipped from the jar and the liquor burned into his stomach.

In the movies, when outlaws ordered whiskey at a bar, they made it look good. But if this jug was any example, liquor must be what his mother had called "an acquired taste," like anchovies and raw oysters. Just to be sure it was as bad as he

thought, Wally took another sip. It was better than the first sip.
So he took another.

After a while his toes wiggled without command. They didn't
look right and that horrified Wally until he realized his ankles
were crossed. He took another swallow . . . bared his teeth . . .
exhaled.

Out of curiosity he opened all the barrels. They contained
sugar mostly, and corn. He discovered a shotgun and boxes of
ammunition. In another barrel were matches, and more fatback
which he ate.

He thought about the hounds, but by now he was sure he
could outrun the dogs. In fact, he didn't care whether he did or
not. He imagined reaching down a dog's throat, seizing the animal by the tail and snatching him inside out.

Sip . . . sigh . . . .

He couldn't bare his teeth anymore because he couldn't feel
his lips. Nor the tips of his fingers.

Somehow—he didn't remember how—Wally got back into the
crawl space above the ceiling. He reached the pallet of burlap
sacks and fell onto it, peering under the flap of roofing.

On the lake, a gray heron moved with long-legged majesty,
lifting one foot carefully to place it before the other. The sky had
never been more blue nor the clouds whiter. The air had been
washed by rain and suddenly all that had been ugly became
beautiful. If there were mosquitoes, Wally didn't feel them. But
then he didn't feel anything. Not the ovenlike heat of the attic or
his own perspiration soaking burlap bags upon which he rested.
He hadn't slept well last night, constantly alert for the return of
the Festers. Right now he felt as if he could sleep forever.

He roused with a jerk, bashing his elbow on a rafter. For one
terrible moment he thought the whiskey had made him go blind.
But no, he'd slept away the day and night had fallen. His crocus
sack bedding was drenched and soured. His teeth wore lichen
sweaters. Pain shot through his brain from temple to temple.
Every burp brought a new flavor of old whiskey. Thinking of the
whiskey made him queasy.

The sound of voices rose from the lake and Wally shoved up

the loose roofing. He saw lanterns, heard the bark of a hound. The Festers were coming again. Sickly, he lay back on the sacks.

Wally heard the clatter of a barrel lid and Ike Fester swore coarsely. "Which one of you morons left this barrel ajar? The sugar is full of ants."

"Not me, Pa."

"Me neither."

"One of you did! We'll have to build a fire under each barrel to drive out the ants and—" He paused, then in the silence that followed, Ike said, "Somebody has been eating fatback and sampling our shine, boys. I'm going to catch me a thief."

Wally heard the snap of a breached shotgun and the crisp click of hammers drawn.

"I think I'll take a look in the attic," Ike said. "Cole, you check the whiskey under the house."

Wally pulled burlap over himself and pressed flat as he could between rafters.

"Pa, I hear the boat coming."

"First I'm going to shoot me a thief."

A lantern came through the access hole.

"Yo, Ike!" a man yelled from the lake. The rumble of a boat motor idled down to a putter.

"Pa, you've got to answer, or they'll leave."

"I know that, Aldo. I'm going to find the man who—"

"Yo, Ike!"

"Pa?"

"I'll burn this shack to the ground if I have to." Ike spoke to the shadows, "I'll feed your carcass to the gators."

Then he said to Aldo, "Chain them dogs."

The other son returned from beneath the house to report, "The whiskey is there, Pa."

Wally dared to breathe. Through loose roofing he saw a spotlight scan the shore and come to rest on Ike and his sons.

"Are you ready for us, Ike?"

"Ready as I'll ever be. Come on in."

The spotlight extinguished and the motor died. As they waded ashore, their lanterns looked like fireflies. *Cousin*, they called one another.

Including the Festers there were now five. They came to the shack to "taste test" the whiskey.

Wally was amazed to hear his own name: "Wally McManus is missing, Ike."

"I heard."

"By this time tomorrow, the law will be combing swamps and dragging canals. You better clear out."

The Fester boys and their cousins went to load moonshine into the boat, leaving Ike and the other man on the porch sipping whiskey. "I can't believe the white folks of Belle Glade abide that nigger-lover," Ike said. "If it was up to me, I'd burn him out and hang him too."

Their voices receded as the men stepped into the yard. By the glow of a lantern, Wally saw money change hands. The boat motor sputtered to life. After the vessel was gone Ike called out to the house, "What you saw, you best forget, Wally McManus! And best be gone too, or that'll be the end of you."

Mosquitoes buzzed Wally's ears.

His mother had once said, "Sometimes you have to reevaluate a situation." She was talking about Wally going to live with his father.

"Anthony can be a thoughtful loving person," she'd said. But he wasn't.

Trying to think of positive things to say, she finally said, "I'll make a list! The good things about Anthony Edward McManus." She managed to come up with a few: *witty, charming, a nice smile*. But Wally had seen none of the attributes his mother mentioned.

Nevertheless, it was time to reevaluate. He had no friends. He had no other place to go, except to his father. This was home now, as Jeremiah would say, *like it or not*.

Wally crawled across the rafters, feeling his way. He was about to drop his money coat when Cole Fester suddenly spoke in the darkened hallway. "He ain't here, Pa."

Wally shrank back. Ike struck a match and lit a lantern which he held high. He turned in a circle.

Beyond Ike—it was a miracle they didn't see her—stood the woman who had beckoned Wally from the lake. She waited outside a window, then slowly faded from view as Ike lowered the lantern.

"Okay," Ike said. "Let's go home."

chapter seven

The next morning when Wally arrived home, a crowd was waiting in the yard. They hustled him inside where he was confronted by Sheriff Leon Posey. Posey was really a deputy, but people called him "Sheriff." He wore a wide leather belt hung with holster, pistol, and handcuffs.

"You got any idea what all this activity has cost the community, son?"

"No sir."

"Manpower lost, time wasted. Most of these niggers need to be bringing in crops." The deputy shot an apologetic glance at Hattie and Minnie Lou. To Wally he said, "Over at the airport they were about to put up crop dusters to look for you."

Wally scratched a forearm already bloody from scratching. Out on the porch another deputy dismissed search parties, thanking them for coming to volunteer. Most of the men were black, marshaled by Hattie's father, but there were a few whites too. "Rednecks and idlers," Wally's mother would've called them.

"Is the boy all right?" somebody called.

"Chigger chewed and thirsty, but he's all right," the outside deputy replied.

Wally's throat was so dry his breath whistled. He scratched his other arm.

"You being a city lad," Posey said, "maybe you don't know about gators, snakes and quicksand bogs. Rats the size of cats. Panthers bigger than a dog. Bears."

He put hands on knees and bent to be nearer Wally. There was one hair like a unicorn's horn growing out of the tip of his nose.

"Saw grass that will rip you to shreds," Posey said. "Thorn

trees with poisonous barbs. One prick, a dip in stagnant water, and the next thing you know a doctor is chopping off an arm or leg to stop the spread of gangrene."

Out front, people started their motors. "Some of you men give those niggers a ride back to town," the yard deputy hollered.

Inside, Deputy Posey moved away then returned to stand over Wally. "Some dangers are so tiny you can't see them with your bare eyes," he said. "Every drop of swamp water is alive with germs looking for a young body. Walk around barefoot and you'll get ringworm. The Everglades is hostile, boy. You understand me?"

"Yessir."

"That's why folks came rushing to hunt for you. A few hours can mean life or death. Lost is bad enough, but running away was foolish."

"Yessir."

Behind the lawman, Jeremiah chewed off a fingernail and spit it on the floor. When Wally met Minnie Lou's gaze, she looked away.

"We're doing what we can to tame this godawful place," the deputy said. "Every day they're pumping off water, dredging canals and building dikes. But when you get beyond the paved road, it's a jungle. Am I right, Mr. McManus?"

"Right you are," Anthony said. He sat at the kitchen table wearing a long sleeve white dress shirt as if going to town. His fingers trembled and he slid them off the table into his lap.

"Folks in Belle Glade say you're a wealthy man, Mr. McManus. Is that true?"

"Define wealthy, Sheriff."

Posey's eyes narrowed to slits and he looked around the room. "I wouldn't define it as living like this, Mr. McManus."

"Our needs are simple," Anthony said.

"You prefer to live without modern conveniences?"

"We appreciate the aesthetic, Sheriff."

Wally saw the lawman's face flush. "Writers talk smart mouth, don't they, Mr. McManus? You think because I'm a county law officer I don't know the meaning of words like *aesthetic*?"

The other officer entered and Leon Posey waved him away. Posey stood at the door peering out. He spoke to Hattie and Minnie Lou behind him. "Y'all mind if I have a word with Mr. McManus alone?"

"I'll take Minnie Lou home," Hattie said. "Jeremiah, you and Wally come with us."

"Not Wally," the sheriff said. "What I have to say pertains to Wally. Is that the word, Mr. McManus? *Pertains?*"

Wally noticed a twitch under Anthony's right eye. Anthony rubbed it away while the deputy's back was turned, then sat up straighter as the lawman faced him. Posey put a hand on Wally's shoulder. "Are you this child's father, Mr. McManus?"

"I am."

"Look at him. Looks like he's been bagging bobcats. He needs a haircut and decent clothes. I've seen white trash take better care of their children. School starts in two weeks. Has this youngster had his shots?"

"His mother was a conscientious woman. I'm sure she took care of that."

Posey's hand slid off Wally's shoulder. "I've seen this boy all over town with Jeremiah, and where Jeremiah goes there's trouble. Don't you have any pride, Mr. McManus? When people judge this lad, they judge you too."

Anthony's gaze fell to the floor.

The deputy stooped to Wally's level again. "Why did you run away, son?"

Wally shrugged.

"When a boy runs from home, he's got a reason. What was your reason?"

"I don't know."

The sheriff stood up, adjusted his belt of hardware. "The last thing y'all need is public attention, Mr. McManus. But I'm going to report this to child welfare. I can't ignore these conditions, and this boy is headed for trouble."

He went outside to join the other deputy and they drove away in a patrol car. Wally waited for Anthony's wrath.

Anthony rubbed his eyes with a thumb and forefinger. "I hope you never do this again, Wally." Still massaging, he said, "Go take a bath."

"Yessir."

"There's a bottle of calamine lotion in the bathroom. Rub it on the insect bites."

"Yessir."

It was too early in the day for water to be hot. Shivering, Wally scrubbed himself, then smeared chalky pink lotion over stinging welts. He combed his hair, cleaned fingernails, and applied more medicine to places that itched most fiercely. He dreaded facing his father again, but he couldn't hide in the bathroom forever. Wrapped in a towel, he went to the kitchen.

He was alone.

Anthony was gone.

"You know how long I'd be gone before anybody came hunting for a body?" Jeremiah said. "There wouldn't be two bones touching by the time somebody found me. My granddaddy might give up a pine coffin to bury me, but he wouldn't come looking, unless I had his money in my pocket."

Hattie was standing at the stove cooking.

"But for your lily-white behind," Jeremiah said to Wally, "Granddaddy sends out a call for help and two hundred folks show up. Where's Precious? Precious is gone!"

"Jeremiah," Hattie said, "sweeten the tea."

"I'll do it," Wally offered.

"No, you won't," Hattie snatched the spoon from Wally's hand. "I told Jeremiah to do it."

"Now, now," Anthony soothed.

"And you shut up!" Hattie yelled.

She stirred potatoes and onions in a skillet. Fire flared and she sprinkled water on the coals to dampen the flames. "Jeremiah," she said, "if I have to ask again—"

Jeremiah scooped sugar, stirred the tea. "Everybody wanted to know why you didn't show up to sell sandwiches like you promised to do," Jeremiah said evenly. "Like you begged to do."

"I didn't beg, Jeremiah."

"Begged! Wanted to make money."

"I said, I'd rather sell than stand there."

"So they made more sandwiches than I could handle by myself. Where is Precious? I said you was sick. Then my grand-daddy sends out a call for help because you ran away. It was embarrassing to get caught lying like that. Brings shame on all of us. Everybody's asking, How come Precious ran away?"

"Jeremiah," Hattie pointed with a spatula. "Sit down, and no more talk about this mess."

She served their plates from the skillet.

"No meat?" Anthony asked.

"No god-damned meat."

"I was only asking, Hattie."

"I was only telling you."

"Next time you decide to run off," Jeremiah said, "ask me. I'll give you better ideas how to spend two nights."

Outside in the night, insects shrilled. Jeremiah chewed food noisily, and no one spoke again. After supper, Hattie went to her room, Anthony to the front porch swing. Wally cleared the table and washed dishes.

"Where did you go?" Jeremiah questioned him.

"It was where the Festers were moonshining."

"Kramer's Island? Did they see you?"

"No, but I ate their food and they know I was there."

"If the Festers caught you," Jeremiah said, "you'd be fish bait. You couldn't sleep on the ground. Did you climb a tree?"

"There's a shack out there."

Jeremiah took a plate from Wally's hand and dried it. "You could be dead, you know that? I've heard of the Festers killing people. You could be dead!" He took another plate and dried it. "So, what happened?"

Wally told about the shack and arrival of the Festers. He described the taste of whiskey and the headache which lingered even now as a dull throb behind his eyes.

When the dishes were finished and Anthony had gone to bed, Jeremiah led the way to their own bedroom. "Then what?" he whispered.

Wally spoke of Ike Fester's search for him, interrupted by the motorboat and the sweeping spotlight. He embellished it a little, describing Ike's raspy voice as he threatened to burn the shack, and the snarling dogs bounding at the attic. He added the scream of a panther for effect.

Jeremiah shivered.

Wally thought about asking for a quarter to continue, but in truth he enjoyed relating the story. He talked of water snakes and alligators, rats swimming toward cattails. He told about the storm and the discomfort of his hiding place. Wally deliberately lowered his voice, drawing Jeremiah nearer. Coming to the end of his story he recounted the moment when he was ready to climb down from the attic and realized Cole Fester was hiding in the dark hallway. *He ain't here Pa. . . .*

"Ike Fester's match spewed and the smell of sulfur rose toward the ceiling. He lit his lantern and held it high. It was a miracle they didn't see the woman," Wally said.

"What woman?"

"She led me to the shack."

"What woman?"

"I don't know her name."

"A woman at Kramer's Island?" Jeremiah said. "What did she look like?"

"She had blond hair, braided, and it fell over her shoulder. She was wearing jodhpurs—pants that fan out at the thigh, which is what a lady wears to ride horses."

"Riding a horse at Kramer's Island?" Jeremiah scoffed. "Where does she live?"

"I don't know. She never spoke to me."

"What!"

"She motioned me to come on, but then she hid."

"And she drew the Festers away from you."

"I didn't say that."

"She got on her horse and drew them off."

"I didn't say that, Jeremiah."

Jeremiah threw himself on his bed. "You had me for a minute. Sounded like Mr. McManus telling one of his lies."

"I wasn't lying."

"You must think I'm stupid," Jeremiah said. "A woman in riding trousers out at Kramer's Island? A horse would break a leg running in a bog."

"She was there, Jeremiah."

"Sure," Jeremiah sneered. "Sure she was...."

They lost their jobs selling sandwiches, and Jeremiah blamed Wally. In fact, it was a consequence of the changing season. Temperatures hovered at ninety degrees before daybreak, a promise of scorching heat by midmorning. Laborers balked at working the black muck fields longer than half a day, so sales of sandwiches plummeted.

Thereafter, Wally and Jeremiah went to town together but soon parted company. Wally's favorite refuge was an icehouse in the packing district. He enjoyed watching men make winter on the hottest days of summer. Huge blocks of ice slid out of a freezer through rubber flaps, down a chute to a screaming machine that reduced the blocks to snow. Ice crystals were blown through a large flexible hose into boxcars filled with crates of vegetables ready for shipment.

Wally grabbed a handful of crushed ice and retreated far enough to be unnoticed, near enough for second helpings.

"Did you pay for the ice you're eating?" Cole and Aldo Fester had caught him unawares. Cole's fingers dug into Wally's arm. "Did you steal the ice?"

"I don't think so," Wally stammered. "Who would I pay? It was going to melt anyway."

"Thing is," Cole said, "everybody does things other folks might not like. It's none of my business if you stole the ice, ain't that right?"

"Who should I pay?" Wally asked.

"What Cole is saying," Aldo said, "we'll mind our business and you mind yourn. We don't tell people you're swiping ice and you don't talk about us."

"Another thing," Cole said, "it'd be smart to stay away from Kramer's Island. Ain't nothing there that belongs to you."

The screech of the snow machine ended conversation for a moment. Ice melted in Wally's numbed fingers. "Are you going to hurt me?" he questioned.

"Now why would we do a thing like that?" Cole said. "We're buddies, ain't we?"

His eyes were yellow as milkwort. "Do we have us an understanding, Wally?"

"Yessir."

A packing house guard came over. He was so large his stomach strained his shirt buttons. "You Festers got business here?"

"No siree," Aldo said. "We was doing some business with our little buddy here, but that's finished now."

"I've told you before," the guard said, "I don't want you hanging around the packing houses."

"We was on our way, weren't we, Cole?"

"On our way," Cole said. He smoothed Wally's sleeve and smiled. Even his teeth were yellow.

They sauntered off, the guard watching. They stopped to read the label on a hamper, then paused again to leer at women sorting vegetables on conveyor belts. They eased down on the dock and hopped to the ground.

"Those men friends of yours?" the guard asked Wally.

"No sir."

"If you roost with buzzards, people will believe you eat dead meat. You understand what I mean?"

"Yessir."

"Who's your daddy?"

Before he had time to think, Wally lied. "My daddy is dead."

"Who's your mother?"

"She's dead too."

"Where do you live?"

"Atlanta. I'm an orphan. Visiting here."

"Who are you visiting?"

"I don't know their names. They're thinking about adopting me."

He'd gone too far. The guard said, "Get along home, boy."

Wally jumped from the platform into blistering sunshine.

Across the street the Festers were selling jars of whiskey to workers. When the packing house guard went to a telephone, the
Festers got into their truck unhurriedly.

"Hey Wally!" Aldo hollered. "Need a ride?"

"No," Wally said.

Aldo cranked up and slowly drove away, fenders of the pickup
rattling, muffler rumbling. The bottoms of Wally's feet were too
hot to stand still. He had no particular place to go, nothing to
do. He considered circling the packing house so he could return
from the other side. The guard was too rigilant.

Wally started toward home. He'd be glad when school began.

Wally was sitting at the kitchen table helping Minnie Lou shell butterbeans into a bucket. He had just mastered "unzipping" pods when the Fester hounds announced an approaching visitor.

He went to the front door as a red Chevrolet pulled into the yard. Out of the car stepped an attractive, young, slender, short woman with curly blond hair. She carried a clipboard, and seeing it, Minnie Lou said, "Mmmm-mmm-mmm."

When the woman saw Wally, she spoke from the yard below. "Wally McManus?"

"Yes ma'am."

"Is your father home?"

"He goes for a walk after work."

The woman studied her clipboard. "Hattie Willoughby?"

"She works at the colored funeral home."

She came up the steps on stumpy high-heel shoes; her legs glistened because she wore nylon hose. From the porch, she peered inside at Minnie Lou.

"Nobody here but me and the boy," Minnie Lou said.

"That's all right. I'll have a talk with Wally."

"Be best if you come back when folks be home," Minnie Lou advised.

The woman moved to the porch swing and sat down. She dabbed her forehead with a neatly folded white handkerchief. When she smiled, her eyes sparkled. She patted the swing beside her.

"Do you mind sitting with me, Wally?"

"No ma'am."

"My name is Edna Lanier. I want to be your friend."

"Precious ought to fetch his papa," Minnie Lou called.

"We're all right," Miss Lanier said.

Wally heard Minnie Lou, "Mmmm-mmm-mmm."

Miss Lanier said, "Tell me about your mother, Wally."

"She died."

"I'm sorry. Who looks after you now?"

"Hattie and my father."

"Precious, get you papa!" Minnie Lou demanded.

To Wally, Miss Lanier said, "Who is she?"

"Minnie Lou."

"Minnie Lou," Edna Lanier said sharply, "do your work and stop worrying about us."

She redirected her attention to Wally again. "School starts next week. Have you registered for classes?"

"Not yet."

"What grade are you?"

"I don't know. At Montessori we didn't have grades."

Miss Lanier made a note on her clipboard. "If you could live anywhere you wanted, Wally, where would that be?"

"With my mama."

"But she's dead."

"I know."

"No screened windows or doors," she observed. "Does this house have electricity?"

"No ma'am."

"What do you use for light?"

"Kerosene lamps."

"Did your mother have electricity?"

"Yes ma'am. Refrigerator. Fans."

Minnie Lou loomed in the door. "You oughtn't be asking this boy such questions when his papa is gone."

"We're having a nice visit, aren't we, Wally?"

"No ma'am," Minnie Lou said, "you knocking on the front door, but coming in the back. You got to leave now."

Edna Lanier's face flushed. She produced a business card and extended it to Minnie Lou. "I'm with the Department of Social Services. We've had a report of child neglect. Tell Mr. McManus

I'll be back this evening and I expect him to be here. I also expect Hattie Willoughby and Jeremiah."

Minnie Lou didn't take the card so Miss Lanier gave it to Wally. Then she put a hand on Wally's shoulder and he walked with her to the Chevrolet. "I'm your friend, Wally," she said. "I'm the best friend of little people everywhere. I'm a person who can get you out of here, if you wish to go."

"You can?"

"Tell your father I'll be back this evening."

As Wally watched her drive away, Minnie Lou said, "Fetch you papa, Precious."

Waiting for the social worker, Hattie demanded that Wally and Jeremiah take baths, then she complained there was no hot water for her. She changed clothes only to have them soaked with perspiration as she labored over the hot stove.

"There's no excuse for squalor," Anthony said. "What does Minnie Lou do around here?"

"She puts away clothes and sweeps floors," Wally said. "She makes beds and scrubs the bathroom. She—"

"Obviously she doesn't do it adequately," Anthony said. He pushed dust between the floorboards with one foot. "I think you should speak to her, Hattie."

They were helping their plates at the dinner table when the red Chevrolet arrived. Cicadas and tree frogs played alto as Miss Lanier came up the steps with her clipboard. The door was opened. There they sat in plain view, but she knocked anyway.

"Mr. McManus, I'm Edna Lanier from Child Welfare."

Anthony stood up. "Jeremiah, give the lady your chair."

"What about my food?"

"Take it with you. Have a seat, Miss Lanier. Would you care for supper?"

"No thank you." She pulled a chair away from the table and brushed it off.

"Iced tea?" Hattie offered.

"Nothing." Miss Lanier sat down, slender ankles almost

touching, the clipboard on her lap. "Will you verify information for me, Mr. McManus? Is Wally your son?"

"He is."

"You became his guardian upon the death of his natural mother?"

Behind her, Jeremiah slurped and chewed louder than usual.

"Does Wally suffer any physical or mental impairment which would excuse him from public schooling?" Miss Lanier asked.

Jeremiah returned to the table, standing between Anthony and Miss Lanier to dish up more of everything.

"I presume," Miss Lanier said, "this is Jeremiah."

She flipped pages on her clipboard. "Jeremiah attended school a total of ninety-four days last year. He has twice failed the fourth grade and is about to repeat the fifth. Is that right, Jeremiah?"

"I don't know," Jeremiah said, "and I don't care."

"Does anyone know?" Miss Lanier inquired. "Does anyone care?"

"You sure don't," Jeremiah accused. "You're not here about me."

"Jeremiah," Hattie said mildly, "don't be rude."

"It's not me she wants, Mama. I'm a little pickaninny. Pick that cotton, shoulder that bale."

Miss Lanier's eyes were blue ice. "The State of Florida requires citizens under age sixteen to attend school," she said.

"White children," Jeremiah countered.

"All children."

"Get educated so I can crawl a muck row weeding celery? What good is an educated nigger anyhow? My mama went to college and she can't get a job except with my granddaddy."

"This year the system will not be as forgiving of truancy," Miss Lanier warned.

"Not so long ago," Hattie said, "it was against the law to educate a Negro child."

"Fortunately, those days are past," Miss Lanier said. "A lot of people fought for your right to be educated. Are you about to thumb your nose at them?"

Miss Lanier turned to Anthony. "Mr. McManus, the State of Florida requires immunization against communicable diseases before a child enrolls in school. If you do not have validation of immunization, your son is required to take shots again. Perhaps you could contact his family physician and get a record of past inoculations."

"Wally," Anthony said, "do you know where you got shots in Atlanta?"

"No sir."

"In which case," Miss Lanier said, "you may get free shots at the public health clinic in Belle Glade. School starts next week, Mr. McManus. If these boys are not enrolled, they must appear before a juvenile court judge to determine if they are uncontrollable. Should the court decide the problem is with the parent, fines and jail time may be mandated."

"Jail?" Hattie yelped. "What if Jeremiah won't go?"

"Then he becomes a ward of the state and will be sent to a home for wayward boys," Miss Lanier said. "He will attend school one way or another."

"Not me," Jeremiah said defiantly.

Miss Lanier stood up. She stroked Wally's head. "These boys need shoes, Mr. McManus. Health laws prohibit bare feet in public buildings."

"Shoes!" Jeremiah wailed. "Forget it."

"If money is a problem," Miss Lanier said, "you may apply for public assistance at our office."

A kerosene lamp flickered and a wisp of smoke curled up from the globe. Without another word, Miss Lanier walked out into the night.

"I'm not wearing shoes," Jeremiah seethed. "They can hang me."

"All right, Anthony," Hattie snapped. "Now what?"

"Well," Anthony said, "this is what happens when we fall under the thumb of a bureaucrat."

"I want to know what you're going to do," Hattie cried.

"Whatever you want to do, Hattie. Buy shoes. Get shots. Whatever you want."

Hattie threw back her chair and ran to her room. Jeremiah said, "I'm not wearing shoes!"

Anthony followed Hattie to the bedroom. Wally heard his name, Hattie weeping. Astonished, he realized Jeremiah was on the verge of tears, too. "Don't nobody give me any trouble until you start messing up, Precious. I'm not wearing shoes. I'll move to the Bahamas first."

Jeremiah went to his bedroom and slammed the door so hard the house shook. Alone at the table, Wally watched a moth fall into mashed potatoes. He scraped food into bowls and covered them, stowing perishables in the icebox.

Out on the porch he sat in the swing. The smell of camphor overpowered decomposing hyacinths. The sky was so clear stars spread over Lake Okeechobee like rock salt on black silk.

He tried to visualize his mother and couldn't. She had been gone only three months and already he was forgetting her face.

Then he had a memory of her when she was healthy, working with potted plants in their Atlanta apartment. He recalled how hair fell around her face as she sat on the floor, leaning over the pots on an oil cloth. She didn't know he was watching and she was talking to herself.

That must be how she had looked as a little girl, playing on the floor.

Holding the memory, Wally dozed in the swing.

While he slept, somebody put a blanket over him.

The next morning Wally awoke on the swing as Jeremiah whispered, "Get up."

Fog enveloped the house. Wally couldn't see the ground for the mist. Hattie's voice rose angrily in the kitchen. "I will not take that child to get his shots, Anthony."

"Suit yourself, Hattie."

"You never had to take Jeremiah to school and I'm not taking Precious. When they ask about his mama, what do I say?"

"Say she died, Hattie."

"Then they want to know what am I, the maid?"

"Don't be ridiculous."

"Doesn't it bother you that I have to go tail-tucked and head hung, shuffle foot and hangdog, yassuh dis and yassuh dat?"

"If you don't want to do it, then don't do it, Hattie. Things have a way of working out anyway."

"If those boys are not registered for school," Hattie said, "welfare will be coming for them. I'm supposed to buy shoes, get their shots and have them enrolled all by myself?"

"Do as you will, Hattie, I don't give a damn."

"Nothing would please that welfare woman more than taking these boys," Hattie said.

"She's bluffing, Hattie."

"She's not bluffing! She's got the power and you know it."

Wally drew up his legs, making more room for Jeremiah to share the swing. Hattie came to the door and screamed, "How many times I have to say get dressed, Jeremiah?"

"I am dressed, Mama."

"Where are your shoes? Didn't you hear the woman say you need shoes?"

"I'm not going to wear shoes."

That response was lost on Hattie. She was in the kitchen again, yelling at Anthony. "They'll ask questions I can't answer. What is his blood type?"

"I don't know, Hattie."

"If they ask about brothers and sisters, what do I say?"

Their voices drifted to Anthony's office, then they were on the porch and into the yard, still arguing. Anthony terminated the debate by strolling down the lane toward his lonely retreat.

Hattie returned, hair askew, face drawn. "Where are your shoes, Jeremiah?"

"I've outgrown them."

"And yours?" she asked Wally.

"They're too small, Hattie."

She put a hand over her eyes. "Jeremiah," she said finally, "give Wally your shoes from last year. Wally, see if you can wear them just for today."

Jeremiah's Buster Browns looked new, but the insides were velvet with mildew. Wally dipped a rag in Clorox bleach and washed them out. The shoes were so narrow his instep curled, but he got them on.

The "free" clinic had been set up for migratory workers who otherwise would have no medical services. Wally accompanied Hattie and Jeremiah through an entrance marked "colored."

"You're on the wrong side," a nurse spoke to Wally.

"He's with me," Hattie said.

The nurse gave Hattie a form. "Fill this out." She took Wally by the wrist and led him into an examining room. The dread of inoculation was made worse by the shrieks of children in the hallway getting shots. After each injection, a raspy voice said, "There now, that wasn't so bad, was it?"

In hope of avoiding his turn, Wally tried to remember the name of his doctor in Atlanta. He could recall his mother's physician, the names of people at Emory Hospital, but not the person who had given immunizations. Therefore, he received shots in both arms and his rear end. Typhoid-tetanus stung the most, and the smell of alcohol made him dizzy. A doctor peered into his ears, down his throat, and thumped Wally's back. A nurse checked his blood pressure, height and weight. Then she said, "Wait outside for your nanny. I'll give her the papers."

Sweltering, Wally sat in the Ford coupe with both doors open while waiting for Hattie. He watched the procession of ill and wounded come and go. After an hour, Hattie emerged with Jeremiah in tow. Jeremiah squeezed into the passenger seat with Wally and stared straight ahead.

"Now," Hattie said, "the hard part."

All twelve grades of Belle Glade's white school were on one campus. The building was brick and stucco with columns on either side of a double front door. Hattie stopped across the street, motor idling. High school boys in short sleeve shirts and neatly pressed slacks sat with girls who wore full skirted dresses. Benches girdled the trunks of oak trees, and the aroma of mown grass made the air sweet.

"Not one broken window," Jeremiah observed. "Cement sidewalks and shady places to sit."

"Damn Anthony," Hattie said. "I'm not going inside. See the malt shop next door?" she directed Wally. "After you register, go there to wait for us. Watch for me. When we get back from the colored school, I'll park across the road, so pay attention. Don't make me come for you."

She gave him twenty-five cents and Jeremiah said, "You never paid me to wait for nothing!"

"You'll have to order something to sit there," Hattie instructed Wally. "First, go into the school office and tell somebody you came to register. Tell them your father's name. Miss Lanier might be there, or she might have told them to watch for you. If anybody asks about your father, say he's a little bit sick."

"He's a little bit sick a lot," Jeremiah said.

Wally got out. His trousers were too short, exposing socks that drooped for want of elastic. His last haircut was three months ago. When a breeze blew, the long hair made him feel something was crawling on his ears. The shoes were so tight he had to take little steps, and the bleach had begun to burn his feet.

He walked with arms close to his sides hoping nobody would notice him. Inside the building students clustered in a wide corridor. Now and then laughter reverberated down the hall. The office was there at the entrance.

He told a receptionist his name and she said, "Oh," and summoned a teacher.

"So you are the young Mr. McManus," the teacher said. Her name was Mrs. Bullock. She wore a print dress with frolicking Scotch terriers as the pattern. "Where is your father?"

"He couldn't come. He's sick."

"I had hoped to meet him," she said. "I've read his books."

Mrs. Bullock led Wally to a room where dust rode shafts of sunlight entering a high window. "I've spoken to the faculty at the Montessori school in Atlanta," she said. "They suggest I test you at a ninth grade level, but that would make you the youngest child in class. I must decide what to do with you."

On multiplication, division, fractions, and percentages, Wally did well. He faltered at second year algebra. Then Mrs. Bullock changed subjects. "I will say a sentence and you fill in the blank," she explained. "Aristotle was—"

"A Greek philosopher who studied under Plato, and who taught Alexander the Great. He died 322 BC."

Mrs. Bullock sat back to look at him. "My father used to get sick too," she said. "I told fibs to hide his troubles. Then my mother died when I was about your age and a court decided my father could not care for me."

She gazed at particles of dust climbing rays of sunshine. "They took me away from my father and sent me to a foster home."

"Did you like it?" Wally asked.

"Nothing is perfect."

"Was it better than your real home?"

"The court thought it was. However, with my help you can avoid such unhappiness, Wally." She patted his arm with a cold hand. Her lips stretched. It was meant to be a smile. "If you need anything," she said, "come talk to me."

By the time Wally got to the malt shop, bleach in his shoes had set his toes afire. He ordered Coca-Cola with a lot of ice and put cubes between his toes. In maddening irony, Sons of the Pioneers sang "Cool Water" from the jukebox.

When Hattie arrived, she pulled up across the street. Jeremiah was slumped in the seat beside her. Wally got in and Hattie jammed the car into gear and turned toward home.

That evening they ate in silence. An amphibian chorale serenaded the night and katydids replied from stands of bamboo.

"Tomorrow I will have to buy clothes for these boys," Hattie announced. "They need haircuts. There are no free clinics for shoes and haircuts."

"If that is a reference to the inoculations," Anthony said, "they aren't free. We pay for them with our taxes."

After a heavy lull, Anthony asked, "How did enrollment go?"

Wally realized the question was for him. "It was all right."

"What grade will you be in?"

"I don't know yet."

Anthony pushed back from the table. "Whatever is required, Hattie. Get what is needed." Then he went out to the Ford and drove away.

Jeremiah stood at the stove helping himself to stew. Hattie slumped in her chair, her head down, food uneaten.

"Hattie," Wally said, "thank you."

She nodded, but she didn't look at him.

chapter nine

When they wanted to exclude the boys, Hattie and Anthony spoke French and Wally hated it.

"*Pourquoi pas?*" Hattie snuggled in Anthony's lap at the breakfast table. "*Petit vin, chanson d'amour? Pour de bon,* Anthony."

"I don't think so, Hattie."

"Come on sweetheart," she teased. "We'll go to *Coq du Village,* enjoy a fine meal, dance a dance or two."

"I don't think so, Hattie."

"Anthony, why not?"

"I can't allow myself to be distracted, Hattie. I'm at a critical juncture in my work."

"Fine. Show me. Let me read what you've written."

"You know I don't show my work until editing is complete."

"One paragraph. Read me that. One sentence then!"

Irritably, he pushed her, and Hattie got off his lap. "A day away from work won't hurt you and it might help, Anthony. How long has it been since we saw Pierre Arneaux?"

Jeremiah leaned toward Wally. "This Pierre walks like he's holding a nickel between his knees. Kisses everybody, men and women."

Conversation between Hattie and Anthony escalated to rapid French and Jeremiah continued, "At this place, *Coq du Village*"—he exaggerated the pronunciation—"the menus are in a foreign language so nobody knows what they're ordering. Customers talk in low voices like the cook is laid out dead in the kitchen. Waiters stand around watching you eat."

"*Qui est fait est fait!*" Hattie yelled.

"They sell gray meat sprinkled with yard grass," Jeremiah

said. "People will eat anything if it has a fancy name. They call chicken *poulet* and a pig is *cochon*. Look out for anything called *foie*. The safest bet is the gray meat and grass."

"*Quoi bon*, Anthony?" Hattie demanded. "Are we to avoid a good friend of long standing just because he knew Kathryn?"

Wally jolted.

They were back to French again, even more angrily. Anthony stormed out onto the porch, wheeled and shook a finger in Hattie's face. Even in French, Wally recognized vulgarities.

Anthony went down the steps two at a time and from the porch Hattie hollered, "I'm taking the car, Anthony. I'm going to Palm Beach, you hear me? I'm going to *Coq du Village* whether you like it or not."

She returned to the kitchen, shouting, "Take a bath, both of you! Scrub your feet with a brush. Trim your toenails."

Wally bathed while Jeremiah sat on the closed lid of the commode hugging one knee, cutting his nails. A sliver flew into the tub, others to the floor. "Last time we went to *Coq du Village*," Jeremiah said, "there was an old man at the next table. He must've been eating boiled cabbage and butterbeans. One fart after another, and you know what? People acted like they'd gone deaf and their noses died. I couldn't stand it. Mama sent me out to sit outside, and it was a merciful thing to do."

"You'd better not repeat that performance, Jeremiah," Hattie called from the kitchen.

Wally changed places, clipping his toenails while Jeremiah bathed in the tub.

"If you say one negative word," Hattie warned from afar, "you will suffer, Jeremiah, and I don't mean maybe."

"Another thing," Jeremiah whispered. "Going to *Coq du Village* makes Mama walk funny and talk funny."

They had to have shoes to go shopping for shoes. Hattie bought two pairs of tennis shoes at the five-and-dime in Belle Glade. The smell of canvas and rubber brought back memories of the last time Wally had gone shopping with his mother. Last school year. So long ago.

Jeremiah chose to ride in the rumble seat, so Wally was up front with Hattie. "How long have you known the man at *Coq du Village?*" Wally asked.

"A long time. Before the war."

Hattie wore sunglasses that mirrored muck fields and Brahman cattle grazing beside hyacinth-choked canals. The wind whipped her scarf.

"In Paris," Hattie said, "Pierre Arneaux owned another place called *Coq du Village,* which means 'cock of the town.' It was where writers, artists, actors and playwrights went for a drink. I was a child, although I didn't think so then. I wanted to sing and be treated like—"

Hattie thrust her arm out the window and banged the car door. "Jeremiah, stop kicking the wall!"

Then she said, "He drives me crazy kicking."

"Did you like my mother?" Wally asked.

"Listen, Wally, nobody plans these messes, they happen. Your daddy fell into the bottle and I kept trying to bail him out. Then war came and we got caught up in the Resistance."

"Where was my mama?"

"She wasn't there when Anthony needed her, that's all I know."

It had been so long since Wally was in a department store he'd forgotten the soft ping of bells, the quiet dignity of customers. But he hadn't a moment to enjoy the experience; Jeremiah raced up and down escalators, yelling for Wally to join him. Meantime, Hattie sauntered the cosmetics aisle sampling colognes and sniffing her wrists.

Jeremiah collided with a mannequin and, temporarily chastened, apologized. Then he realized it was a dummy and stuck his head up her skirt. A floorwalker told Hattie to "curb" her child or leave.

In the clothing section, a saleswoman challenged Hattie icily. "Is there something you want?"

Hattie's reaction was more that of Minnie Lou than herself. Her shoulders slumped, her voice got small. "We need school clothes for this child," she said, pushing Wally forward.

The clerk looked past Hattie at Jeremiah circling a rack of trousers. "Is that colored boy with you?"

"Yes ma'am."

"He shouldn't touch things you aren't buying."

"Jeremiah," Hattie said tonelessly, "don't touch things."

Buying Wally's clothes took time. He had to try on each garment and model it for Hattie. Now and then she told the clerk, "Give us a second one of these, a size larger."

"Isn't Jeremiah going to try it on?" Wally asked.

Jeremiah effected a drawl, "Us colored folks can't try on nothing! Might give white folks the epizootics."

"Is that true?" Wally asked.

Leaving the store, Jeremiah said, "Precious, you don't know nothing about nothing."

From there they went to colored town in West Palm Beach. The sun was so hot, spit sizzled on the sidewalk. The streets were narrow lanes between tightly clustered garishly painted buildings. Storefronts were sulphur yellow with vivid red signs advertising shoes, three dollars and up. Below that offer: GOOD CLOTHES NEW AND USED.

Walkways were shaded by sheet metal awnings. Street musicians played homemade contraptions designed more for rhythm than melody. There were cigar box banjos, paper-covered combs, and oil can drums. Grinning boys tap-danced on an improvised stage, their taps made of soda bottle caps nailed to toes and heels of their shoes.

Vendors sold sugar cane stalks and sausage sandwiches. The air was filled with the smells of sauerkraut, popping corn, and meat sizzling over open grills. Children ate cones of shaved ice flavored with grape, cherry or orange syrup.

Following Hattie and Jeremiah, Wally met the stony gaze of black men who assessed him, then laughed contemptuously. Inside the clothing store, it was Jeremiah who got preferential treatment this time.

"That white boy with you?"

"Yes," Hattie said.

It was obvious they didn't like him, and Wally told himself he didn't care. He didn't like them either. Not their raucous music or their raucous laughter.

He watched Jeremiah being fitted and fussed over. The trousers Jeremiah selected were baggy at the thighs but pegged above his ankles. His shirt was a blouse with balloon sleeves. The costume was testimonial to a tasteless lifestyle. The shirt was purple, socks canary yellow, leather shoes dyed red, green and brown. Added to this, Jeremiah selected a yellow silk scarf which he wrapped around his neck and tucked into his shirt like an ascot.

A salesgirl arched her back and cried, "Oooooh-eeee! Look at this boy. Going to turn some eyes in this outfit!"

It was the wardrobe of a clown, but Hattie did not protest. If that's what Jeremiah wanted, that's what she bought.

Black children peeked through opened front doors, watching Wally. On the street, youths tap-danced and musicians pounded their instruments in a monotonous shivaree, the audience clapping hands to keep time.

Jeremiah strutted over and turned before Wally. "What do you think?"

"It's okay, I guess."

"Okay is right!" Jeremiah examined himself in a full-length mirror. "Womens, cross your legs, here I come!"

But that was not what he wore to *Coq du Village*.

"White boy's rags," Jeremiah disdained his slacks and dress shirt. "Argyle socks and a necktie!"

They'd gotten their haircuts in colored town, shaved on both sides three fingers above the ears and cropped close on top. Wally itched from clippings that slid beneath his collar. At *Coq du Village*, a valet took the Ford coupe to park it. Wally tasted sea salt in the air. Gulls squealed above the boom of the surf. Hattie led them down a flagstone walkway beneath a canopy with scalloped borders that rippled in the breeze. She placed each foot precisely before the other, her shoulders back, head high.

"Have you reservations?" the maitre d' inquired.

"No," Hattie said.

He looked at a datebook, pondered a moment, then took them to a small table in a distant corner. It was perfect, Wally thought, right next to the swinging doors of the kitchen. But a moment later a stocky man, no taller than Wally, rushed toward them as if he truly held a coin between his knees. He swooped up Hattie, as well as a short man could, and kissed her cheeks left-right-left. Tears glistened in his eyes, more kisses left-right-left. Then he snapped his fingers and waiters came running.

They were moved to a large table with a glass top beside a fountain which overlooked an indoor courtyard, an oasis of palm trees and flowering plants. A string quartet played classical music. Pierre Arneaux seated Hattie, kissed her hand and held it. He had a tiny mustache beneath a large hooked nose and very white teeth.

When menus arrived, Pierre waved them away and briskly issued orders. Only then did he seem to notice Jeremiah and Wally.

"Jeremiah! *Bonjour.*"

"Hey, Mr. Arneaux."

"And this, your friend?"

"Pierre," Hattie intervened, "this is Kathryn's son, Wally."

The man's eyelids fluttered.

"Kathryn died," Hattie said.

He reverted to French, and Hattie interpreted. "Pierre is sorry," she said to Wally. "Your mother was a handsome woman. He will remember her soul in his prayers."

"Thank you," Wally said.

"I hope for these years she was happy," Pierre said to Wally. "Paris was *sans contentement* for Kathryn. She did not like it. Not the river Seine, or the Eiffel Tower, or the art, or Debussy. She did not like my food!"

Wally remembered his mother's favorite treat, pimento cheeseburgers from the Varsity Drive-in, in Atlanta.

The Frenchman searched Wally's face. "Ah, yes, I see Kathryn," he said. "The eyes, she is there looking back at me."

It struck Wally that Pierre Arneaux didn't like her, so he asked, "Did my mother like you, Mr. Arneaux?"

"She said I was a frog," Pierre said. "She wanted cowpeas with pork—"

"Black-eyed peas with ham hocks," Hattie explained.

"And for my musicians to play songs of the mountains—how do you say it, Hattie?"

"Hillbilly music."

"Paris was not for her the place to be."

Waiters delivered food and Pierre lifted lids of covered dishes, reciting the contents while Hattie murmured appreciatively.

"I have a picture of your mother," Pierre said to Wally. "I will show it to you, but you may not have it. Many people in the photograph are dead, and it is all I have to remember them."

After Pierre left the table, Hattie spoke as if Wally had asked. "I was a singer in Pierre's place. Anthony and Kathryn were frequent customers, so I saw them often."

Pierre Arneaux returned with a framed black-and-white photograph. It was a group of people standing around a piano. Pierre put a finger on a stranger's face. "My beloved Anton, dead by execution during the war." He touched another image, "That is me. This is Hattie—"

She was even more beautiful then.

Pierre identified Anthony, a thin young man with a cigarette in one hand. And Kathryn....

She seemed unprepared to be captured on film, her eyes wide as though startled. She wore a long dress covered with sequins, her hair was short with finger waves. Wally studied her for a sign of pregnancy—was he in the picture, too? But no, the dress was tight over a flat tummy. Her arms hung straight by her sides, and she was pigeon-toed, which made her seem vulnerable somehow.

"The Nazis were coming," Pierre said hoarsely. "We clung to one another, didn't we, Hattie?"

"Yes, we did, Pierre."

He took back the picture. "Friends were tortured, loved ones executed. But for you, Hattie, and Anthony, I too would be dead."

Pierre used a napkin to polish glass covering the photograph.

"Tell Anthony I love him, Hattie," he said. "Tell him come to see me."

"I will, Pierre."

Music rose as the string quartet bent to their task. Wally thought of his mother, homesick for America and southern ways. In Pierre's photograph she'd been dressed for fun, but she alone was unsmiling. She wore a shiny dress and high heel shoes, a feather boa around her neck. Everyone looked toward the camera except Hattie and Anthony.

They were looking at one another.

During the forty-five mile drive back to Belle Glade, Jeremiah was in the rumble seat again, this time to sleep. The moon hung low and stars winked on the horizon. Warm air swept the interior. Hattie's face was illuminated by lights from the dashboard.

"Hattie," Wally said, "will you tell me the truth about something, or don't tell me at all?"

After a moment, she said, "All right. What is it?"

"Did my mother leave Anthony because of you?"

Hattie hesitated so long Wally thought she'd decided not to answer. Then she said, "We always have excuses to offer, and others to blame for our troubles. Kathryn accused me in the beginning, but she knew I was not the trouble between them."

Insects dappled the windshield, others swerved and survived. "Did she know about Jeremiah?" Wally asked.

"She knew I was pregnant. Everybody did. What did Kathryn tell you?"

"She didn't tell me anything."

"Well," Hattie said. "She told Anthony she wanted a baby and then she wanted to leave him. That was after Jeremiah."

Wally yearned for a pal like his friend Randall Carney in Atlanta. Smart in class, but not a smart aleck, Randall said funny things and was quick to laugh. He enjoyed Monopoly, Chinese checkers, and chess. He invited Wally for overnight visits and his mother treated Wally as her own.

They had a lot in common. That's what Wally wanted in a new friend—things in common.

He and Randall had been close, until Mr. Carney got in trouble with the law. Suddenly one morning without notice the Carneys were gone. If Wally knew where they were, he might consider living with Randall and his parents today, but he'd never seen them again.

He reminded himself that school in Belle Glade wouldn't be like Atlanta. Nothing in Belle Glade was like Atlanta. At Montessori, he stayed with the same teacher all day. She knew his interests and abilities. He wasn't required to compete with other students and there was no such thing as *average*. He was expected to do the best he could and advance at his own pace.

In Belle Glade, eighth graders began the school day in a "home" room. On the hour a bell sounded, signaling change in location and subjects. Students from class to class were not always the same ones as in homeroom. But Naomi Noonan shared every hour with Wally except gym class. She was a skinny girl with a sunken chest. Her arms were so long her fingertips almost touched knees that looked like oranges stuffed into stockings. While she talked, she twirled her long straight auburn hair, and when she put her elbows on the desk her shoulder blades stuck out like wings. She wore eyeglasses that magnified an unblinking stare.

"See the gap between my teeth," she said. "That's called 'diastema.' Did you know that?"

"No."

She removed her spectacles and chewed a well-gnawed piece that hooked over her ear. "The boy who sits behind you in homeroom has diastema. What's his name?"

"I don't know."

"He looks older than us."

"Yes, he does. I think they put him back a couple of grades because he doesn't speak English very well."

Naomi twirled her hair and chewed her glasses. "Do you think he has hair in his armpits?"

Wally couldn't imagine the relevance of that information. "I don't know," he said.

Naomi pondered the thought with blue eyes wide. "If I knew for sure he has hair in his armpits, I'd know a lot of things," she said. "You could find out."

"Me? How?"

"As we pledge allegiance to the flag, when he salutes, turn around and look up his sleeve."

But the boy didn't salute like a soldier. He put a hand over his heart, elbow down. "Well," Naomi said, "I'll have to ask somebody in his gym class. Do you have hair in your armpit, Wally?"

"No."

Two weeks after school started, a hurricane swept South Florida and rain fell in torrents. Minnie Lou came to keep house, arriving in the same hearse that took Hattie to work. The driver was Minnie Lou's husband, Ezekiel "Eazy" Jackson. He was Minnie Lou's opposite: She was tall and thick-bodied, Eazy was short and wiry; she was utterly black, he was the tint of cinnamon; she was dour, he wore a constant grin that exposed buckteeth.

Riding to school, Wally and Jeremiah sat in the rear between a coffin and a curtained window. Hattie rode up front with Eazy.

"They can't bury the decedent," Eazy explained. "The grave gets so full of water a coffin bobs right up again."

Wally was dreading his arrival at school in a vehicle marked THREE PALMS FUNERAL HOME. "Dig two feet down and you're going to hit water in the Glades," Eazy continued. "We have to heap a heap of soil on a grave as it is. During the hurricane of nineteen and twenty-eight before they built the new shell dike around Lake Okeechobee, floods caused caskets to pop up everywhere. In those days a corpse didn't carry identification with him. Nowadays we put that in a casket for just in case."

Eazy pulled into the school driveway behind a bus, as near a breezeway as possible. Wally dashed for cover and Naomi appeared beside him. "You rode in an undertaker's car? Is there a body in there?"

"Yes."

She gripped his arm. "Man or woman?"

"I don't know. The casket is closed."

For the rest of the day Naomi wouldn't leave Wally alone. "Did it scare you, riding beside a dead person?"

"No."

"Was there an odor?"

"No."

The storm lasted three days and the news of Wally's transportation had spread. Naomi walked along beside Wally and fielded questions from other students on his behalf. "There was a body in the hearse," she announced, "but the casket was closed and we don't know the sex."

Wally tried to ignore Naomi, pretending to be engrossed in a book or distracted by unfinished homework. He didn't linger in the library or dally after lunch. But Naomi was not to be discouraged.

In history class, she slipped him a note. "Somebody said your mother is—" she had erased various words and settled on "not white."

Wally penned a careful reply. "My mother died."

"Is your daddy white?" she wrote.

He nodded curtly.

"But your brother is colored?"

He was deciding whether to answer when the teacher confiscated their messages. She stood over Wally and silently read the notes. "Suppose you two save this discussion until after school," she suggested.

That afternoon, gusting winds hurled rain onto the breezeway where students gathered and Wally waited for the hearse. "Oh, W-a-a-a-l-l-y," somebody called. "Yooo-hooo, W-a-l-l-l-y! Here comes the nigger digger."

Eazy stepped out of the hearse, opening an umbrella, but Wally bounded for the rear door, instantly soaked and miserable. Eazy got back in, joking, "You won't need a bath this night."

Sitting behind the casket, Jeremiah asked, "How do you like school, Precious? Being with your own kind, how do you like that?"

Eazy slammed on brakes and the casket shot forward dumping Wally and Jeremiah on their backs. "Whew!" Eazy whistled. "It wouldn't do to hit no white boy. They'd skin me alive."

A student stood in front of the hearse, his clothes drenched. He posed with arms extended like a looming skeleton, mouth agape as he wiggled his fingers.

Finally, the boy moved and Eazy shifted gears with a quivering hand. "Look at this rain," Eazy said. "Going to have some flooding if this keeps up."

Answering Jeremiah's question, Wally said, "I don't like this school."

Jeremiah nodded. "At least you got that much sense."

Wally knew when Jeremiah planned to skip school. He put on his gaudiest blouse and pegged trousers. He even wore shoes, "Because womens likes them."

He preened and strutted and neither Hattie nor Anthony seemed to notice.

"Nobody cares whether I go to school," Jeremiah said. "The thing I keep wondering is why you go to school if you don't like it."

"It's better than a reformatory."

"I hear they've got swimming pools up at reform school."

"It's a prison, Jeremiah. Besides, I need an education to get out of here."

"If education would get me gone," Jeremiah said, "I'd be studying every minute."

They parted company at the footbridge leading to colored town. "Loan me two dollars, Precious."

"I don't have two dollars."

"You lie." Jeremiah squinted toward the packing houses. "Here comes that girl."

Naomi's feet flopped sideways as she ran toward them.

"See you later," Jeremiah said, and he hurried across the bridge.

Naomi arrived breathless. "Was that your colored brother?"

"He's not my brother. Where are you coming from, Naomi?"

"I live upstairs at the packing house. My daddy is the guard. Remember the day he chased off the Festers and told you to leave? I was watching. Daddy asked if I knew you. I didn't then. Do you like comic books?"

"Some of them."

"Bugs Bunny, Porky Pig, Daffy Duck," she recited subjects as they strolled. "Captain Marvel, Superman, Superboy, Superwoman, Batman, Green Hornet—"

"I usually read books," Wally said.

"What about your brother? Does he read comics?"

"Jeremiah doesn't read much of anything."

"Have you seen him naked?"

"Why do you ask that, Naomi?"

"Is he colored all over?"

Irritated, Wally said, "Are you white all over?"

They walked a short distance before she spoke again. "It doesn't matter to me if your family is colored."

"Yeah, well," Wally said. "Thanks a lot."

It became a regular pattern on days when the weather was good. Naomi would wait for Wally and Jeremiah at the footbridge.

"Is there something wrong with her?" Jeremiah asked.

She *was* different. But she was the only person in school who sought Wally's company. And she *did* invite him to her home.

Wally had never seen so many comic books. Stacked from floor to ceiling, sorted by subjects and the number of publication, pulpy paper filled the apartment with a musty smell like old newspapers.

"What do you do with them?" Wally asked.

"Daddy and I read them," Naomi said. "We trade with other collectors. I have every edition of some of these. Want to read any?"

"Not right now, thanks."

Naomi's father had been watching Wally since his arrival. He said, "Don't I know you?"

"No sir."

"Where do you live?"

"Out at Chosen."

"Who are your parents?"

"My mother died."

Mr. Noonan shifted in his sturdy overstuffed chair, eyes darting as he tried to make a mental connection. Naomi said, "Now, Daddy, stop being a guard. This is my friend, Wally."

Friend.

It sounded wonderful.

Changing classes, Naomi adjusted her stride to match Wally's. "Never mind about the boy who sits behind you in homeroom," she said. "He does have hair in his armpit."

"How did you find out?"

"I told him I saw a spider go up his sleeve and helped him hunt for it. Looks like a swamp in there."

"So now, what do you know?"

"He can make babies. It takes a boy and girl with hair in their armpits. My mama told me that. She's a midwife so she knows all about babies. If you'd like, I can get you in to watch a birthing sometime. It's real exciting."

Naomi described the position, legs up, mother wailing.

"There's a lot of pushing and heavy breathing and out comes the baby. It's sort of messy."

Now it was his turn to follow her.

"It starts with sex," Naomi expounded. "The boy gets on top and the girl on the bottom. He sticks his peewee inside and squirts juice which goes to an egg and makes a baby."

As he listened, Wally didn't have to ask about "peewee"; his pounded to attention.

"Not every woman can have babies," Naomi continued. "My Aunt Rowena never did. Mama said it's because Aunt Rowena is too stingy to give up an egg."

Naomi interrupted Wally's thoughts. "Haven't you ever seen anybody do it?"

"No."

"Not your mama or anybody?"

"My mama wouldn't do that!"

"She did it with somebody. That's how babies are made."

It was a disturbing thought.

"How about your daddy and your colored mother?"

"I've heard the bed knocking in the room next to mine."

"That's when they're doing it!" Naomi said.

It became their major topic of conversation. Contemplating who had hair and who hadn't, who probably did and who didn't do it. Naomi claimed most women and all men had probably done it at least once. That knowledge gave new dimension to nearly everybody, including Wally's teachers.

He tried to imagine them doing what Naomi so graphically described, but he'd never seen a woman nude and wasn't sure just where the peewee went. Naomi drew pictures and Wally developed a constant ache. During the change of classes he walked with one hand jammed in a pocket, groaning. He didn't dare go to the bathroom for fear other boys would see his problem.

At night, he lay awake and listened to the rhythmic thump of Anthony's bed and suffered unrelenting pressure and pain. By day he spent an awful lot of time looking at armpits. For the first time he noticed Jeremiah's curly fuzz. Not much, but more than Wally's own armpit which was smooth as a puppy's tongue.

He pulled Naomi aside to share the information.

"Curly?" she said. "You saw it?"

"I did."

She peered at him with eyes the blue of burning gas—something he'd witnessed in science class.

"What we need to do," Naomi said, "is get Jeremiah to my place."

"What for?"

"To look at comic books."

"What for?"

"Just do it, that's all. I'll take over from there."

"If he does it," Wally said, "I want to do it too."

"But of course," Naomi said.

Getting Jeremiah to Naomi's was not as easy as Wally might have thought. There were restrictions, she said. "It can't be when my parents are home. And Jeremiah can't suspect what we're planning. I want to know him first."

"What do you want to know? I'll tell you."

"Just tell him he can come read comic books. Why are you shaking?"

"I don't know."

"Are you cold?" She put a hand on his leg and stroked. "Your poor little peewee feels like a thumb."

Suddenly he squirted on himself. Wally tore away from Naomi and ran. He ran all the way to Chosen and hid beneath the bridge. He pulled down his pants and examined the sticky mess.

Dreadful as it was, there'd also been an exhilarating sensation. At last, the peewee was tamed and lay docile and unthreatening.

Wally didn't tell Jeremiah exactly where they were going, or why. "I want to show you something," he said.

They scaled a fire escape, crossed a roof over the packing house, and walked a ledge to Naomi's window. She'd helped map the route a day before. Wally squeezed inside and Jeremiah followed. Immediately, Naomi closed the shutters and latched them.

"Jeremiah," Wally said, "this is Naomi Noonan."

Jeremiah looked around the darkened room. Comics were

stacked higher than their heads.

"Want to read some funny books?" Naomi offered.

"No," Jeremiah said. "I reckon I better go."

"Don't you want to stay and have a cold soda pop?" Naomi tempted. "We have orange and ginger ale."

When Naomi returned with the drinks, she watched Jeremiah with her unblinking blue eyes. "Wally and I were talking about sex," she said.

"You didn't tell me that," Jeremiah accused Wally.

"Talking about people with hair in their armpits," Wally said.

"How babies are made," Naomi added.

Jeremiah handed Naomi his empty soda bottle and stood up.

"Wally has never seen anybody do it," Naomi said.

"Precious never saw nothing," Jeremiah noted. He looked from her to Wally and back to her again. "I know the games some womens play," Jeremiah said. "It wouldn't be smart to diddle with me like you maybe diddle with Precious. On account of, I know what's what, whether he does or not."

Then he said to Wally, "Let's go."

"You don't have to go," Naomi insisted.

"Yeah we have to," Jeremiah said. "Get up, Precious. Let's go."

They left the way they'd entered, by way of the roof and fire escape.

"You are so dumb," Jeremiah said.

They walked railroad tracks toward the Chosen road. The smell of axle grease and creosote mixed with smells of vegetables from the packing houses.

"So dumb!" Jeremiah said.

"I may be dumb, but you were too scared to stay, Jeremiah."

Jeremiah wheeled and hit Wally's chest with a fist. "You wouldn't know smart when you see it! That girl will get you whipped. But *me,* she'll get me killed. Her daddy comes upstairs and catches me there, he'd shoot me and not one white man in Belle Glade would hold it against him."

"But she wanted to, Jeremiah."

"Like that counts for something," Jeremiah said. "I heard

about a colored yardman did just what a white lady wanted. She came to him and peeled off his clothes. Know what they did to him? Tied one leg to a tree, other leg to a car, and drove off."

The thought was so atrocious, Wally halted between rails. "Is that true?"

"It's told for true. I reckon it is."

They slid down a cinder hill to the underpass. Wally said, "If I got caught with Naomi, what would happen?"

"Probably nothing," Jeremiah said. "You can do anything you want and pretty much get away with it. That's what I hate. A white boy is just being a boy even if he's with a colored girl. But let a black boy look at a white girl and they'll hang him."

When they reached the dike, Wally sat in the shade of an Australian pine while Jeremiah threw sticks into the water. A breeze from the lake brought a murmur from boughs overhead.

"Next time you go back," Jeremiah said, "look at those comic books. There isn't a colored person in them."

Moorhens squawked and walked lily pads below. Ospreys soared overhead.

"Me, I'm a nigger," Jeremiah said. "No amount of reading or going to school will change that. I'll always be a nigger."

chapter eleven

Next day at the footbridge, Naomi was waiting. "Uh-oh," Jeremiah said. "I'll see you later, Precious." He scampered up cinder beds of the railroad and took a long way to colored town.

"All right, Wally," Naomi demanded, "what did you tell him about me?"

"I didn't tell him anything."

"You must've told him something. What did you talk about after you left my place yesterday? Talked about me, didn't you?"

"Only for a minute."

"What did you say in a minute?"

"Jeremiah said he was afraid you'd get us in trouble."

"He knew what we planned to do?"

"You practically told him."

Naomi walked slowly, head hung, hair making an auburn curtain around her face. "I want you to tell Jeremiah I'm glad he ran off," she said. "Then tell him you and I did it."

"He knows better than that, Naomi. When we left your place I went with him."

"He doesn't know what we're doing right now. Or during lunch. Or after school."

Wally hugged his abdomen and bent forward. "Naomi, I can't keep talking about this. It makes me hurt."

There was triumph in her expression. "Mama said it's better if you wait, but waiting too long makes a man sick. That must be what's happening."

Then, she said, "Get Jeremiah to come see me. After him, you and I will do it."

"Why can't I be first?"

"Because you don't know how, and neither do I. Tell Jeremiah the best time is mid-morning because that's the shift that keeps my daddy busiest at the packing house. Tell him my mother makes her rounds between breakfast and lunch."

That night, Wally told Jeremiah, "Naomi wants to see you. She won't do anything with me until you show her how."

"She must think I'm stupid," Jeremiah said. But there was a gleam in his eye that Wally had never seen before.

A nickname could be the worst thing that ever happened to a person. Wally had seen it with his friend Randall Carney in Atlanta.

> "Randy Candy sweet and dandy
> When the girls come out to play
> Randy Candy runs away."

From then on, Randall Carney was renamed. Another boy at Montessori had never been bad until people called him "Terrible" Terrell. He began to wear a leather jacket and combat boots, hair flung carelessly over one eye. He swaggered and took up smoking cigarettes. Within a year, Terrell Thompson had quit school and was twice arrested for stealing bicycles which he chopped up for parts.

So Wally knew the power of nicknames.

"Where's Nutty Naomi, Polly Wally?" Danny Weiderman taunted.

Danny Weiderman had pimples on his nose and earlobes. His knuckles were skinned from shooting marbles on concrete. He suffered a lumbering gait and short attention span. If ignored, he often forgot his subject. Wally ignored him now.

"You hear me, Polly Wally? Where's Nutty Naomi?"

She hadn't been in school for three days.

"I don't know where she is, Danny Dumb-dumb."

Students laughed and Danny shoved Wally against the lockers. "Watch your mouth, Polly Wally."

"You too, Dumb-dumb."

There had been times when Danny made fun of the hearse or Wally's black chauffeur. Now and then Wally overheard whispered references to "nigger lovers." In Naomi's company it was easier to ignore ugly remarks as if out of respect for her. But by himself silence seemed cowardly. By the end of the day he'd been in one wrestling match and twice more he'd been shoved hard enough to fall.

The next morning when Wally reached the footbridge, he sat on a rail waiting for Naomi. A slate blue heron stepped gingerly across hyacinths in search of frogs and minnows.

A few minutes later Jeremiah arrived. "You're going to be late for school," he said.

"What about you?" Wally countered.

Jeremiah leaned over the rail and spit at his reflection in inky waters. "Maybe I'll play eightball, or a few hands of poker. I haven't decided."

"I'll go with you," Wally bluffed.

"Better get your education, Precious."

"You're going to see Naomi, aren't you, Jeremiah?"

"Do I look stupid?"

"That's what you've been doing the last several days, seeing Naomi."

"You must think I'm an idiot," Jeremiah scoffed.

But for the fourth day, Naomi was not in class.

During recess, Wally ran to the packing houses. Women in rubber aprons stood beside a conveyor belt culling overripe fruit. Wally was halfway upstairs when Mr. Noonan called from below. "Hey, kid! What do you want?"

"Looking for Naomi."

"She's in school." Mr. Noonan paused. "Isn't she?"

Flustered, Wally said, "I didn't go to school this morning. I wondered if Naomi could give me our homework assignments."

Mr. Noonan waited as Wally descended the stairs. "Where did you say you live?"

"Out at Chosen."

"And who is your father?"

Wally used the hubbub of voices and a rattle of equipment as an excuse not to hear. "I'll see Naomi tomorrow," he yelled.

He jumped off the platform, strolled to a far corner and

walked out of sight. He circled back on the railroad side to the
rear of the building where he sat on the fire escape. He did not
have long to wait. Jeremiah almost fell over him.

"So," Wally said.

Jeremiah shrugged, looking sheepish. "Been reading comic
books, Precious."

"Don't lie, Jeremiah. You don't have to lie to me. I don't
care."

"Let's get out of here," Jeremiah said.

They retreated down railroad tracks, ducking under idle boxcars. "Okay, so what?" Jeremiah challenged. "Naomi wanted me
to come see her and I did. It's not like I broke in."

"You've forgotten the man with one leg tied to a tree, his
other leg to a car?"

"I'll be more careful than he was. That man got caught with a
naked woman in a wheelbarrow. What could he say? Taking her
where to do what? He wasn't too smart."

They slid down the embankment, thoughts of school forgotten.
A fluttery coo of waterfowl rippled the bogs. Frogs gulped, not in
chorus—one here, another there. "Truth is," Jeremiah confessed,
"I planned to go once and never do it again. I thought, hey, why
not? I never been with white womens before. Never saw one
naked except when I snuck in a carnival show last year. And she
wasn't really naked, wearing stretch tights the color of skin. I
thought she was peeling, but it was a hole in her tights."

Jeremiah threw an arm around Wally's shoulder, grinning.
"She likes me, Precious. First white person ever liked me. Lots of
white folks say they do, but step over a line and see what happens. Naomi likes me, no lie she does. She feels different, which I
didn't expect. Smells different too."

He squeezed Wally playfully and released him. "She was waiting for me when you went to school the next day. Hiding so you
wouldn't see her. She said I was the prettiest man she ever saw.
Don't laugh, Precious."

"I'm not laughing."

"You're right, I don't have to lie to you. No need saying I
won't go back, I will. I'll be careful, but I'm going back."

Naomi didn't play chess or checkers, Wally reminded himself. She did not read books, she looked at comics. Her favorite subject was body parts and their secondary functions. She would never be the friend to him that Randall Carney had been in Atlanta. But for the moment, she was Wally's only friend and he missed her. Worse, he was jealous.

When he thought of Jeremiah and Naomi together, his belly ached, and hot prickling sensations raced across his shoulders. The mental image of them intertwined was so upsetting it made him ill. But mostly Wally was jealous of Jeremiah's happiness.

Oh, he was happy. Jeremiah whistled while he dressed in the morning. He laughed easily and was quick to cuff Wally's shoulder in a gentle gesture of affection. He trimmed his own hair, took more baths, brushed his teeth vigorously. When Hattie asked him to burn the garbage, Jeremiah did so cheerfully, and he teased her, "You're looking good this morning, Mama!"

After Jeremiah went outside, Hattie said to Anthony, "What's gotten into him?"

Wally wished it were happening to himself.

In the second week of Naomi's absence, a note was tacked to the cafeteria table where she and Wally usually ate lunch together. It read: COLORED ONLY. He sat there anyway.

Mrs. Bullock, the school counselor, joined him. She removed the message and put it under her tray. "How are you doing, Wally?"

"I'm all right."

"Getting along with other students?"

It was apparent he was not, but Wally said, "Yes ma'am."

Without asking if he wanted it, she put a cupcake from her tray onto his. "Watching my weight," she said. Wally was aware of other students smirking.

"You remember when we first met I said I'd be available if you had a problem?" Mrs. Bullock reminded. "Anything we talk about is between you and me, Wally. Nobody else will know."

"Yes ma'am."

"I received a report that you left school in the middle of the day last week. I waited for you to come tell me why."

He really didn't want the cupcake. It had vanilla icing, his least favorite. He ate it to be polite.

Mrs. Bullock's smile faded. "Since it is obvious something is wrong," she said, "I can only assume you don't want to discuss it with *me.*"

"There's no point talking about things nobody can change, Mrs. Bullock."

"Discussing misfortune is a way of coping with it," she replied. "A good listener is the next best thing to good advice. But I can't help you if you won't confide in me."

Students chattered, lunch trays clattered.

"Where is Naomi?" Mrs. Bullock questioned.

"She's out of school today."

"I know, Wally. That's why I'm asking."

"At home, I guess."

"She's not at home. Her father telephoned to see if she had been attending school. He thought she might be with you. He said you've been coming by the packing house to see her. He also said you told him you are an orphan being adopted. Do you often invent stories about yourself?"

He didn't think so.

"As for Naomi, she never had a boyfriend before, and you needed a chum. I didn't think either of you would be a bad influence on the other. But now I'm not so sure."

The lunchroom was almost empty which somehow amplified sounds from the kitchen.

"It's my job to spot trouble, Wally, and I see trouble coming. Child Welfare has entrusted you to me, did you know that?"

"No."

"Miss Lanier telephones to ask about your attendance and deportment. You can't afford to make a mistake. For example, the colored boy I've seen you with. What's his name?"

"Jeremiah."

"It's true he lives in the same house, so you're forced to spend time with him. But you invite contempt if people think you prefer Jeremiah over them. Child Welfare is looking for any reason to take you out of your situation. Let me tell you, no matter how bad it is at home, it's better than foster care. I speak from experience. At the mercy of strangers. Wearing hand-me-down clothes. Living with people who keep you only for the money they're paid. I'd hate to see that happen."

Wally swallowed so hard it made a noise.

"You would be wise to be forthright with me," she said. "I will stand by you."

Mrs. Bullock put a hand on Wally's arm. "Now tell me about Naomi and Jeremiah."

She knew. How could she know? But she knew!

"You see," Mrs. Bullock said, "I already know things you thought were secrets. After I checked on Naomi, I telephoned Mr. Noonan to say she had been skipping school. He said he'd just found that out. Evidently he discovered the door to their apartment was locked. He assumed you were in there with Naomi. He went around to the fire escape—"

Wally's chest constricted. "He caught Jeremiah?"

"Almost caught him. Jeremiah jumped off the roof and got away. But they'll catch him eventually."

"What will happen?"

"If this insinuates what I think it does, he will certainly suffer the consequences. The sheriff is coming to talk to you, Wally. I want to stress the importance of truth. The last thing you want to do is give an impression you are protecting that colored boy."

Wally stood up.

"They'll be here soon," Mrs. Bullock said. "You may wait in my office."

He stumbled toward the hall.

"Wally, don't leave the school grounds," she called from behind.

Danny Dumb-dumb blocked Wally's way. "No running in the hall, Polly Wally."

Wally moved left and Danny sidestepped to stop him. He moved to the right and Danny did it again. Anger and frustration erupted. He hit Danny as hard as he could and the stunned boy stood on tiptoes and fell backward.

"Wally!" Mrs. Bullock cried.

He bolted into noonday sun past students sitting beneath oak trees. When he ran out of breath down the road, he paused, hands braced against his knees, gasping and sick with worry. He imagined hooded men closing on Jeremiah as he screamed for mercy.

A police car pulled beside Wally and Deputy Leon Posey spoke through the open window. "Why aren't you in school, son?"

"I don't feel good."

"Get in." It was an order.

The car smelled of leather, machine oil, and sweat. The police radio hissed and crackled. "Were you with Jeremiah this morning, Wally?"

"No sir."

"When did you last see him?"

"On the way to school."

"Did he say where he was going?"

"No sir."

The car moved slowly, Deputy Posey looking this way and that across bogs and along the canal bank.

"What will happen to Jeremiah, Mr. Posey?"

"I thought you hadn't seen him, Wally. What makes you think that anything will happen?"

"You're looking for him, aren't you?" At the crest of the dike, Posey stopped the car. In the distance, a flock of egrets circled hummocks then settled like flower petals from the sky.

"Mr. Posey, I think I'm going to throw up."

"Then get out of the car, son."

Wally leaned out and lost Mrs. Bullock's cupcake. Deputy Posey gave him a handkerchief. "You haven't been swimming in canals, have you?"

"No sir."

Posey drove down the lane through saw grass higher than the car. At the Fester house, hounds bayed and chickens ran. The Fester men stood beside a truck they were repairing. As the lawman passed, the Festers watched deadpan.

Posey pulled into the shade of Anthony's oak tree. The Ford coupe was gone. Minnie Lou came onto the porch wiping her hands with a dishtowel. "Nobody here but me," she called. "That boy be in trouble, his daddy gone to Palm Beach."

"Wally is all right, Minnie Lou." Deputy Posey got out. "I'm looking for Jeremiah."

"What he do?"

"Have you seen him?"

"Not since he went to school."

"He didn't go to school, Minnie Lou. He went to the barbershop in colored town."

"Playing hooky," Minnie Lou concluded.

Posey looked around the yard, up in the oak and under the house.

"What it be, Mr. Posey?" Minnie Lou asked. "With your hand on that gun. What Jeremiah do?"

"He went to the barbershop in colored town," Posey said. "Jeremiah said he needed money. He claimed he'd been cheated at cards."

"They did cheat him," Wally said. "I saw them making signs when Jeremiah wasn't looking."

Minnie Lou pulled Wally beside her. He felt her hand tremble.

"Jeremiah grabbed the owner's pistol," Posey said. "He shot two men."

"Oh, Lord. Are they dead?"

"They were alive the last I heard," Posey said. "That doesn't mean they won't die. Jeremiah still has the gun, Minnie Lou. This is bad, but it could get worse. You still say he's not here?"

"Not here," Minnie Lou said. "His mama and Mr. McManus gone to Palm Beach until late tonight. You wouldn't shoot that child, would you, Mr. Posey?"

"I wouldn't," Posey said. "Unless I had to."

chapter
twelve

For supper, Minnie Lou served fried bologna, cornbread and buttermilk, none of which Wally liked. She lit a lamp and sat at the table with him, the whites of her eyes like tiny crescent moons set in a black sky. When the Fester hounds began to bark, she said, "Here they come," meaning Anthony and Hattie.

But it was Jeremiah's grandfather.

He came up the steps hurriedly. "Where are they, Minnie Lou?"

"Gone to Palm Beach, Mr. Willoughby."

Mr. Willoughby doused the lantern, plunging them into darkness. "Has Jeremiah been here?"

"Not since break of day."

The floor creaked as he moved to a window. "Jeremiah shot two men at the barbershop in colored town," Mr. Willoughby said, "but that's not all. He was caught with a white girl."

"Aw naw, pshaw," Minnie Lou said.

"A drunken guard from the packing house is prowling colored town looking for that boy. He might come out here, Minnie Lou."

"If he does, what I do?" Minnie Lou asked.

"I'm sending you home with Eazy," Mr. Willoughby said. "I'll stay with Wally."

Hastily, Minnie Lou gathered a bag of clothes that needed repair. She felt her way down the steps, going to the hearse. After she left, Wally sat at the supper table in the dark. He knew Mr. Willoughby was still there by the smell of wintergreen.

"What do you know about the white girl, Wally?"

"Her name is Naomi Noonan. She's in my class at school."

"Was Jeremiah with her?"

Wally repeated Jeremiah's planned defense—"Reading comic books."

"How did this come about?" Mr. Willoughby questioned.

"Naomi wanted to know Jeremiah. She has a room full of comic books and she doesn't care if somebody reads them. I introduced them. Then when Naomi didn't come to school, I went by the packing house to see why. It made her daddy suspicious."

After a moment, Wally said, "It's my fault they got caught."

"It's nobody's fault," Mr. Willoughby said.

"If I hadn't introduced them. If I hadn't gone by the packing house—"

"It's nobody's fault!" Mr. Willoughby said. "God gives little boys a leash by which little girls can lead them. The brain doesn't work until the boy's hair goes gray."

The Fester hounds set up a racket and a pickup truck roared into the yard, headlights on high beam.

"You in there!" a man yelled.

"Who is it?" Mr. Willoughby called.

"Send out that nigger boy to get what he's got coming."

"That's Mr. Noonan," Wally said. "Naomi's daddy."

"Sir," Mr. Willoughby yelled, "there's nobody here but a grown black man tending a white child whose parents are out of town."

"You got a firearm in there?" Mr. Noonan shouted.

"No sir."

"Then I'm coming in."

Mr. Willoughby lit a lamp.

Mr. Noonan had a gun and he was drunk. When he saw Wally, he waved the pistol. "You lying punk kid. You're no better than these niggers. What were you doing coming to my home anyway?"

Willoughby seized the man's wrist and held the gun steady. "Mr. Noonan, sir," he said, "I'm staying with this boy while his parents are away. You're welcome to look around the house. There's nobody here but us."

Noonan's shadow loomed and retreated, enlarged and diminished as he lurched from one room to the next holding the lamp in one hand, his gun in the other. He returned to the kitchen and stuck the revolver in Mr. Willoughby's face. "And who the hell are you?" he said. "Are you related to the nigger kid Jeremiah?"

Sweat traced Mr. Willoughby's cheek.

"He won't get away with this," Noonan promised. He pressed the muzzle under Mr. Willoughby's eye and cocked the hammer. Wally heard Mr. Willoughby groan.

"Mr. Noonan," Wally said, "Jeremiah is not here. He ran away this morning. We haven't seen him."

Noonan slowly lowered the firing pin. He turned aside and paused as though reconsidering. Finally, he stalked out, got into his pickup truck and drove away.

Mr. Willoughby eased into a chair. He stared at Wally, then blinked his eyes rapidly. "I expect," Mr. Willoughby said, "it is your bedtime."

Wally had hardly dozed when he awoke to the slamming of car doors and Hattie screaming, "They'll kill him, Anthony! They'll kill my boy."

Her shrieks roused the Fester hounds to frenzied barking, yelps rebounding across the lake to echo back like two more hounds afar.

Anthony came into the bedroom and pulled Wally's toe. "Get up," he said. "We're going to the funeral home."

Wally rode in the rumble seat. As they passed the Fester house, a lamp was lit and Ike Fester stood in the door. Hounds lunged at the car, fangs flashing in headlights, snapping at the tires. After crossing the bridge, Anthony picked up speed. The air in Wally's face was cool and moist. A sliver of moon cut a slice in the star speckled sky.

Anthony parked behind Three Palms Funeral Home out of sight from the street. They entered a rear door and walked the long hall to Mr. Willoughby's office. Eazy was there, and men Wally had never seen before.

"McManus, do you know these men?"

Introductions went round but nobody shook hands. Unnoticed, Wally slipped behind a couch to listen.

"We have a dangerous situation," Mr. Willoughby said. "I've spoken to Deputy Posey. He and I believe we can control things if we find Jeremiah soon and send him to the juvenile lockup in West Palm Beach."

"Jail?" Hattie cried. "He's a boy."

"That *boy* shot two men, Hattie, one of whom may die. White folks don't give a damn if one Negro shoots another. But Jeremiah crossed the color line to have relations with a white girl, and for that they'll kill. This evening the girl's father was bursting into bars, threatening to call out the Klan. He came to your house waving a gun, looking for Jeremiah. If we get Jeremiah through this in one piece, it's more than he should expect."

Mr. Willoughby sat at his desk. "What we're here for, is to figure how to avoid a war against colored town. No man of color ever won such a fight in this country. There's talk of nightriders making a house-to-house search for Jeremiah."

"I didn't go ashore at Normandy to come home and be pushed around by a bunch of gun-toting crackers," a man said. "If they come calling at my house, threatening my family, they're in for some of what the German army got."

"We've got to stop that kind of talk, Earl," Mr. Willoughby said. "You want your business burned? Your family shot? There's only one way to defuse this matter, and do it quickly. We must find Jeremiah and get him in the hands of the law. McManus, I want you and Hattie to get out of town until this stink blows off."

"No!" Hattie said. "I'm not leaving without Jeremiah."

"Listen, little missy," Mr. Willoughby said evenly, "you and McManus would be next in line at a lynching. They'll say a nigger boy went with a white girl and how would he know better with you two as an example?"

Hattie was unyielding. "I'm not going without Jeremiah."

"You think you can reason with men blinded to reason? You plan to explain why you and McManus are unique? Talk about love? There's not a thing you can say to a mob, Hattie. I've seen men hanged on nothing but rumor. In this case, even Wally thinks Jeremiah was with the girl."

"Reading comics," Wally said.

A hand reached down and pulled Wally to his feet. All eyes were on him.

"You heard what was said, boy," Mr. Willoughby stated. "You know how serious this is. It is important that we find Jeremiah right away, do you understand?"

"Yessir."

"I want everybody to go out in the community and talk to people. Calm them down. No more nonsense about shooting nightriders. Don't say anything to incite violence."

"You expect us to stand by and take threats?" a man asked.

"I expect you to do whatever it takes to mend frayed nerves, Earl. This is not Germany. These white folks and their children will still be living right across town after this is over. If it comes to shooting, they'll never forget it."

Riding home, Wally shared the front seat with Hattie. Not a word was spoken until they reached the house. Then Hattie said, "I'm not leaving without Jeremiah, Anthony. You can take Precious and go, but I'm not leaving."

"We'll sleep on it, Hattie."

"I don't have to sleep on it," she said. "If that child comes home, I'll be here. And despite what my father said, if Klansmen show up I'm going to shoot some hotheads."

She went to her room and shut the door.

Lying in bed, Wally lay wide-eyed in the dark. The night was turning cool and insects caroled weakly. Colder weather would hold down mosquitoes in case Jeremiah was sleeping outdoors. But if he were up a tree somewhere, he'd be chilled. And hungry. He'd have to steal food and for that he'd need to be near a town.

Anthony came in and sat on the side of Wally's bed. "Are you all right?"

"Yessir."

Anthony rearranged the sheet around Wally's shoulder. "Good night," he said.

"Yessir," Wally replied. "Good night."

The next day was Saturday, the first of November. In Atlanta the trees would be wearing red and gold, drizzling rain signaling an imminent end of fall. In south Florida, packing houses ran shorter shifts as crops diminished, and that marked the main change in seasons. Less work meant migrant workers moving elsewhere. Cars and trailers and stakebody trucks rumbled past Wally as he walked through the packing house district.

He considered approaching Naomi's place by the front door, but the prospect of meeting Mr. Noonan helped him decide against it. He went around back and climbed the railroad trestle where he sat on the railroad tracks staring at her bedroom window. She had said mid-morning was the best time and it was still early.

Hattie and Anthony had gone to meet Deputy Posey to ask if there was news of Jeremiah. Hattie wanted Wally to go with them. He didn't want to, and Anthony said he was in no mood to argue. "Besides," Anthony had reasoned, "nobody is angry with Wally. He'll be all right."

Crows the size of chickens strolled the cinder strewn tracks selecting gravel for their craws. Cars passed below, the families crowded inside, their belongings strapped to the roof and bumpers. They looked like motorized beetles covered with camouflage as they puttered away north.

Wally saw Mr. Noonan walk from sunshine to shadow going to the packing house office. In the next moment, Naomi waved from her window. She slowly climbed onto the fire escape and descended one step at a time.

If Wally had met Naomi anywhere else, he might not have recognized her. Her lips were so puffy they didn't move when she spoke his name. Her eyes were slits in discolored flesh. Her arms were bruised purple and sickly green.

"Daddy beat me, Wally. First with his belt, then his fist. I wouldn't tell him Jeremiah's name. He hit me so hard I couldn't breathe."

She lifted her skirt to reveal gashes swabbed with iodine. Even her feet were swollen, the toes like peas bursting from a pod. Wally put his arm around her.

"I had to tell him," she moaned. "I had to say Jeremiah's

name. I couldn't breathe."

"Did they take you to a doctor, Naomi?"

"Daddy won't take me until I look better. He broke my teeth. I can't chew. Did Jeremiah get away?"

"Yes."

"Don't squeeze me, Wally."

She sucked air in short gasps, the taut skin of her face a mask of misshapen features. "I told Daddy we were reading comic books, Wally. No matter how much he beat me, I said that's all we did. Tell Jeremiah."

"I would if I could, Naomi. But he's gone. Everybody is looking for him."

"Everybody," she agreed. "My daddy hates the Festers, but he went to them for help."

"The Festers? Help do what?"

"Find Jeremiah. Hurt him."

"How many people does it take to hurt Jeremiah? He's not much larger than me."

"Daddy says they'll kill him." Then she said, "You have to move your arm, Wally. It's pressing my shoulder."

He sat away from her.

"I never thought Daddy would whip me like this," Naomi said. "I can't believe Mama let him. She kept screaming that he was killing me, but she didn't make him stop."

"How could she make him stop, Naomi?"

"Shoot him. If I could've gotten to his gun, I would have shot him. I told him if he ever hit me again I'd kill him, and he knows I mean it, too. Nobody should beat somebody like this. Can you see my teeth?"

She tried to bare them and Wally said, "I see," but he didn't. He smelled her breath though, like stale meat in a warm icebox.

They sat there so long the sun rose over the roof of the packing house. "Want to get in the shade, Naomi?"

"The sun feels good."

"Hey! Hey!" Mr. Noonan yelled from the platform.

"Run, Wally!"

"I have nothing to be ashamed of, Naomi."

"Run!"

Mr. Noonan sat on the edge of the platform and then jumped off. His weight made him stumble, but he got up, face beet-red, and came toward Wally.

"Mr. Noonan," Wally said, "I don't have any reason to be in trouble. Naomi and I were just talking."

Naomi stood up, groaning, and tried to run, but she couldn't.

"Mr. Noonan," Wally reasoned, "this is all a mistake. Jeremiah and Naomi were only reading comics and—"

The man hit Wally's face so hard it knocked him down.

"No, Daddy! No!"

He grappled for Wally, but Naomi held his arm and Wally twisted away.

"What's the matter with you?" Wally screamed. "I told you, it's a mistake."

Noonan had Naomi by the blouse dragging her backward, her heels bumping the railroad ties. When she struggled, he cuffed her head, hit her shoulder. Wally seized the man's arm and Mr. Noonan hit him again.

"Are you crazy?" Wally yelled. "You beat Naomi like that. Are you crazy?"

"Get out of here boy, before I hurt you."

"You fat slob, I keep telling you it's a mistake."

"Run, Wally! Run!"

Noonan slapped Naomi, then slapped her again. Wally dived for the man's leg and bit his thigh. Noonan grabbed his holster, but the pistol was not there. He kicked Wally away and dragged Naomi beside the high platform to a set of steps. Wally followed.

"Oh, God, Wally!" Naomi was shouting and weeping. "Daddy, stop!"

But Noonan hauled her up the steps and when Naomi held on to the rough wood railing, he snatched her and splinters stabbed into her hands. Wally beat the man's back. He looked for a club.

At the stairs leading to their apartment, Noonan turned. "I'm going to get my revolver," he said. "If you're here when I come back, I'll shoot you dead so help me God. And if you ever come around here again, I'll kill you."

"Wally," Naomi wailed. "Run, Wally. Run."

"And tell your no-good, white-trash father and that nigger woman, their day is coming," Noonan said.

Wally watched them ascend the stairs, Naomi delaying her father by grabbing the banister. "Run, Wally! Run!"

Mrs. Noonan was at the top of the steps, begging her husband to stop. He shoved Naomi past the woman, and Naomi hobbled inside.

Wally backed away, the cries following.

He heard the mother scream, "No! No!"

Curses.

"No! No!"

And a gunshot. Then another.

chapter thirteen

A guard from another packing house came running with pistol drawn. He vaulted onto the platform from street level and stood at the stairs yelling up, "Everything okay? Hello?"

Wally heard Mrs. Noonan scream her husband's name.

The screened door opened and the guard below crouched and aimed his gun. It was Naomi. She said, "My daddy is dead." The guard climbed steps in long bounds. When he passed Naomi, she called to Wally, "I shot my daddy."

It seemed a long time before police and an ambulance arrived. Then suddenly there were people everywhere: medical personnel dressed in white, Deputy Posey and other lawmen, Miss Edna Lanier from child welfare, a couple of students from school who had been riding by on bicycles. Migratory laborers paused to gawk.

Four men brought Mr. Noonan down the steep steps. He was covered from head to ankles, his booted feet sticking out. He was strapped to a stretcher, a motionless mound that had been living a short time ago. They put him in the ambulance and it pulled away slowly, red lights revolving but without using a siren.

Miss Lanier accompanied Naomi, taking tiny steps because Naomi was hurting. As they passed him, Naomi said, "'Bye, Wally."

"Bye," he said.

Then Deputy Posey came to Wally. "You seem to be right in the middle of trouble lately. What are you doing here, Wally?"

"I came to see Naomi."

"What for?"

"To ask about Jeremiah."

"Tell me what happened."

"Mr. Noonan was whipping Naomi. She shot him."

"You saw her shoot him?"

"No sir."

"Then how do you know she did it?"

"She said she did."

Deputy Posey took a cigar from his shirt pocket, unwrapped it and licked the tobacco from one end to the other. He bit off the tip, staring across the street at people staring this way.

"Did you send Naomi to jail?" Wally asked.

"She's going to the hospital, Wally."

"Will she be electrocuted for shooting Mr. Noonan?" The deputy looked down at him and put a hand on Wally's shoulder. "Come on, son. I'll give you a ride home."

The police car smelled like last time, leather and sweat, and now cigar smoke. Deputy Posey drove slowly as before, scanning fields and canal banks. He rode with an elbow stuck out his window. His uniform was twisted. Wally could see his underwear.

"What led to the shooting, Wally?"

"Mr. Noonan said he was going to shoot me."

"Why would he say that?"

"I was with Naomi."

"You were with Naomi?"

"Yessir. She came out a window, down the fire escape."

Deputy Posey used a little finger to brush ashes off his cigar. "Wally," he said, "have you and Naomi ever—you know—played with one another? Played house. Doctor and nurse? Mama and Daddy."

"Naomi hurt too much to play anything."

"I mean, did you and the girl get intimate in a boy and girl way?"

"You mean sex?"

"Yes. Sex."

"I don't have any hair in my armpits."

The lawman stared through the windshield.

"I guess sex is bad," Wally said.

"It's natural as a heartbeat," Posey said. "But most folks think you should wait until you're married."

"Naomi says it's better if you wait, but waiting can make a man hurt. She was right about that."

The deputy leaned across Wally and opened the door. "After I talk to Naomi," he said, "I'll come see you. I want to know everything you can remember about today. Try to recall what Naomi said and the way things happened. I'll be seeing you, Wally."

Watching the deputy drive away, he realized Mr. Posey had not answered about whether Naomi would be electrocuted.

Wally had once seen a squirrel walking a power line that swayed between poles. The animal flicked his tail this way and that to keep his balance. Then when his line swung near another, the squirrel reached out. There was a flash of light and a vicious crackle. Smoke rose from the charred body which, for a moment, clung to both electric lines before burning in two.

He'd asked his mother if she thought the squirrel felt pain. "Probably not," she'd replied. "That's why governments use electrocution to execute criminals. It's more humane than hanging or shooting."

Wally mounted steps to the cooling shade of the house. He realized he'd watched Naomi's life change forever. There would be no more talks with Naomi about sex or anything else. He would never have a chance to teach her chess. None of that mattered anymore.

In the kitchen, Wally discovered food uncovered, cockroaches feasting. The icebox was ajar—he never did that.

"Jeremiah?"

Wally's dresser drawers were opened, his clothes ransacked. "Jeremiah, are you here?"

Even the chifforobe had been searched and Wally's mattress was askew. For fear he was being watched, Wally casually straightened the chifforobe, looking for his money coat. It was there undisturbed.

Was Jeremiah watching?

"You might as well talk to me," Wally said aloud. "You can't go anywhere without help."

It was like speaking to the spirit of his mother, and apparently just as futile. "Jeremiah," Wally called, "if you are staying at Kramer's Island, watch out for the Festers. Naomi says they plan to kill you."

The whisper of bamboo in a freshening breeze was his only answer. Not long afterward, Anthony and Hattie came home.

"We went to West Palm Beach and hired a lawyer," Hattie said. "Pierre Arneaux recommended the man we saw. Pierre said he's the best lawyer in Florida."

She was talking more to herself than to Wally and Anthony. She wiped the table and cupboard as she spoke. "Because Jeremiah is only twelve, there may not be a trial," she said, "just a hearing. The judge will take into account the stability of Jeremiah's home life, and our reputation."

Was that good?

"We couldn't have hired a better lawyer. That's what Pierre said, isn't it, Anthony?"

"That's what he said."

"The lawyer said all this might go away if the men at the barbershop don't die. He said we should go by the hospital and show that we're concerned about the wounded men. That's what he said, wasn't it, Anthony?"

"He did, yes."

Wally was bursting to speak. "I went to see Naomi today."

"No, no," Hattie said, "don't do that. Sheriff Posey thinks Mr. Noonan is not a man to mess with. Stay away from there."

"I already went," Wally choked back a sob. "Naomi shot Mr. Noonan."

"The girl—Anthony, do you hear this?"

"Will he be all right?" Anthony asked.

"She killed him."

"Shot and killed her own father?"

"Yessir."

"You were there?" Anthony asked.

"Yessir."

"But, why did she do it?" Hattie questioned.

"Mr. Noonan beat her real bad. He even broke her teeth. He

hit her so hard she couldn't breathe, because Naomi wouldn't tell him Jeremiah's name." Wally could hardly breathe himself in the retelling of it. "That was yesterday. Today, when he saw me with Naomi, he started hitting her again. So she shot him."

"Oh!" Hattie writhed. "Is there no end to this?"

"Mr. Noonan said he was going to get his gun and shoot me," Wally said. "Naomi shot him first."

"You're certain he's dead?" Anthony said.

"Yessir, he's dead. They carried him out with his head covered."

"Does Deputy Posey know you were there?"

"He brought me home."

"What are we coming to, Anthony?" Hattie wailed. "What is happening to us?"

Sunday was Hattie's day to sit with her mother, and Anthony went along to tell Mr. Willoughby what the West Palm Beach lawyer had said. They asked Wally if he wanted to go, and he said no.

He thought Jeremiah might come back.

Last night had been cold and by day the wind came in short chilling gusts. The sky filled with birds in migratory flight, tens of thousands of them, passing on their way elsewhere. Jeremiah couldn't sleep in a tree all winter, and if he was at Kramer's Island he couldn't stay long because of the Festers. He'd need blankets, matches for a fire, and more clothing.

So Wally sat in the front porch swing reading to catch up on school work he was sure he'd missed on Friday. He spied a movement at the edge of the front yard. Without looking up, he called, "You might as well come in. I see you there."

He was flabbergasted when Aldo Fester stepped into view.

"Who'd you think I was?" Aldo asked.

"I saw it was you."

"Thought it was the little nigger come sneaking back, didn't you?"

"He's probably in Georgia," Wally bluffed. Sweat zigzagged down his spine.

Aldo was barefoot, unshaven, wearing dirty overalls and no

shirt. He peered under the house. "Naw," he said, "Jeremiah ain't in Georgia. We got friends who work the railroads, so he didn't hop a train. Police are watching the highways. He can't hitch a ride."

"Jeremiah knows a lot of workers leaving town," Wally said. "He could be in any one of those trucks going north."

He saw by Aldo's expression that thought hadn't occurred to him. But Aldo said, "We've been watching them too. We know Jeremiah is still about, and like as not he'll be coming here for food."

"Well," Wally closed his book, "he hasn't been here yet."

Aldo came up the steps, yellow eyes darting left and right. "We'll catch him. He'll get caught stealing something, and if he ain't shot, he'll go to prison. Me and my brother know such things, don't we, Cole?"

Cole spoke from inside the door. He had come in the back way. "We know about police," he said. "Even they're scared of the Klan."

"What do you want?" Wally asked.

"Being friendly. Neighbor in trouble. Checking to see that you're all right."

"And that's the truth," Cole said. "Me and Aldo like you, Wally. We don't want you hurt."

"You got guts," Aldo walked the porch looking in windows. "We admire guts. You can't help if your white-trash pappy took up with a high-yellow nigger. That's not your fault."

Cole spoke from within. "Aldo, come look at this. Got them a outhouse inhouse. A tub and hey! Is this where your daddy writes books, Wally?"

"Come out of there," Wally said. "This is wrong and you know it."

They returned to the porch. "Like we said, Wally, we're being neighborly. Before long, the welfare people will come calling. They already ask us what kind of life you live."

Both men laughed at that.

"What we're here to say," Aldo said, "is that you should leave when you get a chance. Bad luck is about to settle on this place.

Your pappy needs to learn, it's against nature for a man to take up with dumb animals."

"We've had an eye on you, Wally," Cole said. "You don't spend any time with them you don't have to. You never said a word about us out at Kramer's Island, so we figure you're due a warning. But only this once. Get out while you can."

They went down the steps, bare feet slapping wood, crossed the yard and walked toward home.

If the Festers were watching the house even while everybody was away, they were bound to see Jeremiah sooner or later. He had to be warned.

Wally rolled two blankets and tied them with a belt. He was putting food in a burlap sack when he glanced out the kitchen window. Ike Fester had climbed the water tank and was looking at the house.

If Wally left now, he'd be seen.

He put away the blankets and food. He had to be smarter than this.

Anthony and Hattie arrived home before dark and Wally ran to meet the car. "The Festers were looking for Jeremiah," he said. "They were in the house."

Anthony rolled up windows of the coupe and shut the doors. "Hattie," he said, "we'll be back shortly. Come with me, Wally."

"Anthony—"

"We won't be long," Anthony said. "Start supper anytime."

Walking toward the Fester house, Wally had to trot to keep up. His heart tried to beat free of his rib cage. "I did tell them to come on in," Wally admitted. "I thought it was Jeremiah sneaking around."

The Fester hounds scrambled from under the stoop, charging. Anthony walked up to and between the snarling animals as though they didn't exist. He stopped at the front porch.

The house was dark. *Please be gone*, Wally prayed.

"Ike Fester!" Anthony yelled.

The hounds nudged Wally's quivering knees, bumping him off-balance. "Ike Fester!" Anthony hollered.

The elder Fester emerged onto the shadowed porch hitching up straps of his overalls. Wally saw Cole and Aldo at the windows.

"You came calling on me?" Anthony questioned.

"A friendly visit, Mr. McManus."

"Your boys walked through my house, Fester."

"The boy said 'come on in,' Mr. McManus. A neighborly thing. Heard about your troubles, that's all."

"What trouble is that, Fester?"

"The nigger boy is missing, ain't he? It's all anybody talks about in town."

"I'll tell you, Ike," Anthony said, "I'd be obliged if you tend your problems and I'll tend mine."

"Whatever you say."

"Don't come to my house while I'm away."

"As you say, Mr. McManus."

Wally's father turned to walk away and Ike Fester make sucking sounds to call his hounds. Halfway home, Wally said, "Aldo said it's against nature to live with dumb animals."

Anthony halted and for one dreadful moment Wally thought they were going back.

"There's a breed of man who needs somebody to look down on, Wally. It's their proof that they're not the lowest members of society."

"I read that in your book."

Anthony walked more slowly. "You read one of my books?"

"When I found out I was coming here, I read them all."

After a moment gazing at him, Anthony said, "Well, are you going to maintain this pregnant pause, or tell me what you thought of what you read?"

"They were okay."

"Okay?"

"Your worst is good," Wally quoted his mother, "your best is unforgettable."

"Kathryn," Anthony said.

"Yessir."

chapter fourteen

Walking to school alone, Wally reached the footbridge where Naomi usually joined him. He wondered if she awoke this morning as he had awakened so many mornings, believing his mother's death to be a bad dream. Perhaps Naomi stayed in bed, half asleep, nurturing the delusion that everything would be as it had always been. Then would come the sick realization that death was absolute; nothing would be as it had been.

At school, students stared but stepped back to let Wally pass as he walked toward homeroom. Their ranks closed behind him and he heard their whispers.

It was Danny Dumb-dumb who finally made rude inquiry. "Were you there when Nutty Naomi shot her old man?"

Wally opened a book as if to read, but he couldn't focus his eyes.

"Was there a lot of screaming?" Danny probed.

"Hold down on the talk back there," the teacher chided.

"Is it true she killed him to save you?" Danny persisted. "Did you see him die?"

The bell rang. Time to change class.

Students looked at Wally, but upon his notice they turned away. He saw notes traded from desk to desk. In the lunchroom, even teachers cast lingering glances his way. The kitchen sounds were louder than usual. Pans and trays clanged, voices reverberated. Chairs scraped the floor. Laughter was piercing.

Mrs. Bullock seated herself at the table, across from Wally. "I'm sorry you ran away Friday," she said. "I had to tell the sheriff you disobeyed me."

"He found me," Wally said.

"We do not solve our problems by running from them," Mrs. Bullock said. "Getting drunk does not relieve a parent of his responsibility, and running away merely delays your acceptance of the inevitable."

She separated English peas from carrot salad, pushing macaroni and cheese to one end of her tray. "I had to be truthful with Miss Lanier, Wally. I told her that you knew the sheriff was coming and ran anyway. She will be here this afternoon, and Wally, you *will* be here."

"Yes ma'am."

"I can help only to the degree that you help yourself," she said. "There is nothing I can do to overcome self-destructive behavior."

"Yes ma'am."

"Now then," she said, "where is Jeremiah hiding?"

"I don't know."

"I don't believe that, Wally. A Negro boy without money or food cannot hide without help. He'll become a thief because what else can he do?"

Wally chewed dry food, took a sip of milk.

"I've urged the authorities not to take action until I could talk to you," Mrs. Bullock said. "I assured Deputy Posey and Miss Lanier that you would confide in me. Now then. Where is Jeremiah?"

"I don't know."

She peered past him, her lips compressed. Then, with a quick nod, she said, "Very well, Wally. I will try to convince them on your behalf, on one condition—when you see Jeremiah, you will come tell me immediately."

Wally pushed away his tray. He couldn't take another bite.

"Better run along now," Mrs. Bullock said. "You'll be late for class."

In the hallway, Danny Dumb-dumb wrapped an arm around Wally's neck. "Listen, Wally," he said, "I'm not angry about the poke in the nose."

Wally didn't care whether he was or not, but he said, "Okay."

"So where'd they send Naomi?"

"To the hospital."

"Was she shot, too?"

"She was beat up."

"Beat by who?"

Wally shrugged off his arm. "I've got to go now."

"Yeah, hey. You can't blame Naomi's old man for laying into her. She was giving it to the nigger, wasn't she?"

"They were reading comic books."

"Is that what she said? Her old man caught them naked."

"That's not true, Danny."

"How would you know? Was she giving it to you too?"

"I have to go. I'll be late for class."

"The bell hasn't rung."

At that instant it rang.

Danny shouted as Wally walked away, "You were getting it from Nutty Naomi, weren't you?"

During science class, the principal summoned Wally. Edna Lanier from Child Welfare and Mrs. Bullock were waiting in the vice-principal's office, which had glass walls, making them visible to passersby in the hall.

Miss Lanier smiled. "We've had a rough weekend, haven't we, Wally?"

"I don't know where Jeremiah is."

"I didn't ask."

"You sent Mrs. Bullock to ask."

Miss Lanier looked at the school counselor. Mrs. Bullock shuffled papers in a file folder.

"Actually," Miss Lanier said, "I came to tell you we're going to have a custodial hearing about your family situation. The court will try to determine the best place for you to live.

"Will I go to a foster home?"

"That depends on several things." She paused. "Where would you prefer to live?"

"Not in a foster home."

"Very well, suppose you tell me why you want to remain where you are."

"The food is good. I like living by the lake."

She wrote a note which Wally read upside down, *food and location.*

"I enjoy the birds, especially egrets. Egrets nest in hummocks along the lake."

"I think the judge will be more interested in whether you feel loved, Wally. What sort of things do you do as a family? Do you go on picnics? To the movies?"

A lump formed in his throat, larger than a grape and hard as rock candy. "We play games," he said.

"You play games with your family? What kind of games?"

"Monopoly. Chess. But mostly we talk. Philosophical stuff."

Miss Lanier laughed. "Philosophical?"

"My father is a writer," Wally said. "He thinks philosophical thoughts. His worst thoughts are better than anyone else's. His best thoughts are unforgettable. Have you read his books?"

"No," Miss Lanier said, "I haven't."

"His first novel was wonderful," Mrs. Bullock said.

"Before you judge my father," Wally said, "you should read his books. They tell more than anything I can say."

"For example?" Miss Lanier prompted.

"He has insights into people," Wally could hear his mother's voice assessing the Anthony Wally had never met. "He may not see himself clearly, but he sees you and me, and the world. He doesn't love like you might want him to. He loves Hattie. She loves him. They went through the war together in France. It isn't easy being a colored woman living with my father, but Hattie stays because she loves him. She loves Jeremiah and won't leave town without him, even though she's scared."

"What does your father feel for you, Wally?"

"He—I—he's getting to know me."

"What does Hattie feel for you?"

"People have to—" he fought a tremor in his lip. "People have to learn to love you, Miss Lanier. It doesn't happen just because it's supposed to."

Miss Lanier closed her notebook. "I can hardly wait to present this to the judge," she said. "This will give him cause for thought."

Beyond the glass walls, a crowd of students stared at Wally and the adults. He clamped his teeth, forced his chin up.

"Now let's talk about Jeremiah," Miss Lanier said.

The same questions were redirected: Was Jeremiah loved, happy, a part of this "close" family?

Behind Miss Lanier, Deputy Posey entered the principal's office, hat in hand.

"When you are with Jeremiah," Miss Lanier asked, "does he set a good example, or a bad one?"

After a few words with the principal, Deputy Posey came to knock on the glass door. Miss Lanier motioned him in. "I'm through, Leon," she said to Posey. "Wally was telling us what a wonderful life he has at home."

"I need to ask Wally a couple of questions," Posey put his hat on one chair and sat on another. "I want to confirm something Naomi said to me."

"I'm due to interview her this afternoon," Miss Lanier commented.

Posey leaned toward Wally, elbows on his knees. "Wally, you told me Mr. Noonan threatened to shoot you."

"Yessir."

"But then you said, Naomi shot him first."

"Yessir."

"Was Naomi trying to keep her father from hurting you? Or was she trying to stop him from beating her again? What do you think?"

Wally pondered so long, Mrs. Bullock said, "Does it make a difference?"

"She can't claim self-defense if she was thinking of Wally," Miss Lanier said.

Sheriff Posey tried to stop the remark, but it was out. Wally said, very cautiously, "Mr. Noonan was hurting Naomi and he had already hurt her a lot. She said if he beat her again she would shoot him. But he did say he was going to get his gun and shoot me, too. Maybe Naomi shot him for both reasons."

"Do you understand the difference between self-defense and manslaughter, Wally?"

"No sir."

"Don't bank on it," Miss Lanier said.

Before the meeting with Wally had ended, students packed the hallway and gazed at Deputy Posey, Miss Lanier, and Mrs. Bullock. The principal went out to send them on their way, but within minutes others had gathered to stand and stare.

When it was over, Deputy Posey said, "Thank you, Mrs. Bullock. I appreciate your help."

She stood behind Wally's chair, holding his head between her hands. "Knowing the problems of students is my job, Sheriff."

Then she followed the other adults out of the room, where she stopped to speak to the principal.

It was more difficult for Wally to seem preoccupied while sitting alone. He stretched one arm overhead and scratched his ribs with his other hand, playing to the student audience like an animal in a glass cage. He couldn't hear them but he saw them laugh. He hunched his shoulders and put his tongue under his upper lip like a monkey. They laughed again.

He would have extended the act, but the principal went into the hall once again to disperse the students, and Mrs. Bullock returned to Wally.

"Since your presence has become disruptive," she said, "I've convinced Mr. Hobarth that you should go home for the remainder of the day. I'll give you a ride."

"That's all right. I'll walk."

"I'll take you home, Wally," she said sternly. "Get your books."

Leaving the office, a student yelled, "Hey, Polly Wally! Are you under arrest?"

"You people be about your business," Mrs. Bullock commanded. She held Wally's arm as though she expected him to flee. They went down the corridor, past a dozen classrooms, out the breezeway to the parking lot.

Her car was as no-nonsense as Mrs. Bullock—gray, with fabric seat covers. Pieces of carpet had been cut to cover the floor where feet might soil the rubber mats. She emptied an ashtray that appeared new and unused to Wally. It contained a single crumpled gum wrapper, nothing else. Then she pumped the accelerator three times and pushed the starter button with her foot.

Watching her drive reminded Wally of Jeremiah at the wheel of the Ford coupe. Mrs. Bullock sat forward, clinging to the steering wheel with both hands.

"I still have not met your father," she said. "You may recall, I said I've read his books. Is this the right direction?"

"Yes ma'am."

She shifted to a lower gear, looking at the steep rise of the dike. "We have to go over that, don't we?"

"I don't mind walking from here," Wally offered.

But before he could reach for the latch, Mrs. Bullock gunned the engine and they went up the incline to the top, and then with lifting stomachs plunged down the other side, brakes locked, wheels scratching dust, as they made the bridge and flew into the lane beyond.

Saw grass enveloped them. Dust roiled. "I expect he's an intriguing person," Mrs. Bullock said.

It took a moment to realize she meant Anthony.

Driving on, Mrs. Bullock saw the Fester house and recoiled. "Is that your home?"

"It's the next place."

When she saw it, she said, "Slightly better."

Wally stepped out and Minnie Lou appeared, her head wrapped in a bandanna. "What is it, Precious?"

"Minnie Lou, this is Mrs. Bullock from school."

"What is it, Precious?"

Mrs. Bullock waved away dust and gnats. "Is Mr. McManus here?"

"They gone to Bean City looking for Jeremiah."

"I am Wally's school counselor. May I come in?"

"Nobody to home but me and y'all," Minnie Lou said, uneasy.

"Nevertheless," Mrs. Bullock climbed the steps, "I'd like to see inside the house. Have you anything to drink?"

"Like shine?"

"Like water. Or iced tea."

"Get the lady some water, Precious," Minnie Lou said.

Wally had to go through a window because Minnie Lou blocked the door.

"Has Jeremiah been here today?" Mrs. Bullock asked.

"Nare hide nor hair," Minnie Lou said.

Wally rinsed a glass and brought lukewarm water to the teacher. She held it but didn't sip.

"Be best you wait on the porch until Mr. McManus come home," Minnie Lou said.

"Fine," Mrs. Bullock said. "Wally, while we wait, let's play a game of Monopoly."

"I don't know what we did with it."

"Then we'll play chess."

Mrs. Bullock returned the glass of water to Minnie Lou, then brushed the tips of her fingers with her thumbs. "You have been less than truthful with me, Wally. My job is to know the difficulties of students so I can help them. It is more and more obvious you continue to prevaricate. You have such a wonderful vocabulary, do you know the word *prevaricate*?"

"Lie."

"Such an intelligent child," Mrs. Bullock said. "But you are slow to recognize who your friends are, Wally. You need something I can give you and you haven't recognized that yet. Do you know what it is?"

"No ma'am."

"I've told you often enough," she said. "I can be your ally. You need a stable adult on your side, but you continue to resist my offers of help. That makes me seem inept at my job. How can I befriend someone who conspires to make me look bad? Walk me to my car, Wally."

In the yard, Mrs. Bullock turned to look at the house and Minnie Lou still in the doorway. "Oh, yes," the teacher said. "I know this dwelling well. I know the emotional turmoil that is here. I grew up in a place like this. There are no games played in this household. Just an unhappy existence. But I'm going to give you one last chance to accept my friendship, Wally. When you see Jeremiah, and you *will* see him, I expect you to come to me at once. That will be my proof that you have met me halfway. Otherwise, I will not be your friend, Wally. And if I am not your friend, I am your adversary. Do you know *that* word?"

"Enemy."

She got in her car, furiously pumped the gas pedal, then pressed the starter. She backed into the lane and turned toward Belle Glade.

"They spelled you from school, Precious?"

"I'm not expelled, Minnie Lou."

"How come that lady brings you home then?"

"I'm not sure," Wally said. And that was the truth.

Every morning Hattie and Anthony left early to drive around Lake Okeechobee searching for Jeremiah. And every day after they left, Cole and Aldo Fester and their dogs stood in the road waiting for Wally. It took courage to leave for school.

Cole and Aldo fell into step beside him. They smelled moldy. "Any word on the little nigger?"

"His name is Jeremiah."

"That's the one. Any word?"

The hounds lifted their lips in silent snarls, nuzzling Wally's hands which left his fingers slick with slobber. He switched his school books to an underarm.

"See, the thing is," Aldo bumped him, "we don't have any choice about this. Do we, Cole?"

"No choice at all."

"Let one nigger get away with something," Aldo said, "and next thing you know there's two to fight, then four. It's best to send a message right off. If a colored boy messes with a white girl, he's headed down a gator's gullet and he needs to know it."

"That little nigger has got to be learnt a lesson," Cole agreed.

"It's the only way to keep white blood pure," Aldo said. "This ain't the first time the Klan has had to deal with the problem in this family."

Wally halted. "What do you mean?"

"It started with the little nigger's grandmama," Cole said. "She's pretty near white because her mama was white trash. She got caught naked in a wheelbarrow with a nigger yardman. The Klan tied that nigger to a tree by one leg, and one leg to a horse, and rode off at a gallop. My daddy said you could hear him screaming all the way to Pahokee."

"That would've been at least sixty years ago," Wally said. "Your daddy couldn't have been there."

"He heard the story from *his* daddy," Aldo said. "Even that didn't stop niggers from lusting after white women. That's why the Klan is going to do something about this. The little nigger has got to pay, and the message has got to be clear."

Wally quickened his step and at the Chosen bridge the Festers fell away behind him. It was the start of a bad day. Danny Dumb-dumb and his pals were waiting at the footbridge. Some of the boys smoked cigarettes. "Ho, Polly Wally!"

He tried to go by but Danny blocked his way. Wally smelled hair tonic. Danny liked to comb his hair a lot.

"I heard that Naomi is carrying a black baby," Danny said.

"It's only been a week, Danny."

"Yeah, so?"

"A woman doesn't know she's got a baby in only a week. If you ever went to biology class you'd learn that it takes nine months to make a baby."

Wally had made it a point to find out about that, anticipating meetings with Naomi yet to come. He'd studied "gestation" and "lactation" and "menstruation." The book said that many times a woman didn't know she was pregnant until she'd missed one or two menstruations. Wally told that to Danny.

"Yeah, well, nigger babies are wigglier than white babies," Danny said. "A woman could tell."

Wally sidestepped to pass them. He was blocked again. He thought the hair tonic was Wildroot Creme Oil.

"You told a lie, Polly Wally," Danny said. "You told me Naomi went to the hospital because she was beat up. Truth is, she went to have a baby, didn't she?"

Wally sidestepped again, and somebody shoved him. Then somebody else. He dropped the books he carried. When he bent to pick them up, Danny kicked him and he sprawled to the pavement. Wally came up swinging, blind with rage.

The other boys finally stepped in to stop the fight when Danny sat on the ground, nose bleeding. "I'm going to kill you," he said, so they let Wally go again.

They wrestled and boxed and kicked across the road onto the footbridge, back into the road, and once more the other boys separated them. The flesh of Wally's ears burned from being smashed by a fist. He had to look through the slit of a swollen eye. He tasted blood, and his knees and elbows were raw from being thrown to the pavement. But Danny was no better. He sat with legs spraddled, testing his mouth with a finger.

"I lost a tooth," Danny said. "Does anybody see a tooth?"

"You want it for the tooth fairy?"

Danny's friends laughed at that, and for a moment it looked like the fight would continue. But Danny settled back again. "I just got braces off my teeth last spring," he said. "My mama is going to be mad as wet hornets."

They found the tooth, and Danny retreated, clothes torn, incisor in hand. The other boys drifted toward school, leaving Wally at the footbridge. His clothes were ripped and stained. Blood spotted his shirt. He limped toward the packing house. Maybe he could get ice to ease the throbbing of his jaw.

The icehouse was closed. The packing house was empty, conveyor belts motionless. A black crepe paper wreath hung on the office door. Wally sat on the platform, aching from ankles to eyebrows. He heard an upstairs screen door slam.

"Wally?" Naomi came down the steps, her face still puffed and misshapen. "I can't see you without my glasses," she said. "They took my glasses at the hospital, then couldn't find them. But I knew it was you."

She eased down to sit beside him. She took his hand. "I wish I hadn't caused this trouble," she said. "I wish I hadn't shot my daddy." Her lips were still so swollen they hardly moved when she spoke. "How did you know I was here, Wally?"

"I didn't. I came to get ice. Danny and I had a fight."

"Come on," she said. "We have ice upstairs."

"I don't think I'd better, Naomi."

"It's all right. Mama is here. She knows about nursing."

When Wally entered the apartment, Mrs. Noonan took one

look and went for medicine and a pan of water to bathe his face. She dabbed Mercurochrome and applied unguents. Wally flinched and Mrs. Noonan made sympathetic clucking sounds. The room was full of hampers and orange crates. Only then did he realize she and Naomi were packing to leave.

"The apartment was part of my daddy's pay," Naomi explained. "Now that he's dead, we have to move out. They're sending me to a detention home in West Palm Beach. I'm leaving my comic books, Wally. You may take as many as you want."

"I don't have a place to keep them."

"I'd send some to Jeremiah," Naomi said, "but I don't know what kind he likes."

"Maybe you could store them until you come back."

"If they don't send me to jail, we're moving to Tennessee to live with my uncle," she said. "He goes to church twice a week and preaches once a month. He doesn't approve of comic books."

They sat beside one another on the couch, her leg warm against his. After a while, Naomi said, "Miss Lanier said the detention center is real nice. There are six girls who share a room. She said it's like a hotel except for the fence and bars on the windows."

Wally heard Mrs. Noonan sob.

"If I could see Jeremiah," Naomi said, "I'd tell him how sorry I am. Sheriff Posey told Miss Lanier that things are apt to get ugly. He asked me where Jeremiah went, and I didn't know."

"He asked me too."

Naomi held Wally's hand. Her fingers were cold. "I'll miss you," she said.

"I'll miss you too, Naomi."

That night at supper, Anthony noted Wally's swollen eye, Mercurochrome splotches and Band-aids. "So," he said, "who won the fight?"

Wally was stiff and sore, but Danny had a missing tooth and an angry mother. "I think I did," he said. And that ended the discussion.

For eleven days Jeremiah had been gone, and every morning the weather was colder. Wally awoke hugging his pillow for warmth, thinking of Jeremiah hungry and miserable. In the kitchen, Hattie rattled the grate to shake out ashes, preparing to stoke the fire.

"I think when we find Jeremiah we should go away," she said to Anthony.

"Go where?"

"We were happy in Paris even during the war."

"It won't be the same," Anthony said. "Food is scarce. Our friends are gone or dead. Reconstruction has barely begun and most of Europe is in shambles."

"It can't be worse than this," Hattie argued. "We never should have sent Jeremiah to live with my parents."

"Hattie, I'm tired of hearing you say that. Belle Glade was better than the middle of a war."

"The minute we find him, we should run for it."

Lying in bed listening, Wally heard Anthony say, "The real issue is the Noonan girl. Your father is right, the only way to defuse this mess is by putting Jeremiah in the hands of the law and let the community know that's where he is."

"Are you joking? We can't trust the law."

"We haven't much choice, Hattie."

"What's gotten into you?" Hattie said. "Those white men will find Jeremiah and whip him on general principle. They'll chain him and drag him around like a dog. They'll talk about castration and lynching and maybe go through with it, depending on how liquor flows and tempers flare."

"I pray that doesn't happen, Hattie."

"It won't happen if I can help it, but I'm not depending on anybody else. I'm going to find Jeremiah, and we are headed for Paris."

Anthony came to the bedroom and looked in. Wally pretended to be asleep until the door closed.

"What about Wally?" he heard Anthony ask.

She replied in French and Anthony said softly, "I see."

Wally heard fire roar in the flue. He smelled coffee. A skillet banged on the stove as Hattie cooked breakfast.

"I can't live without you, Hattie."

"Then come to Paris."

"I have an idea for a new book," Anthony said. "It'll be a kind of follow-up to the *Grapes of Wrath*, about changes that have taken place in migratory labor since the Depression."

"You can write it in Paris."

"Being in Belle Glade gives me a unique perspective, Hattie. Here I am living with one foot in the white community and one foot in the colored section. This is the location of Eleanor Roosevelt's pet projects: the migratory camps, free medical clinics, child labor laws—that's what my book would be about. I can't write that in Paris."

Minutes passed in silence, then Anthony said, "I've been suffering writer's block. I've agonized over Kathryn, and now Wally, but I'm getting a grip on myself, Hattie. I can write this migratory labor thing."

"I'm going to find Jeremiah and we're leaving, Anthony."

"What about me?" Anthony said. "My whole life hangs on getting published again."

"That book means more to you than Jeremiah and me?"

"Of course not."

"Then come with us."

"I've worked a long time to regain equilibrium," Anthony said. "Now this."

"Will you stop that?" Hattie said. "If you want to stay and write a book, then stay! But I won't leave Jeremiah in jeopardy by staying here with you."

"Then take Wally with you."

"He's your son, Anthony, not mine."

"Are we family, or not?"

Fire droned in the flue. Bacon sizzled. Wally lay abed, heartsick.

"If we were married," Hattie said, "*then* we'd be family."

Rumors at school grew more bizarre.

"Hey, Wally, we heard that Naomi and your colored brother

are living together, is that true?"

"It's not true."

"Somebody said her baby was born black as soot with one gold tooth."

Even Mrs. Bullock added to the gossip. "Wally, what is this I hear about Jeremiah running naked through the swamps?"

"I don't know, Mrs. Bullock."

"Trying to be a colored Tarzan," Mrs. Bullock said. "There was a photograph in the Clewiston newspaper, I was told. Have you seen it?"

"No ma'am."

With notoriety came a strange popularity for Wally. Students overcome by curiosity began to sit with him during lunch. Girls in giggly groups of three or four would ask questions while their boyfriends leaned against walls nearby.

"Were there really twins, one black and the other white?"

"No."

"I heard the Ku Klux Klan plans to burn crosses against y'all and they held a prayer vigil where they called you by name. Are you scared?"

He was, but Wally said, "No."

Every hour, in every class, somebody had something outrageous to say about Naomi or Jeremiah. Finally, the principal, Mr. Hobarth, took up the subject in assembly.

"I have been hearing unkind stories about Naomi Noonan," Mr. Hobarth said. "Stories that are cruel lies, and I mean to put a stop to it."

He glared at the students from under bushy eyebrows. "Naomi is not pregnant," Mr. Hobarth said. Students all around recoiled at the word.

"She is in a doctor's care because of a whipping, which everybody knows," he said. "She is staying at a juvenile facility in West Palm Beach."

The audience sat motionless under the principal's stare. "As for the colored boy," Mr. Hobarth said, and a titter rippled through the student body. "That unfortunate colored boy is not our concern," he said. "The law will tend to him. Now, students, if I hear anyone talk about this pitiful girl, I'll suspend him for three days with no chance to make up work. For some of you that would mean failing."

As Wally walked the corridor after assembly, his name was a whisper on the lips of students behind him.

Mrs. Bullock stopped him in the crowded hall. "You've missed several days of school, Wally. Do you have an excuse?"

"No ma'am."

"Tell your father to come see me," she said.

"He won't come, Mrs. Bullock."

Her face reddened. Students were listening. Mrs. Bullock scribbled a note and folded it twice. "Give this to your father," she said. "Tell him I shall expect him."

"He won't come."

"He'll come, or you can expect consequences when I make a report to Miss Lanier. I've told you the importance of my friendship, Wally. So far, I have gotten nothing from you but trouble. Tell your father he'd better be here."

Walking home, Wally's shadow fell long behind him. It was too cool for insects to sing and silence was like a blanket. He carried class assignments he had no intention of doing. His grades were falling and for the first time in his life he expected to fail.

"Psssst! Psssst!"

At first, Wally thought the sound was the hiss of a bobcat. Then Jeremiah laughed.

"Jeremiah, are you all right?"

"I was until I tried to get home to eat," came the answer from shifting saw grass. "The Festers are watching our house. Hey, Precious, I need food and something to drink. Can you bring it out to the Fester shack at Kramer's Island?"

"How will you get past the Festers to go there?"

"I got a boat. They won't see me."

A truck approached going toward the dike. Seeing Wally staring at the canal, the driver slowed in anticipation of alligators maybe. Wally shifted his gaze upward as though a bird had taken flight.

The driver picked up speed again, and Wally called,

"Jeremiah! Hey, Jeremiah!"
    A breeze responded, a murmur in foliage.
    Hurriedly, Wally walked toward home.

Wally didn't tell Hattie and Anthony he'd spoken to Jeremiah. Hattie was planning to leave him behind when she and Jeremiah went to France; if she didn't care about Wally, why should he care about her? There had been more talk of military boarding schools, too, so Anthony certainly didn't want a son to worry about.

Day after tomorrow was Thanksgiving, and there'd been no mention of it by anybody. Wally missed his mother's exuberance as she recognized red-letter days on the calendar. "A holiday!" she'd exclaim. "A reason to celebrate!"

She taught him the history of each commemorative date as they observed birthdays of dead Presidents, Flag Day, Fourth of July and Labor Day. But Thanksgiving was extra special.

"We have a lot to be thankful for," his mother would say. "Why don't you prepare a Thanksgiving prayer, Wally. List the things for which we are grateful." It took a while, but they worked on the list together. It was always surprisingly long, and when they read it over, Wally's mother added a blessing or two he'd forgotten.

Wally thought of this as he packed food in a burlap sack for Jeremiah. He tried to think of a blessing for this year. Well, yes; he could be thankful things weren't worse. Imprisoned in a military boarding school would be worse. So he felt justified not telling Hattie and Anthony about Jeremiah, who was safe and sassy. They were being selfish, thinking about expelling Wally from the family, so he would be selfish also, and for the moment he felt as if he had some control over his life.

Mama used to say, "Always help others to the degree that you might wish them to help you." The trouble was, Wally was not sure Jeremiah would do anything for him. Nevertheless, he was filling two large bottles with drinking water when Minnie Lou arrived.

"What's this you do, Precious?"

Wally placed the water bottles in a second sack and tied the two bags together. He slung them around his neck so most of the weight rode his shoulders. "I'm going camping, Minnie Lou."

"You daddy know this?"

"He wouldn't care."

Minnie Lou examined the food he took. "What about school?"

"Day after tomorrow is Thanksgiving," he said, as if that answered her question. "I'll be home before dark, Minnie Lou."

Wally went to the road and looked for the Festers to be sure the way was clear. Minnie Lou stood on the porch watching. Then he ran down the lane toward Anthony's retreat. Waterfowl clucked in the hummocks, disturbed by his passing. He heard the clickety-clickety of duck bills chittering nervously in stands of cattails. It was still half an hour before sunrise, and Lake Okeechobee was the color of platinum.

To Wally's surprise, he found he was enjoying himself. The air smelled fresh. There was a peacefulness in the setting and the hour, and he felt good skipping school. He was relieved to be going away from taunting classmates and dominating adults. He was glad to be where creatures existed without interference from man.

He saw an owl tearing the wings from baby birds still in their nests—awful, but understandable. Out here there was a reason for everything; even terrible things had reason. When death came here, it served a purpose.

He rolled his trousers above the knees and waded away from shore, the food and water he carried pulling hard on his shoulders. Mist spread across the lake like a gossamer sheet. Frogs leapt from lily pads to watery depths, each plunge a liquid gulp surrounded by ripples. A long-legged blue heron skimmed low, near enough for Wally to see the yellow of its eyes. A moment later the mighty bird extended his feet as though braking to a halt, and settled gently into the shallows.

The trek was farther than Wally remembered. Or maybe it was the weight of his burden that made it seem so. He stumbled and soaked his trousers, then splashed onward. Offshore, ducks preened, then upended themselves with tails high and heads submerged as they foraged for food underwater.

He began to worry that he might have passed the site. There was no dry place to stop and rest, the shoreline choked by water grasses, a natural haven for snakes. Despite the cool of morning air, he was perspiring, his cargo cutting into his shoulders. Surely by now he'd gone several miles!

Again he staggered and quickly snatched up the bags to keep them dry. He stopped to catch his breath, legs spread, so weary he considered dumping part of his load.

Then he saw her—

The woman stood where she'd been the first time, at the edge of the lake. The long braid fell over her shoulder. She still wore jodhpurs, and now Wally saw she was wearing riding boots too. She beckoned to him. *Come on*, her motion insisted. *This way!*

He trudged toward her on leaden legs, algae clinging to his calves. She was at the top of the dune now. Wading out of the water, Wally dropped the bundles and fell to his knees, breathless. Over the dune, up at the shack, she stood on the porch. Wally waved a greeting, but she turned and went inside.

He gathered the sacks and continued forward. He climbed onto the porch and walked down the breezeway past empty rooms. In the rear where the Festers kept their barrels, Jeremiah was asleep on a pile of gunny sacks, one arm beneath his head, chest bare and feet unshod. The woman knelt beside him.

Wally dropped his bags on the floor, and she looked up at him. Her eyes were blue as a summer sky.

"I brought food," Wally said.

And she disappeared.

Wally yelped and hurled himself backward. Jeremiah vaulted upright.

"Did you see that?" Wally screamed.

"See what?"

"The woman! Did you see the woman?"

"Are you trying to scare me, Precious?"

"She was beside you, Jeremiah. She was right there!"

"Will you quit that?" Jeremiah demanded. "Giving me goose bumps the size of marbles."

Wally ran out back, then in again. He peered behind empty barrels and across the hall where firewood remained. Jeremiah poked through the sack of food. "I hate sardines," he said. "Potted meat is okay. Peanut butter is good."

Wally jumped off the rear porch to peer beneath the house where the Festers kept their liquor. No jars now. Nothing.

"You brought water?" Jeremiah yelled. "You couldn't bring sweet tea?"

Wally circled the shack. There was no place to hide. Besides, she didn't walk out or run, she *disappeared!* Like smoke, she was there and then she wasn't. A shiver tickled his spine and hair rose on the nape of his neck.

Returning to Jeremiah, Wally said, "I'm telling you, Jeremiah, she was clear as my hand one minute and gone the next. I'm not joking. While I was looking at her, she dissolved."

"Sure she did," Jeremiah scoffed. "Sit down, Precious. How are things at home?"

While Jeremiah ate potted meat and saltine crackers, he told Wally how he'd been hiding with a grown woman in Bean City south of Lake Okeechobee. But Wally could think of nothing but the vision—whatever it was. Every shadow quickened his pulse. Who was she? *What* was she?

"Know how many friends I've got?" Jeremiah lamented. "None. I thought this Bean City woman was my friend, but when she found out the police were after me, she told me to get out. I wouldn't go until her husband came home and made me. He drives a long-haul truck from Bean City to California. I asked him to give me a ride back to Belle Glade, but he said he didn't want the law coming after him too. They brought me back to the migratory camp and threw me out."

A breeze made the sheet metal roof crackle, and Wally jumped to his feet. He stared at a hole in the ceiling.

"If you're trying to scare me home," Jeremiah said, "it won't work. I know the Klan is looking for me, and I'm not going to get lynched by the Klan, no thank you. I'm hiding from the law on one hand, Naomi's father on the other—"

"He's dead," Wally said.

"Who's dead?"

"Naomi shot her father."

"Naomi killed her daddy?"

Wally related the story from start to finish. "Naomi is locked in a detention home in West Palm Beach," he concluded.

Jeremiah cleaned out the potted meat can with a finger. "I still have the gun from the barbershop," he said. "Shoots bullets bigger than your thumb and kicks like a pool hall bouncer. I didn't mean to shoot nobody, but the gun shot twice. I don't know how it happened. Are they dead?"

"Last I heard they were alive. In the hospital."

"Dirty lying card cheats," Jeremiah said. "But I didn't mean to hurt nobody. I needed money to get away, that's all. When I asked for my money back, they laughed at me. I knew where he kept his gun, so I grabbed it from under the cash register. I swung around and it went off—twice!"

Wally sat on the floor again, alert for every sound or movement. He heard saw grass rasping in a breeze. "Jeremiah," he said, "do you believe in ghosts?"

"Quit your talking like that."

"I'm telling you, she was in this room. She looked up at me and melted away."

"Precious, you aren't scaring me."

"I was looking right at her," Wally marveled.

Jeremiah reached under the gunny sacks and pulled out a pistol. "Don't come back tonight trying to scare me, Precious. Anybody comes messing about here and I'll shoot."

"Or get shot," Wally said. "Deputy Posey is looking for you. He walked around the house with a hand on his gun, ready to draw because he knew you had a gun. Having that pistol will get you shot."

Jeremiah blinked hard. "The folks in Bean City wouldn't hide me, and I used to run bolita for that woman. I delivered moonshine for her husband, but he told me to get out or he'd call the sheriff. I went to the grocery store where we sold sandwiches, and she told me don't be bringing my troubles to her."

Jeremiah ducked his head and wiped one eye. "What I need is a place to grow up," he said. "If I could get to France, I'd take Naomi with me."

"Do you speak French?" Wally questioned.

"*Mais oui.*"

"All this time you understood Hattie and Anthony?"

"You'd be surprised what they say when they think we don't understand."

Jeremiah turned the cylinder of his pistol, examining bullets. "I'll need help breaking Naomi out of jail."

"You're not going to do that, Jeremiah. Don't be stupid."

"I'll need money to get us to France. Will you help me?"

"I'll help, if you give me the gun."

"First scare me to death talking about ghosts, and now you want my gun, too? No."

"There's no point trying to help somebody who's going to be shot dead anyway," Wally said.

A dirt dauber fell to the floor in the throes of old age, the end of summer, its time to die.

"Maybe your grandfather and grandmother would help us," Jeremiah said.

"My grandparents are dead."

"They live in Indiana," Jeremiah said. "I've heard Mr. McManus talk about them."

"Liar. His parents died when a train hit their car," Wally said.

"I don't mean his parents," Jeremiah said. "I mean your mama's mama and daddy. They got lots of money."

"My mother told me her parents are dead."

"But they're not. Mr. McManus wrote them a letter after your mother died. I read letters that your mama wrote about them. Your mama said she couldn't send you to her people because she never wanted to talk to them again. She said there was only one place for you to live and that was with Mr. McManus."

"You're lying, Jeremiah."

"Get the letters and read for yourself! Mr. McManus keeps them in his desk drawer. If your grandmama and granddaddy would help us get to France, I'd be a new man. Grow me a mustache, get fancy clothes. French womens aren't like American womens. They'll curl your toes and make your eyeballs cave in."

Too many things were happening. *Grandparents?*

"I stole a boat to get out here," Jeremiah said. "We'll use it to go around the lake and catch a bus to Indiana. I know you've got the money for tickets. I couldn't find it, but I know you got money. When we get to Indiana, I'll teach you how to get money out of rich people. And they *are* rich, Precious. Mr. McManus has money, but he said your grandfather is *rich!*"

Afternoon shadows bowed to the east. The cries of waterfowl became peeps in settling rookeries. Somewhere an alligator bellowed.

"I have to go, Jeremiah. Give me the pistol."

"When you come back tomorrow," Jeremiah said, "I'll give it to you then."

"If you don't, I'm through helping you."

"If you don't help me," Jeremiah said, "a gun won't matter much anyway."

In the violet glow of setting sun, Wally arrived home wet, cold and exhausted. The house loomed on stilted legs, unlighted and uninviting. The Ford coupe was gone, and Minnie Lou had left for the day. Wally lit a lamp and stoked the stove to rekindle the fire. Smoke trickled up from the eyes until he remembered to adjust the flue, then flames flared. While the stove heated, he went through Anthony's desk drawers.

He found the letters in a bundle tied with string. They spanned more years than Wally had lived. Anthony had numbered the envelopes as though to read them again and again in proper sequence.

I will not forgive you, Wally's mother had written during her pregnancy. *You refused to come home to America, denied you wanted a family, and all the while betrayed our vows by sleeping with another woman. You are without honor, Anthony. I would no more name a son for you than call him Judas Iscariot. You will never see the child I carry, nor do you deserve to. I hope you and your colored woman can be content with a mulatto child.*

On tissue-thin paper her bitterness made cruel reading.

A thousand times I wondered if you loved me, she wrote, *and a thousand times you ridiculed my doubts. I worried when you stayed out all night, never thinking that you were safe in the arms of another woman. I despise her, Anthony.*

In other letters, Kathryn recriminated even as she asked for money. *The least you can do is provide an income sufficient to support me as I devote my life to raising my precious baby.*

In another letter: *The terms of divorce arrived today. I will need more money than you offer. My attorney here in Atlanta urged me to wait until the war ends so that if you are killed I remain your legal heir. I insisted the divorce be finalized, war or no war.*

Months later she wrote without a hint of forgiveness. *My son will not hear your name until I am forced to speak it. I dread the day when I must admit you exist. I see much of you in this toddling child, and to my surprise it does not revolt me. He has your smile and mannerisms, which must be genetic. I mention this not to please you, but to show what you have forfeited. It should cause you pain to contemplate what you lost.*

Wally wished he could read his father's response. How would he reply to such bitterness? The next letter was dated January 1946, when Wally was nine years old.

Thank you for letting me know you are in Belle Glade, Anthony. I am pleased that you are safe. Despite everything, I wish you no harm. I'm sorry to hear your writing is not going well, but you will overcome that.

Then she got sick.

Anthony, she wrote, *I hadn't been feeling well for a long time and finally went to a doctor. He thinks I have a cancer. It is premature to consider death, but the thought is on my mind. I am terrified, not for myself, but for my precious boy. What would become of him?*

In a subsequent letter, she knew she was dying:

I cannot send Wally to my parents, Anthony, so do not suggest it. They were so mean to us before we married, I can never forgive them. They know nothing of our divorce, or of Wally. However, a child should be raised by blood relatives. That means you. Please do not say no. You would only compound the greatest error of your life. Wally is his father, body and soul. You will adore him. So when the time comes I will send him to you. Please. Anthony. Please.

Wally did not remember ever seeing his mother write a letter, and yet here they were.

And the last one: *If we have done nothing else, Anthony, we produced a fine son. Do not reject him because he is of me, but rather, love him because he is of you. Thank you for that which was good between us. Thank you for the good to come. . . .*

Wally bound the letters in sequence and put them where he'd found the bundle. The chill of night seeped through the house. He took a lamp and went to sit beside the stove.

What kind of people were they, this family of his? Wally's mother, hurt by an unfaithful husband, had also disowned her parents even unto death. Who was right and who was wrong, and what difference did it make?

He thought about going to Indiana to get help from his grandparents for Jeremiah's escape. If the grandparents were as unforgiving as their daughter, there'd be no tearful reconciliation. Besides, what would he say? "Hello, my name is Wally McManus and I am your grandson. And this," he'd introduce Jeremiah, "is my brother. We're wanted by the law. Jeremiah shot two men who had been cheating at poker. He got personal with a white girl and she killed her father. The Ku Klux Klan wants to lynch him and we need money to go to Paris."

They'd probably call the police.

Fire in the stove was dying and there was no more kindling in the woodbox. Wind moaned in the chimney and the damper waggled under pressure. To stay warm, Wally went to bed. He wrapped himself in blankets, his own hot breath trapped beneath the quilts.

His head was a merry-go-round. So many people were angry with him—Mrs. Bullock, Danny Dumb-dumb, even the librarian who still refused him books.

As he drowsed, he dreamed of Jeremiah, out at Kramer's Island tonight, clutching a revolver, afraid of the dark. And there, the woman, kneeling at his side. . . .

chapter seventeen

Everything Wally knew about ghosts he had learned from the movies. Ghosts could seep through keyholes and float in the air. Like spider webs torn from earthly anchors, ghosts were transparent and elusive. So when Wally thought about the woman at Kramer's Island, he couldn't be sure she was a ghost. She did not pass through solid walls, she used doorways. She wasn't wispy, but was firm as flesh and bone. Yet she'd dissolved before his eyes. What could she be but a ghost?

Another thing. If it was possible for a dead person to reappear, why didn't his mother visit him? Didn't she know how lonely he felt, how desperately he needed her? Surely she would come if she could.

Burdened with these thoughts, Wally slept fitfully. Suddenly the ghost of Kramer's Island was in his room, and somehow night became light. Frightened, he tried to flee, but she blocked his escape and herded him back to bed. Cowering under the covers, he felt her weight depress the mattress, her leg against his hip. When he dared to open his eyes and look at her, he saw nothing threatening in her manner, and yet he was terrified. Was she a ghost? he asked himself, and then, if this were his mother's ghost would he insult her by cringing in fear? Wouldn't it be rude to act this way? Thus resolved, he reached out—and the woman melted away.

With a shriek, Wally, threw himself to the floor and scampered to a far wall.

"Precious?" Hattie called from the kitchen. "You all right?"

"I fell out of bed."

"Time for breakfast," she said.

That had been real enough, Wally thought. He had felt the

woman's weight on his bed. Or, maybe he'd been dreaming all along, even out at Kramer's Island. Perhaps the woman was never there.

He dressed and went to sit at the table while Hattie cooked sausage by the dim light of a kerosene lamp. Her head was bound in a scarf and she wore a faded pink chenille robe. She stood with one hand on a hip, lost in thought, turning sausage in the skillet.

"Hattie, have you ever seen a ghost?"

"No." She flipped sausage. "Why do you ask?"

"Your daddy owns a funeral parlor. I wondered."

"I grew up a mortician's daughter and I've been around a lot of dead people," Hattie said. "I never saw one get up and walk. Has Minnie Lou been talking haints again?"

"Has she seen a ghost?"

"I told Minnie Lou not to scare you boys with silly stories."

"Does she believe in ghosts?"

Anthony stood in the bedroom door buttoning his cuffs. "Why are you bringing up the subject?"

Wally couldn't tell them about the woman kneeling beside Jeremiah without telling about Jeremiah. That would be the end of Jeremiah's run. Off they'd all go to France, and Wally would be sent to a military school.

"I read a book," he said.

Anthony pulled up a chair and sat at the table. "Fiction," he said. "Well, that's all it is, fiction. Phantoms and visions are holdovers from primitive cultures searching for a way to explain natural phenomena. Pass the biscuits, Wally. I'll speak to Minnie Lou about scare stories," he said.

"She didn't tell me scary stories," Wally insisted. But as he protested, Minnie Lou arrived and Hattie said, "I told you not to tell ghoulish tales, Minnie Lou."

"What I say?"

To distract them, Wally said, "Are we planning anything for Thanksgiving tomorrow?"

Anthony and Hattie exchanged glances. "We've been caught up in Jeremiah's troubles," Hattie said.

"We lived so long in France we tend to ignore American holidays," Anthony said.

"Precious can take dinner with us," Minnie Lou offered. "I'll send Eazy to fetch him come dinner time tomorrow."

As for today, Hattie and Anthony were going to the north shore of Lake Okeechobee in search of Jeremiah. After they'd left, Wally saw Cole and Aldo stroll past the house, then turn and amble home.

"What's this you tell Miss Hattie 'bout me scaring you?" Minnie Lou accused.

"I didn't say you did, Minnie Lou. I asked Hattie if she'd ever seen a ghost, and she thought you'd been talking about it. Have you ever seen the spirit of a dead person?"

"Haints," Minnie Lou said.

"Ever see one?"

"Can't talk about it. Too scary."

"I'm not scared. Tell me."

"Some haints be good, some make trouble."

"What is a ghost, exactly?"

"They just like live folks even when they dead. White folks stays white, colored come darkly."

"Can any dead person be a ghost?"

"Can't talk about it."

"If I can't talk to you," Wally protested, "who will I talk to?"

"You been poking Indian mounds?" Minnie Lou asked.

"No."

"That's when haints gets mean," she said, "somebody pokes they bones."

Wally looked toward the road. The Festers were still lurking. He began to assemble leftover sausage and cold biscuits for Jeremiah.

"You seen a haint?" Minnie Lou inquired.

"She seemed like a real person," Wally said, "but she dissolved while I was looking at her."

Minnie Lou's eyes widened.

He told her how the woman was dressed in jodhpurs and boots, her blond hair braided, and Minnie Lou's eyes grew even larger. "Where you see this haint?" she asked.

"Kramer's Island," Wally said, and Minnie Lou sucked air.

"That's where I'm going now," Wally said as he stepped onto the porch. The road was clear, the Festers gone. "I'd like to see her again," he said. "I want to ask if she's seen my mother over there where dead people stay."

When he glanced back from the road, Minnie Lou stood on the porch, a hand to her chest, watching him go.

Splashing the lake toward Kramer's Island, Wally passed beneath thousands of high-flying geese spiraling against a cloudless sky. Their wings captured the morning sun only to disappear moments later as they turned in unison. He heard their cries, a plaintive inquiry aimed at flocks below. *Is it safe? May we land?*

Mindful of the ghost, Wally watched for her in the distance. But it was Jeremiah who waited. "What took so long?" he demanded angrily. "I'm out here starving to death!"

He snatched the sack from Wally and pawed through the contents. "Is the tea sweet?"

"It's sweet."

They went into the back room and Jeremiah tore into the biscuits and sausage. "Bring more tea next time and put ice in it," he said.

Wally felt beneath the gunny sacks. "Where's the pistol, Jeremiah?"

"I threw it away."

"I don't believe you."

"I got to thinking what you said about a gun could get me killed, and I threw it away."

Wally jumped up to leave. As he walked down the breezeway, Jeremiah yelled, "Hey! Can't you wait until I finish eating?"

"Give me the gun or I'm going, Jeremiah."

"Don't push me, Precious. I'm not in the mood for much pushing."

"Then I'm going home."

"What if I got attacked by a gator, or a water moccasin

crawled in here? I need protection. What about the Festers?"

Wally strode down the hall.

"Wait a minute, wait a minute. What's your rush, Precious?"

"I told you before, there's no point trying to help somebody who is going to end up dead anyway. I'm leaving. Tomorrow is Thanksgiving."

"So what?"

"I'm eating dinner with Minnie Lou's family."

"Minnie Lou?" Jeremiah grabbed Wally's arm. "Minnie Lou never asked me to come eat at her house."

"Well, she asked me. Let go of my arm."

"You'll be back tomorrow?"

"I don't think so, Jeremiah." Wally jumped off the porch, going toward the lake.

A moment later, Jeremiah ran inside and came back out to yell, "Stop or I'll shoot!"

And he did. The bullet hit water not far from Wally's leg, then skipped farther offshore. The crack of the shot brought geese to flight, piercing shrieks and a roar of thrashing wings. Wally wheeled and screamed, "Are you crazy?"

Jeremiah looked at the pistol in his hand. "This thing goes off by itself," he said.

"Don't point it at me," Wally yelled. "Now give me the gun, Jeremiah."

"I can't, Precious. I'd be scared to stay out here without it."

"Then I'm leaving."

"If you don't come tomorrow," Jeremiah said, "I won't be here the next day. I'll run away forever. I mean it."

"You might as well," Wally hollered. "You aren't doing anybody any good like this."

"Nobody gives a damn about me."

The tone of his voice made Wally halt.

"Nobody cares whether I live or die," Jeremiah said.

"You make it difficult for anybody to care about you, Jeremiah, but they do. Hattie and Anthony go out looking for you every day. I wade the lake all this way to bring food and tea, and you don't even say thanks."

"I might as well be dead."

"Instead of feeling sorry for yourself," Wally said, "think about somebody else for a change. Naomi blames herself for what's happened, but this trouble is really your doing."

"She wanted me to visit."

"But you knew better."

The pounding rush of ascending wings had settled to a whispery return of countless birds. Minnows swam around Wally's legs.

"You shot two men, Jeremiah, and you don't seem to care. You keep that gun and that's sure to mean another shooting before it's over."

Jeremiah made a running start and threw the pistol as far as he could. The lake took it with a splash. "All right! I did what you wanted. Now come on back, Precious."

Wally returned to the porch and Jeremiah cried, saying he never meant to shoot anyone, and then he cursed the "lying, thieving card cheats" he'd shot. After a while they talked about ghosts and Seminole Indians and why frog pee caused warts.

At a distance, Wally heard a motor. "Jeremiah, somebody is coming."

"The Festers, I bet," Jeremiah gathered the last of his food. "Now I need the gun and I threw it away." He jumped off the porch, Wally following, and hurried around back to the flat-bottom boat he'd stolen. He tossed in his provisions, and Wally helped him push away from land. Out front, Aldo Fester hollered, "We know you're here!"

"Jeremiah," Wally confessed, "Hattie wants to take you to Paris."

"Don't lie to me, Precious."

"I'm not lying. She wants to go to France."

Jeremiah poled his boat into a narrow rivulet between tall reeds. The grasses closed behind him, and a moment later Ike Fester seized Wally's arm, twisting it painfully. "Where's the kid?"

Aldo yelled across the grasslands, "Come on out, you little nigger!" His voice echoed away.

"I'm alone," Wally said.

Ike slapped him. "You think we're dimwitted? We heard the shot, saw the birds."

"I heard that shot too," Wally said. "I think it came from west of here."

Ike knocked Wally to the ground, then yanked him up again. He lifted Wally to his tiptoes and dragged him toward the shack. Cole came onto the back porch holding an unopened can of sardines. "He was here, all right. I found this and a bed of sacks."

Aldo crawled under the shack poking at straw with a shotgun. Again, Ike slapped Wally's head. "All this time you've been hiding that nigger."

Aldo fired his shotgun into the saw grass field. The explosion brought up a scream of geese, and the thunder of wings was deafening. Aldo fired again.

"Stop it!" Wally yelled.

Cole shot a pistol here, there, aimlessly.

Once more, Ike smacked Wally with an open hand, and Wally felt blood ooze from his nose. "We ought to kill you here and now," Ike snarled. "You're a worthless piece of trash, just like your daddy."

Ike hauled him to the lake and shoved Wally into their boat. Aldo yanked the starter cord. The motor coughed, spit and caught.

"Don't say you didn't ask for what's coming to you," Ike said. He squinted across the lake. "A man who's not your friend is your enemy, McManus. Did you know that?"

"Yes," Wally said. "I knew that."

He thought they would drown him, or beat him. Wally was so sure he'd be whipped, he prepared himself for pain with a promise not to cry, no matter how much it hurt. But as the boat neared the sandy spit where Anthony went to think, Ike threw Wally overboard into knee-deep water. "Tell your daddy the Klan is coming," Ike said. Then the boat picked up speed and they went around a bend toward home.

Wally didn't see Hattie or Anthony that night or the next morning. He arrived home bleeding and sore from the mauling he'd received. He heated water on the cookstove for a hot bath and went to bed before dark. When he awoke, Hattie and Anthony had come and gone. It was Thanksgiving Day.

He didn't know whether he should eat or stay hungry in anticipation of dinner at Minnie Lou's. Nor did he know how to dress for the visit. He put on trousers so stiff the legs were khaki tunnels, and a shirt that rasped against bare flesh. Minnie Lou used a lot of starch.

For warmth Wally wore his money coat, although the sleeves were now too short. He sat on the front porch to wait for Eazy. The sun was a small ball in an uncluttered sky. He heard vehicles arrive at the Fester house. Minutes ticked away so slowly pale shadows in winter light seemed unmoving. His stomach growled. He wondered if Minnie Lou forgot him.

It was past noon when Eazy arrived in a pickup truck, springs screeching over every bump. In the bed of the truck a dozen children had come along for the ride. They stared at Wally, unsmiling. Eazy said, "Sit up front with us, Precious."

Wally squeezed in with two men, one of whom held a shotgun between his legs. No introduction was offered, the occupants grim.

The Fester's yard was crowded with cars and trucks. Aldo, Cole, and Ike stood over a pit fire cooking slabs of meat. Unfriendly white faces watched Eazy's truck rattle past.

"That's them?" the man with the shotgun asked.

"That's them," Eazy replied.

At Minnie Lou's, well-dressed Negroes congregated on the porch. Indoor furniture had been brought outside to accommodate visitors. Pots of red-blossomed geraniums lined the porch banisters. When Eazy stopped his truck, the children jumped out and ran to the steps where they turned to watch Wally emerge.

"Go on, go on," Eazy prodded Wally's back.

Approaching the house under Eazy's guiding hand, Wally's presence brought conversations to a halt as he was passed among strangers. Eazy urged him inside, out to the kitchen. "Minnie

Lou," Eazy said, and without looking up from food she prepared, Minnie Lou called, "Orlean! Here's Precious."

Whatever her age, Orlean looked mature. She had the bosom
of a grown woman and the manner of a child. "I'm going to see
after you," she said agreeably. "Minnie Lou said I had it to do."

She held Wally's hand taking him from room to room, saying,
"This is him, y'all."

Reactions varied from indifference to resentful acceptance.
"This is him," Orlean repeated, and she led Wally to another
group in the next room.

They ended up at a far end of the front porch, seated with
their legs dangling off the edge. After a long pause, talk resumed
among the adults.

"Black folks in Chicago get treated like anybody else," somebody reported. "I heard tell a Negro got hit by a car and he
snatched the white man out and beat him good. Nobody did a
thing about it either. When I get the money, I'm going north and
beat me a white man."

"How come white people so mean to coloreds anyhow?"

"They say we stink."

"Take a whiff of them sometime!"

"Y'all mind what you say now," somebody warned. "We got
a white boy listening. Unless you want him telling his neighbors,
the Klan."

"He's all right," Eazy said. "But the Klan *was* meeting at the
Fester place when we came by. They got dogs trained to bite
black asses."

"When they talk about hunting coons," somebody said, "they
ain't talking rackety-coons!"

"I'm telling you again, watch what you say in front of this
white boy."

"Neb mind him," Eazy said. "Precious is different 'cause of
Hattie and Jeremiah."

"Jeremiah's the one going to get us killed!"

"Meanness is bred into white folks," another voice said. "I
been working for the same white man twenty years. Last summer
he said, 'Wendell, it's a hundred degrees here in the shade where

I'm sitting, and Lord knows it's hotter than the Devil's pitchfork where you're working in the sun. But sun don't affect niggers, does it?' I got three shades darker working his garden that day. I peeled back my sleeve and said, 'Mister, you see how the sun burnt me?' He said, 'I never knew a nigger could tan.'"

"What makes me mad," somebody else volunteered, "is white women coming up to my child wanting to rub his burr for good luck. Like white people ain't got all the luck there is."

"Rub the baby's burr for good luck, and praise be to God," another mocked. "They believe in God. Try going to church with them sometime."

"Amen."

"You right."

"Right about that."

"A white woman was looking at my toddler one day and she said, 'He's so cute, he's almost human.' Said that to me! What does she think I am?"

"This is why I only work for Mr. Willoughby," Eazy said. "White people are born to be bad. 'Come mow my grass,' they say, and argue 'bout paying a dollar for a day's work. When you agree, they say, 'And while you at it, edge the walk and prune the shrubs, rake the lot and burn the trash.' One thing upon another like that. Then they say, 'You did a fair job, Eazy, but you're awful slow.'"

"Now y'all listen to me," the wary man said. "We got enough troubles with this white boy's *Griqua* brother without having tales get back to the Festers. I don't want no more talk about white folks in front of this Caucasian boy. On account of Jeremiah, the Klan's threatening to burn colored town as it is."

"I got some matches of my own," somebody rejoined.

"The Klan say niggers need be taught a lesson."

Wally sensed their mood turning ugly. "We'll see who gets a lesson," somebody growled.

"I ain't taking nothing off white folks again. I went to war just like they did, and German bullets don't know black hide from white. It won't do to threaten me or my family."

"Amen."

"You right."
"Right about that."
"Amen."

A dults and children ate on the back porch, sitting at a long
table of loose boards with benches on either side. There was
turkey, duck, goose and ham, yams smothered under melted
marshmallows, deviled eggs, sliced tomatoes and potato salad,
and a line of pies down the center of the table. Wally was work-
ing a mouthful of food when Orlean spoke. "Minnie Lou say
you got second sight."
"What does that mean?"
"Seen a ghost."
"It may be a ghost."
"Disappeared while you had eyes on her?"
Wally realized adults were listening.
"Tell them where it be," Minnie Lou spoke from the kitchen
door.
"Kramer's Island."
Naming the place brought a murmur from the listeners.
"He never heard of that woman before, did you, Precious?"
"No."
"You see," Minnie Lou challenged her guests. "Didn't I say he
had second sight? That boy saw Jeremiah's great-grandmother,
and she been dead sixty years!"

The day after Thanksgiving Wally was up before dawn to take food and drink to Jeremiah. Minnie Lou had sent him home with leftover ham and slices of pie. Careful not to wake Hattie and Anthony, he left for Kramer's Island while it was still dark.

The water was cold to his bare legs, and quick sharp breezes swept the lake. Unseen creatures stirred the reeds and ripples of water slithered like serpents. He'd gone about half a mile when he heard a motor. He sloshed toward shore and crouched in water grasses. The sound grew louder and Wally saw the Festers. Their boat passed by, bumping over the lake toward Kramer's Island.

Defeated, Wally trudged home.

The kitchen lamps were burning, and as Wally neared the lane he saw Deputy Posey's car. He crept up the porch and sneaked through his bedroom window. The floor creaked and he waited for reaction.

"As an officer of the court," he overheard Posey say, "it's my job to deliver the subpoena. I don't decide who gets one, that's up to a judge."

"I want to know who is responsible for these charges," Anthony demanded.

"I think you know the answer to that," the deputy said. "Child Welfare warned you, and so did I. The counselor at Wally's school asked for a private meeting and you ignored her."

Wally remembered Mrs. Bullock's note to Anthony and her warning. He tiptoed to the bedroom door and peeked through. Anthony and Hattie were in their bathrobes, seated at the kitchen table. The deputy stood over them.

"Because I didn't go see a teacher," Anthony said, "that gives her a right to meddle in our affairs?"

"Jeremiah hasn't been in school ten days this year, Mr. McManus. He's in trouble with a white girl and he's shot two men over a gambling debt. Now Wally is skipping school too. You can hardly claim things are normal around here."

"We can't bring Jeremiah to court if we can't find him," Hattie said.

"If you don't bring him," Posey warned, "you'll have to admit he's a runaway, and that confirms the worst."

"You couldn't find him," Hattie said. "How do you expect us to?"

"I haven't been looking," Posey replied. "The men at the barbershop refused to sign a complaint, and that ends it so far as I'm concerned. Had somebody died it would be a different matter. If I arrested a nigger every time there's a slash-and-shoot, my jail would overflow."

Posey walked to the front door, his wide body a silhouette in the first light of dawn. "Family court is upstairs in the old post office building," he said. "Be there Monday morning at nine o'clock, and don't be late. Judge William Watson gets a kink in his tail when people are late."

"Should we have a lawyer?" Anthony asked.

"That's not for me to say, Mr. McManus."

Anthony and Hattie remained at the kitchen table until the lawman's car drove away. Then Anthony leapt to his feet and threw open the bedroom door. Wally jumped backward. "Where have you been, Wally?"

"I—I was going camping."

"In the dark and cold? Don't lie!"

Wally agreed the time for lies was past. The Festers had shot at Jeremiah and now they were hunting him. "I was taking food to Jeremiah," he confessed.

"Where is he?"

"He was at Kramer's Island day before yesterday. But the Festers nearly caught him and—"

"The Festers?"

"They said Jeremiah has to be punished or all black men will mess with white women."

"Why didn't you tell us?" Hattie shrilled. "You knew Jeremiah was in danger and you didn't tell us?"

"I'll go rent a boat," Anthony said.

"I can't believe you let us suffer this way," Hattie said.

"I didn't want everybody to run away to France and leave me in a military school, Hattie."

Anthony came out of his bedroom putting on a jacket. "I'll find a boat, Hattie. But first I'm going to have a word with Ike Fester."

"They're on the way to Kramer's Island," Wally said. "That's why I came back."

Hattie sank to her knees moaning.

"At least we know he's nearby, Hattie," Anthony said. "Get dressed. I'll be back in a few minutes."

"Jeremiah is out there terrified and alone!" Hattie agonized.

"His grandmother is with him," Wally blurted. "She watches over him."

"What do you mean?" Anthony said. "Who watches over him?"

There was no better time for truth than now. Wally described the woman wearing jodhpurs and riding boots, her blonde hair falling over one shoulder. He told how he first saw her, and the last time how she knelt beside Jeremiah, then disappeared. "Who told you that story?" Anthony demanded.

"Nobody."

"And yet you say it was Jeremiah's grandmother. Why would you think that?"

"Minnie Lou said she was."

"So Minnie Lou told you the story?"

"No sir. I'd already seen the ghost when she told me."

"There's no such thing as a ghost," Anthony said.

"Then what was she?"

"You tell me, Wally. What *was* she?"

"She doesn't float or go through walls," Wally reasoned. "And except for the melting she seems real. But if a dead person can be seen again, why doesn't Mama come visit me?"

"It was your imagination. Go wash up; you're covered with mud. Be ready to leave when I get back."

In the bathroom Wally sat on a side of the tub and ran water over his legs. Hattie came to stand behind him. "Is Jeremiah all right?" she asked.

"He's not hurt or sick," Wally said.

"Did Jeremiah see the woman you saw?"

"No."

She pushed back his hair. "My mother's mother was a white woman," Hattie said. "She was brought to this country from Sweden to work for a wealthy family who raised sugar cane. She fell in love with their gardener, a young Negro from the Bahamas. When she became pregnant, the Ku Klux Klan learned of it and killed him."

"Tied one leg to a tree and—"

"A gruesome murder," Hattie said. "The woman gave birth to my mother, but by then they say my grandmother had gone insane. Some say she herself was slain by the Klan. Others say she ran off into the swamps on horseback. Her body was never found."

"Hattie, I told Jeremiah you wanted to take him to France. But he didn't believe me."

Anthony drove up and shouted, "I got a boat. Let's go!"

The boat was larger than they needed, a sodden old vessel with a lapstrake hull and doghouse cabin that opened to the stern. Wally knew something about boats because he'd once written a school paper on the history of boat building. This one was a commercial fisherman's inboard with a smoking motor beneath the deck. Nets and corks hung from spars, and the stench of dead fish was choking. The craft was slow to turn and hard to stop, and because it drew so much water, they had to stay well off shore. That's why Wally couldn't get his bearings.

"How much farther?" Anthony questioned.

"I'm not sure."

"I thought you knew the way."

"Nothing looks the same this far from shore," Wally said.

Irritated, Anthony spun the wheel. "Then we'll go nearer land."

The wind had died and the lake was absolutely still. There were no ripples except as they made them.

"What about it, Wally?" Anthony said. "How far?"

"I don't know for sure."

"Damn it! Have you been here or not?"

An instant later the boat plowed into the muddy bottom, throwing Wally and Hattie off balance. Anthony cursed and shifted to reverse. The propeller churned sediment, but the vessel didn't budge. Hattie and Wally went from side to side trying to rock the boat loose while Anthony raced the motor. Still it did not move.

"Must we wait for incoming tide?" Hattie asked.

"There is no tide, Hattie. Are we near the place, Wally?"

"I can't tell."

"You can't tell if it's one mile, five miles, or ten?"

Anthony jumped overboard, put a shoulder to the hull and struggled to lift the boat. He climbed in again, soaking wet and filthy. He revved the motor, and at last they pulled free.

There was no warmth in the sun, but a glare from the lake was blinding. To avoid the reflection, and for a better view of the horizon, Wally stood on the cabin roof, clinging to the mast. He detected a flash in the distance. "I think I see the rooftop," he called.

This time they went aground gently and waded the last thirty yards to shore. "This is where I first saw the ghost," Wally said. "Only I didn't know she was a ghost. Right here is where she waved to me, signaling, *This way, come on!*"

"Jeremiah!" Hattie hollered. "Are you here?"

Anthony joined her. "Jeremiah! Ho, boy!"

Unsettled geese walked on water, running to gather speed as they flapped their wings for takeoff. "Jeremiah!" Hattie cried.

Nearing the shack, Wally said, "The woman was standing on the porch waiting, but then she went inside."

He led Anthony down the hall. "Hello, Ma'am?" Wally called. "Are you here?"

Hattie went onto the back porch yelling Jeremiah's name.

Wally indicated a pile of burlap sacks. "This is where I found Jeremiah sleeping. The woman was kneeling beside him. When I spoke she looked up at me, and then disappeared."

"I don't know what you saw, Wally," Anthony said brusquely. "A bit of fog, sunlight and dust—"

"She looked real until she melted," Wally insisted.

"Whatever it was," Anthony said, "there's a logical explanation. It was *not* a ghost. We don't have time for such foolishness right now."

He opened several barrels and looked in. "Corn and sugar. They were making mash all right."

Outside, Hattie continued to shout Jeremiah's name. Swamp and sky swallowed her voice.

"What lies west of here?" Anthony asked.

"I never went farther than this."

"We'll keep looking," Anthony said. "Jeremiah had to find someplace to stay."

Back in the boat, they chugged westward. Geese bobbed lazily in the wake of the passing craft. An osprey swooped down to pluck a fish from the lake, and it was like watching the bird take food from a mirror.

"Here comes another boat," Anthony said. "Maybe they've seen somebody."

Wally peeked through nets hung from the rigging. "I think that's the Festers."

Hattie stood up and sheltered her eyes. "Anthony, they've got Jeremiah!"

Anthony turned the boat toward the Festers, his jaw clamped. Still peering through the mesh, Wally said, "It *is* Jeremiah!"

Steering with one hand, Anthony took down a long boat hook from the cabin wall. The Festers veered to avoid meeting them head-on. It was obvious they didn't know whom they saw. Anthony was bearing straight for them.

"Hey!" Ike yelled. "Wake up there, boatman! Hey! Pay attention!"

At the last second he recognized Anthony. Ike grabbed a shotgun as Anthony hooked the gunwale in passing. Hattie seized their boat with her bare hands and struggled to hold it alongside. Ike Fester stumbled backward, swearing the most vulgar words Wally had ever heard.

"Unloose us," Ike roared. "Unhand this boat or I'll shoot the lot of you."

"You won't shoot," Anthony said. "And if you do, they'll electrocute you in Raiford prison."

"We're doing the law's work this minute," Ike said. "We're taking this nigger to the sheriff."

"The sheriff doesn't want him," Anthony countered. "I spoke to Deputy Posey this morning. There are no charges against Jeremiah, so let him go."

Jeremiah's face was swollen, one eye bruised, hands lashed behind him. He bled from a cut on his forearm.

"If you want this nigger," Ike growled, "you can get him from the sheriff and not before."

"Ike," Anthony said, "that child is riding with us. If you want to follow, do as you will. But he's coming aboard."

Ike started to lift the shotgun, and Anthony swung the boat hook. It didn't batter Ike so much as it swept him off his feet into the lake. Hattie lunged for Jeremiah and snatched him into their boat.

Aldo had a pistol stuck in his belt, but Anthony stood over him holding the boat hook like a spear. Then Anthony said, "Better fish out your pappy before he gets waterlogged, Aldo. We're headed to the house."

"That nigger was stealing food from fishermen's cabins," Ike hollered. "He was breaking and entering homes of good white folks."

"If they complain," Anthony said, "I'll pay restitution."

Aldo turned off his motor to help Cole pull their father from the lake. Ike had lost his shotgun.

Hattie clutched Jeremiah to her chest as Wally untied Jeremiah's wrists.

"Ike said they were going to kill me," Jeremiah said. "Going to sink me in the lake and let me drown."

Anthony stood braced at the wheel, chin lifted, heading the boat toward home. Behind them, Aldo was trying to restart their motorboat, fruitlessly yanking the cord.

"I practiced holding my breath," Jeremiah said, "counted how many seconds I could live underwater."

Hattie touched his face with trembling fingers. Wally sat on the opposite side. He felt a little ill from rocking the boat, and a little sick with envy, watching Jeremiah in the arms of his mother.

Lying in bed late that night, with the exhausted Jeremiah hard asleep, Wally heard vehicles come and go at the Fester place. The ruckus sounded like a high school football rally, with periodic cheering. The Festers had built a bonfire so large the glow could be seen over tops of trees. Now and then he heard gunshots.

The next morning he awoke to the sound of Mr. Willoughby's voice. "Anybody here?"

"Come in, Daddy!" Hattie said. "Jeremiah is home."

When Wally got to the kitchen they were bent over the table looking at a poster. "These are all over town," Mr. Willoughby said. "Trouble's coming."

Bold letters proclaimed:

SAVE AMERICA!
JOIN THE KU KLUX KLAN

"I don't know who's most angry with y'all," Mr. Willoughby said, "the Negroes or whites. Both sides are making threats."

"Threatening whom?" Anthony asked.

"Anybody not like themselves. But the focus is Jeremiah and that white girl. The rumor is she's carrying his baby."

A snort of laughter erupted from Jeremiah. Mr. Willoughby wheeled furiously. "You won't think it funny if they come to hang you because the law hasn't done so."

Wally stood at the table reading the poster:

JOIN THE KU KLUX KLAN!

Good white men and women, save the
purity of the white race! Fight back!
Protect your wives and daughters!
Hear the Grand Dragon from Orlando
preach the Word of God!
Fight for white!
SAVE AMERICA

Smaller print at the bottom called for a "convocation" at an airfield in Belle Glade "where there are hangars in case of rain."

Moments later, Deputy Posey arrived. "I have another summons," he said to Anthony. "This one is about the Noonan girl. You must appear in West Palm Beach a week from Tuesday."

He spoke to Mr. Willoughby, "Morning, Harold. The judge wants Wally and Jeremiah in juvenile court. He wants to hear from Jeremiah on account of he's the one who started all this. And he wants to hear what Wally has to say since he was there when Naomi killed her father."

"I didn't see her do it," Wally said.

"She told you she shot him, didn't she?"

"Yessir, but—"

"That's what the judge wants to know."

After an awkward moment, Mr. Willoughby said, "Thank you, Deputy Posey. I'll walk out with you."

"Anthony," Hattie said as soon as they were off the porch, "we can take a train to New York and book passage to France."

"What about Naomi?" Wally asked.

"She did shoot her daddy," Hattie said.

"Yes, and Jeremiah shot two men. Naomi's daddy said he was going to get a gun and shoot me. Naomi needs us here to tell the truth."

"I don't need to tell nothing," Jeremiah said.

"We can't let Naomi take all the blame, Jeremiah."

"I'm not to blame for anything."

"You went there, didn't you? You knew better and went anyway."

"And we only read comics."

"Jeremiah, Naomi needs us to speak for her."

"Hush, hush," Anthony said. "We'll think about it overnight."

"We can't leave," Wally insisted. "If we do, we'll never be proud of ourselves again."

"We'll decide tomorrow," Anthony said.

That night after they'd gone to bed, Wally lay awake listening to Hattie and Anthony argue in the next room. Hattie wanted to go now. Anthony said he'd think about it.

Down at the Festers, hounds bayed at the moon.

Only Jeremiah slept, snoring softly.

chapter nineteen

The lawyer Anthony hired arrived from West Palm Beach with Pierre Arneaux, owner of *Coq du Village*. Paul Feinberg was a small man with curly gray hair and brown-flecked green eyes. He wore suspenders and round spectacles.

In the courtroom, Wally sat with Jeremiah, Hattie and Anthony at a long table facing the judge. Every sound reverberated off walls with peeling paint. Overhead fans stirred warm currents from high ceilings. Shafts of sunlight sliced through the windows, and dust motes rode sunbeams like passengers on an escalator.

"What's going to happen to us?" Wally asked.

"Nothing," Anthony said. But he was ashen and shaking. "Everything will be fine."

Wally's impression of courts, like his knowledge of ghosts, came from films. In movies he'd seen Judge Roy Bean dispense justice at the point of a gun, using a saloon as his chamber. He'd watched "A Tale of Two Cities" in which French noblemen were condemned to the guillotine.

He knew judges had great power over the lives of people.

Judge William Watson had tangled brows, and tufts of hair sprouted from his ears. "Are you ready, Mr. Feinberg?" he asked.

"As ready as I can be on such short notice, Your Honor."

"If you can come up with a reasonable excuse for delay, I'll consider it," Judge Watson said. "Otherwise, we're moving ahead with this."

Mrs. Bullock was there from school, and Miss Edna Lanier from Child Welfare. Minnie Lou and Eazy sat in the rear with Mr. Willoughby. Other Negroes were also present. "Two teachers and the principal from my school," Jeremiah informed Wally.

The judge asked everybody to stand at one time, and he said to them all, "If you have business with this court, raise your right hand. Do you each and every one swear to tell the truth under penalty of law if you do not?"

Everybody said yes, except Jeremiah. He said later he didn't intend to say no, but he didn't understand the question until it was over.

"Your honor," Mr. Feinberg said, "I request that this court postpone any action until I have had sufficient time for my own investigation."

"Let's not make a production of this," the judge said. "The case is clear cut, Mr. Feinberg. Do your clients know the miscegenation law of the State of Florida?"

"I'm sure they do, Your Honor."

"Do you intend to challenge that law, Mr. Feinberg?"

"No sir."

"Then everything else is irrelevant."

"Only if this court insists that there are never exceptions to any statute."

The judge leaned to look around the lawyer. "Mr. McManus, are you living with Hattie Willoughby?"

"Yes sir."

"Is that mulatto boy your offspring?"

"I object!" Mr. Feinberg shouted.

"To which question do you object, Counselor?"

"All of them. The only issue before this court is whether custody of these boys shall remain with their blood relatives."

"Very well, Mr. Feinberg. Be seated." The judge turned to Jeremiah. "You are Jeremiah?"

"Yes."

"Are you happy at home?"

"I guess so."

"And you?" he looked to Wally. "Are you happy at home?"

"I don't want to be in a foster home or a military school."

"If you could live anywhere you please, where would that be?"

"With my mother."

"Your mother," the judge said. "Where is your mother?"

"She's dead."

The judge sat back. "Miss Lanier says you were a good student until recently. What happened?"

"Well," Wally said, "Naomi wanted to meet Jeremiah and—"

"I object," Mr. Feinberg jumped to his feet again. "Your Honor, do you intend to pass judgment on this family today?"

"*Family*, Mr. Feinberg? If these people live together as family, that in itself violates laws of the State of Florida."

"Your Honor, we request a trial by jury."

"You have that option, of course, but in the meantime, disposition of these children is my responsibility, Mr. Feinberg."

Judge Watson and Mr. Feinberg glared at one another. Wally heard the tick of a wall clock.

"Miss Lanier!" Judge Watson called. "Step up here, please. Give me your assessment of this mess."

Miss Lanier stood poised with her heels together. She said Wally and Jeremiah were living in a poor environment. She said there was no discipline or affection. That was especially true of Wally, but for Jeremiah, too, she said.

"Do you think I should let these children stay where they are until a trial is completed?" Judge Watson questioned.

Miss Lanier looked at Wally. "I think that would be all right," she said. "The primary abuse is neglect, and both boys are resilient enough to get through a few days more."

"Your Honor," Feinberg said, "I request that I be given time for an independent evaluation."

"Next Monday we will begin, Counselor. After you've earned your fee with this posturing, final judgment will come down to one irrefutable fact: we have before us an illegal interracial cohabitation which has produced one mulatto child. A boy who is a truant, according to all reports. But if he were an altar boy for the Pope, the issue would remain miscegenation. What can you add to that point?"

"The character of the people involved—"

"Their character is self-evident, Mr. Feinberg."

Feinberg strode to the bench, and the men exchanged angry whispers. Finally, Judge Watson waved Feinberg away with the back of a hand.

"Mr. McManus, your attorney has petitioned this court to deliver these boys into your custody. He has also demanded a trial by jury. Do you agree?"

"If my attorney says so, I agree."

"Then, so ordered! We will commence in Courtroom One next Monday morning at nine o'clock." With that, the judge stood up and stalked out.

"He gave me no choice," Feinberg said as he stuffed papers into a briefcase. "This will be an uphill battle, Mr. McManus. The law forbids interracial marriage and cohabitation."

"The law is wrong."

"Perhaps it is," Feinberg said. "We could fight the issue to the Supreme Court and in fifteen or twenty years it might be settled to your satisfaction. But in the short run, we either win or lose in this court, before this judge."

As they walked down a hall to the exit, Feinberg said, "I'll be out to talk to all of you tomorrow morning, Mr. McManus. A trial is not the same as a custody hearing. I'll have to prepare a strategy, and five days isn't much time."

"If you need me, Anthony," Pierre Arneaux said, "call me."

"How can he?" Feinberg mused. "He has no telephone."

Mr. Feinberg, carrying a bulging briefcase, arrived before morning broke. At the kitchen table, he positioned them: Hattie, Wally, Anthony and Jeremiah. His eyes were hidden behind spectacles reflecting lamplight.

He spoke from one end of the table. "When you hired me, Mr. McManus, you indicated money was no problem. I checked on that, and it seems to be true. Do you know your net worth?"

Anthony twisted slightly. "I have no idea."

"More than a hundred thousand dollars?"

"I'm not sure."

"More than half a million?"

Wally saw Jeremiah jolt. "I don't know the exact amount,"

Anthony said, "but what difference does it make?"

The lawyer looked around the room. "A lack of modern conveniences is not unheard of, Mr. McManus. There are religious orders which forsake what society has to offer, cloistered monks for example. But the average person who can afford electricity has it. The Child Welfare people look at your financial worth and perceive the lack of electricity as deprivation. You live without refrigeration, fans or lights. Your hot water comes from pipes heated by the sun. The social worker interprets the absence of electricity as neglect and miserliness. How would you answer that?"

"Why should I have to? Whose business is it?"

"The court is asking; Child Welfare is asking. I would like to say you have good reason not to spend the money. That you live this Spartan existence for some higher purpose. To them it appears you are penalizing your family. Are you penalizing your family?"

"It's himself he wants to hurt," Hattie said.

"Hattie—"

"We came home from Europe and the war," Hattie said, "and Anthony felt guilty because he survived when most of our friends did not. Every day he thought about what they would be doing if they had lived, and his own comfort caused pain."

"Hattie, nobody cares to hear this," Anthony said.

"Pierre Arneaux told me you saved his life," Feinberg related. "Tell me about that, Mr. McManus."

But Anthony wouldn't, or couldn't. It was Hattie who revealed the story. "We had a diagram of a prison where resistance fighters had been gathered for execution," she said. "But the drawing was incorrect. We couldn't locate our soldiers in the confusion. Nazis surrounded the fort with armor, and they were shelling the prison to rubble. We had to grope our way through smoke so thick men were suffocating before we could reach them. The Nazis guards threw flame throwers down corridors and into cells where men were chained."

Wally imagined the screams of people incinerated alive.

"Shackles had to be sawn or shot off," Hattie continued.

"Some men amputated their own feet to get loose. It was a miracle Anthony escaped, but he went back again and again until he found Pierre and brought him out. Fire had burned off their hair and melted their lashes."

Wally visualized Anthony, face blackened, taking a deep breath before entering flames, searching for his friend, Pierre, as shells exploded around them.

"When we got home to America," Hattie said, "Anthony tried to write. Ream after ream of paper went into the trash. He couldn't think. He couldn't compose sentences. His publishers lost faith in him."

Anthony sat with head down, face flushed.

"In France, he had begun to drink, and it got worse here at home," Hattie related. "Then Kathryn was dying—"

Anthony keened, "Hattie. God. Please, Hattie—"

"He never planned to love me, but it happened," Hattie said. "Kathryn wanted Anthony to suffer because he loved me. Even knowing she was dying, she extended his torment by sending Wally to us."

"She had no choice," Anthony said.

"She could have sent him to her own parents."

"No, she could not," Anthony insisted.

"She could have and should have," Hattie said.

Wally was speechless, his eyes darting back and forth as mysteries of his past were revealed.

"Kathryn's father and my father detested one another," Anthony said to the lawyer. "They were violently opposed to our marriage. When my parents died in an automobile accident, Kathryn's parents wouldn't attend the funeral. Kathryn never spoke to them again."

"If you had refused to take Wally," Hattie argued, "what could she have done but send that boy to Indianapolis? They would have no choice but accept him."

"They never answered my letters, Hattie."

"But they would've answered their daughter!"

Feinberg gazed at Wally. "You came here for lack of any place else to go?"

"Yes sir. My mama said this was where I should be."

"What did you think?"

"They didn't want me."

"How did you feel about that?"

"I tried to be good."

"That's enough," Anthony said. "These questions have nothing to do with our case."

"On the contrary," Feinberg said, "they are the essence of our case. The jury will be common folk judging you by the standards they apply to themselves. If they don't sympathize with you, this family will be split up."

"We should leave, Anthony," Hattie said. "We should go now."

"It's too late for that," Feinberg advised. "And if you did, you could never come back."

"Who cares?" Jeremiah sneered.

"What about your grandparents?" the lawyer asked.

"My grandmother hates me! Why should I care if I ever see her again?"

"She doesn't like white people, and who can blame her for that?" Feinberg said.

"Yeah, well," Jeremiah said as he looked to Wally for support, "she hates me, too, doesn't she?"

"Let's talk about the people in this room," Feinberg said. "Jeremiah, what do you feel for Wally?"

"Precious? I feel what he feels. He's stingy though."

"Wally?"

"I feel the same way. Except he's not stingy about Jeremiah— just a bad gambler."

"I'll tell you what I think," Feinberg said. "I believe you people love one another. None of you knows how to say it, and you certainly have a strange way of showing it." He looked around the table at each of them. "This is an unhappy household, but love is here. Otherwise you wouldn't care enough to fight this. What you must do is talk to one another, and do it before court next Monday. When I put you in front of a jury, I want them to see a family struggling to stay together, not one staying together just to struggle."

Wally followed Anthony and Feinberg onto the porch. The sun was half a globe riding a watery horizon. "I should think this place would be conducive to writing," Feinberg commented.

"I had hoped it would be," Anthony said.

Feinberg slapped a mosquito. "I've rented a room at the Glades Hotel where I'll stay through the trial. I'll interview everyone who might appear as a witness. When I come out here tomorrow, I intend to ask each of you a personal question about the others. If you have talked to one another as you should, you will know the answers."

"What kind of questions?" Wally asked.

"Questions like, how did Mr. McManus feel about your mother when they were young? How did your mother discover he'd fallen in love with Hattie? The very things you probably want to know, Wally. And in return, he might ask you, did your mother talk about him?"

"She did."

Anthony blinked.

"I expect your father would like to know what she said," the lawyer said.

He started down the steps and stopped. "Mr. McManus, reporters will be trying to reach you. I contacted magazines and newspapers to tell them you are here and what is happening."

"What should I say to them?"

"Whatever gets good press, Mr. McManus. Exposure is the one thing injustice cannot abide. Publicity. That's my strategy."

Feinberg squinted into the rising sun over Lake Okeechobee. "Publicity is the only hope we have," he said.

Talking was not easy. They had all made several tries during the day, but each attempt was forced and unproductive. Wrapped in a blanket against the evening chill, Wally sat in the front porch swing beside Anthony—close but not touching. Stars were icy diamonds that seemed near enough to pluck. The sound of a breeze in brittle leaves had none of the softness so evident in summer.

"What did you want to know?" Anthony finally said.

Wally had a hundred questions and yet, at the moment, he could think of few. "How did you meet Mama?" he asked.

"I was five years older than she and never paid any attention to her until I came home from college. Then everywhere I went, she was there. Kathryn said she chased me until I caught her, and that was probably true."

"Did you love her?"

"We got married."

"But did you love her?"

"Kathryn married me to defy her parents, Wally. Our parents were enemies in business, politics and socially."

"You never loved her," Wally concluded.

"Love comes in degrees of intensity," Anthony said. "I thought I loved Kathryn. But when I fell in love with Hattie, I realized I had never loved before."

"And you didn't want me?"

"It was a terrible time to have a child, Wally. The world was suffering through the Great Depression. Hitler became leader of Germany, and the Nazis were in power. Kathryn found out about Hattie, and she knew Jeremiah was my child. Nevertheless, she demanded that we have a baby. Our marriage was in trouble, and adding a baby would be irresponsible, I thought. The French were being warned they'd have to protect the Saar Basin from Nazi attack. Europe was headed for war."

"Was Mama afraid of the war?"

"She was very afraid of the war. I think she thought if she were pregnant, we would return to America and I would leave Hattie and Jeremiah. But I couldn't do that."

Remembering Pierre Arneaux's comments, Wally said, "Do you think Mama was prejudiced?"

"Yes, she was."

"She didn't like French people?"

"When Kathryn favored something, it was without reservation. When she condemned, she condemned utterly."

"She really loved me," Wally said. "We went places and did things."

"Yes, she loved you."

"Why didn't you come see me? Why didn't you write to me?"

"She wouldn't allow me to see you, Wally. Kathryn returned my gifts and letters unopened. Only when she was ill did she begin to change."

"She was a good person," Wally said.

"For you, she was good."

Feinberg returned the next morning, and once more they sat around the kitchen table. Wally felt more estranged now than before.

"Tell me, Jeremiah," Mr. Feinberg began, "why did your parents send you here from France?"

"What they say?"

"Yes. What do they say?"

"To keep me safe from war, whether I like it or not. To live with my grandmother who'd as soon sleep with a snake as be in the house with me. They hate Mr. McManus."

"You refer to your father as *Mister* McManus?" the lawyer turned to Anthony. "By what name do you call Jeremiah?"

"I call him Jeremiah."

"Do you ever speak of him as your son?"

"I'm sure I have."

"When we're alone in the bottom of a well, maybe," Jeremiah said.

Feinberg said, "How do you speak of Wally, Mr. McManus?"

"I say 'Wally.'"

"And Wally, how do you refer to your father?"

"Anthony."

"Not papa or father or daddy?"

"My mother always called him Anthony."

Feinberg massaged his eyes with fingers of both hands, then extended the rub to his entire face, his glasses on the table. "Mr. McManus, what does your son Jeremiah want to be when he grows up?"

"I can't say, Mr. Feinberg."

"What do you want to be, Jeremiah?" Feinberg pressed.

"Rich with a mustache, living in Paris, France."

"For an occupation?"

"Rich enough, you don't need to work."

Feinberg faced Hattie, "Did you dislike Wally's mother?"

"I felt sorry for her."

"Mr. McManus, what did you feel for Kathryn?"

"I felt sadness and resentment. Hattie was right, Kathryn wanted to hurt me."

"My mama was a good person," Wally defended. "She did good things. She helped out at Montessori school. My best friend, Randall Carney, thought she was a better mother than his own mother. Mama always dressed up, and she looked good early morning or late night. She cooked meals every day, and she made the table pretty with candles and flowers and dishes that matched. I was with her every minute because that's where I wanted to be. She was always interested in what I'd been doing. She wanted to help me with anything I did. Every single day she asked how my day went. Every single day she was cheerful and we were happy. We laughed—"

Wally choked and stood up, trembling. "She laughed at me because she loved me and she thought I said funny things. We went to movies together. She was my best friend."

"Sit down, Wally," Anthony said.

"And I'm sick and tired of hearing everybody talk bad about her!" Wally screamed. "She was a good person, a good mama. She didn't send me here because she was angry with her parents. She sent me here so Anthony and I would get to know one another. She told me he was wonderful and smart. She said he would love me. You didn't know her. It's not right to talk bad about her if you didn't know her."

Anthony pulled Wally into an awkward hug and Wally sobbed.

The attorney said, "Mr. McManus, henceforth, what will you call this boy?"

"Son," said Anthony. "From now on, I will call him 'Son.'"

chapter twenty

The next evening after supper Mr. Feinberg arrived. The light of the kerosene lamp glimmered on his eyeglasses as he commanded each of them to ask a question of another. For Wally it was an uncomfortable exercise in self-discovery. For Jeremiah it was a chance to make outlandish queries.

"Mr. McManus," Jeremiah said, "did you have other colored womens before my mother?"

"No," Anthony said.

The lawyer pointed at Anthony. "Jeremiah, who is that man?"

"Mr. McManus."

"He's also your father. Refer to him as such. Mr. McManus, what should your sons call you?"

Anthony opened his mouth, twisted a hand. "Dad, I suppose."

"Let's hear you say that, Jeremiah."

"Dad."

Then Wally had to do it, and "Dad" was alien to his tongue. It was as though he'd suddenly begun to call his mother Kathryn.

"What's Precious supposed to call my mama?" Jeremiah asked the lawyer.

"Wally will continue to speak of Hattie as Hattie."

"How come not 'Mama'?" Jeremiah bristled.

"She is not his mother."

"It's because she's colored!" Jeremiah accused. "That's why you don't want Precious calling my mama 'Mama.'"

"A more personal address would not help our cause," the attorney said. "But in the strictest sense, it isn't correct anyway. Hattie is *not* Wally's mother."

The decision was a relief that surprised Wally. He didn't want to replace his mother with Hattie or anyone else. He said,

"Hattie suits me," and Hattie agreed.

The next morning, Feinberg was there during breakfast. "I've finally arranged an interview," he said to Anthony. "The reporter is Pat Bryan from the Baltimore *Sun*. He will meet the family for dinner and drinks at *Coq du Village*, Saturday evening. The boys should get haircuts and new clothes. I recommend conservative suits, dress shirts and ties to make them look like young gentlemen. They can wear the same outfits in court on Monday."

"I ain't wearing a suit for nobody," Jeremiah carped.

Wally watched the attorney's face grow florid. "Certainly nobody can force you to work as a family and pull together, Jeremiah. One smart aleck remark from you, one spark of rebellion, and the jury will be convinced you need to be in a reformatory with other delinquents."

"That's not so bad," Jeremiah said. "I hear they got a swimming pool."

"If you think it will be fun," Feinberg said, "think again. They'll force you to follow a routine designed to teach discipline and respect for authority. You will rise at daylight, work several hours in a dairy barn or hoeing a garden, then take a shower, eat breakfast and go to trade school. When an adult speaks, you will snap to attention, eyes forward, and reply in a loud voice, 'Yes sir!'"

"Like hell I will," Jeremiah said.

"Oh, you will," Feinberg declared. "After you've been whipped and locked in a solitary cell, you'll do anything they say. But if you don't, they will ship you to a grown man's prison; and you don't know what misery is until you do time in an adult prison. They specialize in chain gangs, men manacled to one another, digging ditches as they hobble along. If you continue to resist, they'll shoot you for trying to escape."

Feinberg stood up, eyes cold behind round glasses. "On the other hand," he said, "you might save this family and yourself by growing up. You have until Monday."

The next day was Saturday, stormy and cold in Palm Beach. After buying new clothes which Wally and Jeremiah now wore, they'd gotten haircuts and still had an hour before meeting the reporter. Anthony parked the coupe across the boulevard from *Coq du Village*. He and Hattie stayed in the car. Wally and Jeremiah walked out on a pier to watch the ocean.

Waves rose from leaden depths and like charging rams, the peak of each breaker curled into white horns which bashed the beach. A northerly wind swept rime from the sea and hurled it into their faces.

To be heard above the rumble, Jeremiah stood nearer. "Remember I talked about gigging frogs when you first got here?"

"Yes."

"I never gigged a frog in my life," Jeremiah admitted. "I just wanted to tell you that."

"Okay."

Along the pier, weepy-eyed seagulls faced the wind to avoid ruffled feathers.

"If the judge tries to split us up—send me to reform school and you to a foster home—" Jeremiah said, "let's make a run for it. We can meet Mom and Mr. McManus in Paris."

After a moment, Jeremiah amended, "Meet Mom and *Dad* in Paris. Still sounds funny, don't it?"

The fall of the waves on the sandy shore produced thunderous concussion that put a throb in Wally's bones. Jeremiah slipped closer. "Are you going to call him 'Dad?'"

"I guess so."

"I always wanted to," Jeremiah said, "but now that I can, it isn't easy."

By the time they went across the street to *Coq du Village*, Wally's clothes were damp and his bottom itched from sitting on a wet bench. He saw his reflection in the restaurant door. His hair looked as if he'd gone to bed scared and slept that way.

Pierre Arneaux took Hattie's arm, speaking French as he escorted them to a table. In English he said, "You are my guests. Have anything you wish." Anthony protested, but the owner sputtered indignantly and it was settled.

Then Pierre brought over the reporter who had been waiting in the bar. Pat Bryan of the Baltimore *Sun* was thin and tall, his cheeks hollow. Wally couldn't see his eyes for the squint of them. When Bryan smiled it looked as if he'd rather not.

"This is Hattie Willoughby," Anthony made introductions, "and these are my sons, Jeremiah and Wally."

Pierre hovered. "What may we bring you to drink?"

There was an awkward pause. Hattie pretended to study the wine list, but Wally saw she was watching Anthony. The reporter ordered a dry martini. Anthony requested chablis for Hattie, soda pop for the boys, "And my usual, please, Pierre."

A string ensemble set up instruments on a small stage. A line of customers formed at the door. Every table was occupied.

"Well!" Pat Bryan said. "Here we are. I've been chatting with Pierre since I got here, or more precisely, he hasn't stopped talking. He says the two of you are heroes of the French Underground. Is that the story I'm to write? The war in reprise?"

"What did the editors tell you in Baltimore?" Anthony inquired.

"Said pack my bags and get to South Florida. Said I was to do a feature on a writer who has slipped from the limelight, but they didn't specify what, so tell me—what?"

"We're going to court day after tomorrow," Hattie said. "We have to fight for custody of our boys."

"Yeah?" The reporter accepted his drink from a waiter. He removed the olive and ate it. "Why would anybody try to take your boys?"

"The Florida Department of Child Welfare claims we are unfit to raise our sons," Anthony said.

"Because we are a racially mixed couple," Hattie added.

"That's the only reason?"

"Well, Hattie and I have never spoiled our children," Anthony said. "We've always thought it best to instill a sense of self-reliance. We avoided the excesses that tend to weaken a child's will."

"Excesses like what? Electricity?"

Anthony's eyes darted away. Hattie said, "Being without electricity is not why they're after our boys. It's because Anthony is white, and I am not."

The string ensemble tuned their instruments, making soft discordant sounds. There were so many customers chattering, Pat Bryan had to raise his voice to be heard. "Where does this tale begin?"

Anthony spoke of love "tempered in a cauldron of global conflict." He told how he'd met Hattie in "Pierre's smoky bistro on the Left Bank of Paris," where she was a singer.

"A singer, eh?" The reporter raised a hand and motioned for a waiter. He then tapped the rim of his glass. "Make the next one dry as the Gobi," he said. Then to Anthony, "Let me see if I got this straight. This little family is in jeopardy. It's you folks against unfeeling bureaucrats, and they are motivated by what?"

"They claim that miscegenation is reason enough to tear apart my family," Anthony said.

"It makes me wonder why you reside in a section of the nation with laws against interracial cohabitation, Mr. McManus. If we were sitting in Paris you wouldn't wear a swastika, would you? Yet you came to the Deep South with a Negro woman and child. What did you expect?"

"This is Hattie's home. Her parents live in Belle Glade."

"They must've been overjoyed to have their daughter show up with a white man, living the life of a concubine."

"Now, wait a minute," Anthony said.

"Or maybe there's more to this than we've discussed," the reporter said. "To be honest, I've been in Belle Glade for a few days. I couldn't figure why my newspaper sent me to this godforsaken hole to rehash an old war story. Maybe my editor didn't know you had a colored common-law wife, I thought; or maybe he didn't know you've been swimming in your cups. I talked to a lot of people in Belle Glade, and I couldn't find a single person who was happy you're there. My editor didn't tell me to make this a sympathetic piece, but hey, if it isn't a sob story, what's the angle? My problem is I'm having trouble working up sympathy for you guys."

It was so obvious things weren't going well that Pierre rushed the order for dinner. He even agreed to serve hamburgers to Jeremiah and Wally.

"I did my homework," Pat Bryan continued. "I know you've had five novels published, but the reviews haven't been good since the first one. Your publisher says you're suffering a creative crisis, but he blames it on booze. You haven't done anything of note since 1939."

"Anthony wrote three mysteries since then," Hattie said.

"Oh, yeah, slam-bang-naked-babes-and-crooked cop stories. I read those. I figured you must've needed money. But then your lawyer, whatis name, Feinberg, says you're loaded with dough. Family annuities, inheritance, earnings from your first book."

Anthony held his glass between both hands, but he hadn't tasted it.

"You're living a life of penury, the subject of public ridicule and community censure," Pat Bryan said. "I look at your history and it seems to me you are a man on the run and always have been. You ran from early success as an author, ran from an unhappy marriage. When you couldn't run, you sent your child-out-of-wedlock to Belle Glade, which relieved you of that problem temporarily. You've been running from one thing or another all your life, Mr. McManus."

"You've been talking to Mrs. Bullock," Wally said.

"What do you think she said, kid?"

"She said my dad is not a good father."

"That's what a lot of people think," the reporter said.

"You don't like us because my mama is colored," Jeremiah said.

"I don't know you, son. I never saw you until this evening. But if I don't like you it has nothing to do with your color."

"We're a loving family," Jeremiah quoted Mr. Feinberg.

"Oh, sure you are," Pat Bryan scoffed. "You've been skipping school since grade one. You spend your days gambling. You're a truant on his way to big-time troubles, according to the law in Belle Glade."

"I won't do that anymore," Jeremiah said. "When we get to France I'll go to school and do right."

"What's this about France?"

The musicians had begun to play, but now they quit as Pierre

Arneaux took a microphone. "Ladies and gentlemen," he said, "tomorrow is December seventh. What American among us does not remember where he was Sunday, December seventh, six years ago?"

The audience fell silent.

"I will tell you where I was," Pierre said. "The Nazis had taken Paris without firing a shot. France was face down before her conquerors, and we were ashamed for having surrendered so easily. But there were those among us who decided to fight back, even though every phase of our lives was under Nazi command."

With a lilting French accent Pierre spoke of comrades who died in the quest for freedom, of battles lost and his capture. "But at the moment of greatest terror, facing my own execution," he said, "it was an American who saved me. Anthony McManus and a group of my compatriots stormed the prison and set us free. He is here tonight, my American friend, Anthony McManus."

A spotlight swerved to their table and shone on Anthony. He lifted a hand and waved to a smattering of polite applause.

"And with him at the table," Pierre said, "his sons, Jeremiah and Wally."

Grinning, Jeremiah jumped up and pulled Wally to his feet.

"And lovely Hattie Willoughby, who also fought with the Resistance," Pierre said. "In combat she was a tigress, but before the war we knew her as the nightingale of Paris. It was a rare pleasure to have heard Hattie Willoughby sing *Lili Marlene*. Perhaps she will favor us tonight. What do you say, ladies and gentlemen? Shall we ask Hattie to sing?"

"Oh, no, Pierre," Hattie said. But there was no way she could refuse. In an instant she was transformed. She rose to her feet, tall and graceful, and moved toward the stage with a fluid stride. It was her beauty that made men gasp and women stare, as Anthony had written in his books. Wally glanced at Anthony and saw an expression he'd never seen before—pride, but apprehension too. Even Jeremiah was transfixed.

Hattie spoke to the musicians, then took the microphone from Pierre. The spotlight closed to her face.

Outside the barracks
By the corner light,
I'll always stand
And wait for you at night.
For you, Lili Marlene.
For you, Lili Marlene.

No clink of glasses, no murmuring voices. Wally saw people at the door move inside to listen. Strings of violins and viola quavered as Hattie stood perfectly still, singing:

My love for you
Renews my might,
I'm warm again,
My pack is light . . .

At that moment Anthony seemed younger, and Wally thought he saw how they must've been during the war. Hattie's voice was pure and clear, a plaintive cry from a doomed lover's heart:

My love for you
Renews my might,
I'm warm again,
My pack is light.
It's you, Lili Marlene,
It's you . . .

When she finished, people stood and the applause grew into a roar. Hattie returned to the table slowly, nodding and smiling. Anthony kissed her hand. "It's been a long time," she said.

The reporter's eyes met Wally's and then he looked at a grinning Jeremiah.

"Okay," the reporter said gruffly, "I'll see you guys in court. We'll see how this story plays out."

As he walked toward the door, Hattie said, "What do you think, Anthony?"

"I think you killed him," Anthony said.

twenty-one

Monday morning going to court was the most dreaded day since the burial of Wally's mother. The sun rose colorless and cold. To stay warm in the rumble seat, he'd wrapped himself in a fuzzy blanket that left his new dark blue suit covered with lint.

Downtown, a sign advised, 17 DAYS 'TIL XMAS, and banners proclaimed, *Joy to the World!*

Multicolored lights dimmed by daylight hung in store windows. Artificial snow had been sprinkled over empty boxes wrapped as gifts. A cardboard Santa drove his sleigh up the front of Woolworth's Five and Dime Store. One reindeer had a broken leg; another had lost an antler.

Everyone in town seemed to know what was happening. People on sidewalks stopped to stare as Anthony circled the block a second time in search of parking. The librarian paused to gaze at Wally in the rumble seat beside Jeremiah. In a group of men at the old post office, Ike Fester made vulgar smacking sounds at Hattie as they walked past. Jeremiah said, "Screw you," and defiantly glared back.

Flashbulbs popped. Wally was shoved here and there to pose with Hattie and Jeremiah. More bulbs flared and died with a sizzle. He didn't know whether to smile or not, and it was over before he could decide.

In corridors of the old post office, voices echoed, doors slammed. The air smelled of mold and musk and hot steam from the radiators. People stepped aside to let them pass. Wally shoved his hands into his pockets to hide a trembling. He wanted to be brave, but he was afraid.

This time Judge William Watson was in the courtroom with a

high bench for himself, a place for the jury, and tables for "their side" and "ours." Feinberg asked Judge Watson to dismiss the case because it was based on an unconstitutional law. Judge Watson said, "No." Feinberg told the judge there had been no formal accusations against Anthony and therefore this whole procedure was groundless. The judge denied it. And so it went: Each time the judge said, "No," Feinberg said, "Exception," and Judge Watson said, "Exception noted."

People crowded onto benches already packed with spectators. Ike Fester, Cole and Aldo sat in the back. The judge said, "Mr. McManus, your legal counsel has chosen to escalate this matter to a trial by jury. Until now this was a simple custody case."

"Which Your Honor intended to decide solely on grounds of miscegenation," Feinberg interjected.

"Which must *now* be decided on those grounds," the judge said. "Also, Mr. McManus, your attorney has brought to this court reporters from outside newspapers. Your dirty laundry will soon be hung for all to see."

There were four reporters including Pat Bryan. They occupied the second row, scribbling notes. Another flashbulb went off and Judge Watson shouted, "No more picture taking in this courtroom!"

Then he spoke to Anthony again. "You can stop this now if you wish. We can retire to my chambers and get back to sensible deliberations."

"I will do as my attorney advises," Anthony replied.

"And I will trust to the judgment of a jury," Feinberg said.

Judge Watson slammed down his gavel and ordered a ten-minute recess.

Wally had to go to the bathroom and Jeremiah said he wanted to go too. Feinberg said, "Stay in the building."

In the hallway, an elderly Negro swept with a push broom. He worked his way down the corridor sprinkling oily sawdust which he then swept along. Wally recognized him from Minnie Lou's house on Thanksgiving Day. He was the man who didn't want bad talk about white people in Wally's presence.

"Hi!" Wally said. But the custodian swept by without answer-

ing, going down the hall unnoticed even by those who absent-
mindedly stepped aside to make way.

"What're you staring at?" Jeremiah questioned.

"I thought I knew the janitor."

"That's old Samuel. He's the grin-and-get-it-nigger around
here. I wonder where the colored toilet is?"

Pat Bryan from Baltimore followed Wally into a rest room. He
said, "How do you feel, Wally?"

"Not so good."

"Scared?"

"Yessir."

"I talked to Paul Feinberg. He seems to know what he's
doing." The reporter flushed a urinal. "Did your father or Hattie
give you any last-minute instructions?"

"About what?"

"What to say, how to act?"

Wally thought back as he washed his hands. Hattie had asked
if he wanted biscuits or pan-fried toast, and that was it. "No
sir," Wally said, "they didn't say anything."

Cole and Aldo came in, and Pat Bryan quickly turned away.
"Okay, you worthless white trash," Cole said as he shoved Wally
to a wall. "This is your last chance. Tell that judge you want to
live somewhere else and you'll go to some nice place—"

"No," Wally said.

"Some nice *place*," Cole persisted, "with people of your own
kind instead of folks who just swung in off a vine."

Pat Bryan was busy at the lavatory.

"I want you to tell that little bastard the beating he got is
nothing to the beating he's going to get," Aldo said. "He's a thief
like all niggers."

"Ready to go back, Wally?" Pat Bryan inquired. Aldo said,
"Who are you?"

"Pat Bryan, reporter for the Baltimore *Sun*. I'll make it a point
to mention your names in the article I'm writing. What are your
names?"

"That's Aldo Fester and his brother, Cole," Wally said.

"Shut up, Wally."

"Their daddy is Ike Fester."

"I said, shut up!"

"They live next door to us and belong to the Klan."

Pat Bryan ushered Wally toward the courtroom. "They said Jeremiah has to be punished," Wally said. "Because of Naomi Noonan."

"I'd like to hear more about the Noonan girl."

"We have to go to court for her in West Palm Beach tomorrow," Wally said.

"Which court is that?"

A deputy stepped between Wally and the reporter. "No talking to the witnesses."

The deputy gripped Wally's arm, taking him back to Anthony and Hattie. Jeremiah was already there. "I found the toilet," Jeremiah said. "Did you know blue and yellow makes green?"

"All rise!" a man hollered.

Chairs scraped, seats squeaked, feet shuffled, people coughed, and the judge came in. This time he wore a long black robe and a clerk chanted, "Oyez, oyez, draw near all ye who have business with this honorable court. . . ."

And then he stopped everything. Mr. Feinberg produced a subpoena which said Anthony, Hattie, Jeremiah and Wally had to be in court in West Palm Beach tomorrow morning. Judge Watson was furious, but he granted a delay of one week.

They left at daybreak the next morning for West Palm Beach. Bundled in blankets and hugging hot bricks, Wally and Jeremiah snuggled in the rumble seat to keep warm. Cold air numbed Wally's ears and made his nose run. In the half-light of dawn, cattle stood in their own fog snorting plumes of warm breath. Birds perched on electric lines like knots in twine.

Inside the courthouse, Jeremiah spotted a discarded newspaper and yelped, "Hey! That's us!"

The picture was of them all seated in Judge William Watson's Belle Glade courtroom. The caption read: HERO FOUGHT NAZIS, NOW FIGHTS FOR FAMILY. The story was in the West Palm Beach *Post*. Then they went upstairs to the judge's chambers.

The waiting room was warm and crowded with red leather chairs that squeaked when sat upon. There were magazines and books for children. The floor was covered with plush carpet, the wallpaper printed with cartoon characters. A *Felix the Cat* clock hung on a wall. The pendulum was a long tail which flicked with each tick, and the cat's eyes swung from side to side in syncopation.

When Naomi arrived, Wally hardly recognized her. She wore a burgundy coat with fake fur collar and huge buttons. Her auburn hair was cut short and curled at the ends. She rushed to Wally and hugged him hard. "I missed you!" she said. Then Naomi went to Jeremiah sort of sideways and stood close without touching him. "Are you mad with me?" she asked.

"No."

"I'm sorry for the trouble, Jeremiah."

Naomi's mother said, "Naomi—"

"Listen," Jeremiah murmured, "I told everybody we only read comic books."

"I had to tell the truth, Jeremiah."

Mrs. Noonan beckoned insistently, "Naomi—"

"Don't worry though," Naomi said, "you aren't in any trouble, Jeremiah. The judge promised."

"White judge?"

"Yes, but he's nice. He said for me not to worry about you."

Mrs. Noonan came to take Naomi's arm.

A minute later the reporter from Baltimore arrived. He took off his coat and draped it over a chair. "Did you folks see the local paper?" he asked.

"Yes," Anthony said.

"Hero fights for family," Pat Bryan said. "Nice touch."

Judge Donald Anderton pursed his lips when he listened and closed his eyes when he smiled. He came to the door and said to everyone, "This is not a trial, it is a hearing. Mr. McManus, I sent your attorney back to his office. You do not require counsel in this matter."

"Yes, sir."

"What I have to do," Judge Anderton explained, "is write a report on the incident in question. That means I have to be sure I know what happened. It is important that each of us tells the truth. Do you understand, children?"

Jeremiah said, "What if we don't tell the truth?"

"Why wouldn't you tell the truth?"

"Not me; I'm telling the truth. What happens if somebody else doesn't tell the truth?"

"If it is a mistake and not a lie," the judge said, "then I forgive them. Everybody makes mistakes. If it is a lie on purpose, I'd have to decide what punishment to give. But even if there's no punishment from me, God knows when we lie, and we've made a promise here to God that we will tell the truth. In which case, God will determine our punishment. Do you believe in God?"

"Yeah, I reckon."

"Then you won't lie, will you?"

"Not me, I said not me. Somebody else is who I meant."

Judge Anderton indicated his receptionist. "This is Donna de Vries. If you need a rest room or water fountain, she is here to help you. Please do not talk to one another about anything you intend to say to me, or that you may have said."

He turned to the reporter. "Mr. Bryan has been granted permission to be here, but he has agreed not to question anyone until this case is adjudicated."

He looked at Bryan, and the reporter said, "Just as you said, Your Honor."

"Fine. Naomi, let's begin with you."

She was in the judge's office for a long time, and while she was gone nobody said a word. The Felix clock ticked its tail and tocked its eyes. Jeremiah pretended to read a magazine but stared straight at the page, so Wally wasn't fooled.

At last, the judge came to the door and spoke to Naomi's mother. "Mrs. Noonan, will you join us?"

An even longer time passed, the wagging pendulum and zigzagging eyes making Wally dizzy. He heard Anthony's stomach growl, and when their eyes met, Anthony lifted his brows. The reporter read a *Humpty-Dumpty* book.

When Judge Anderton summoned Wally, Mrs. Noonan and Naomi had left by another door, so he didn't get to say goodbye. There was a large, polished desk in the judge's office, and bookshelves lined the walls. Volumes such as *Florida Tort* and *Florida Precedents* crammed the shelves.

Judge Anderton sat in a chair close to Wally. He smiled and his eyes closed. "Tell me," he said, "what kind of person is Jeremiah?"

Wally had prepared himself by rehearsing answers he'd give to questions he'd imagined. But he had never imagined inquiries about Jeremiah.

"Is he honest?" Judge Anderton queried.

"If he thinks he'll get caught he is," Wally said.

"That's a very wise answer, Wally. How about you? Are you honest?"

"I try to be."

"I want you to be honest with me," the judge said. "Tell me what happened. Start from the beginning."

Which is what Wally did. Judge Anderton listened closely, his hands clasped, leaning forward, elbows on his knees. He would wince sympathetically and nod when Wally felt uncomfortable. Wally recounted Jeremiah's resistance to Naomi's invitation to visit. Then he mentioned school days missed, the discovery of Jeremiah at Naomi's place, and finally he told of the moment when he heard the gunshot and Naomi came down the steps at the packing house.

"She said she'd shot her daddy," Wally concluded.

"That's what she told me," Judge Anderton said. "Now the big question is, why did she do that?"

"He was going to get a gun and shoot me," Wally recalled. "He was dragging Naomi upstairs and she was already hurt."

"Did you see Naomi try to grab the gun from her father?"

"I was on the platform below. I didn't see any of that."

"Did you hear Naomi and her mother screaming at him to stop?"

"I don't remember."

"Was Naomi upset about shooting Mr. Noonan?"

"Yes, sir."

The judge pursed his lips, nodding, nodding, nodding. "Is there anything else you'd like to say to me, Wally?"

"Yessir. Jeremiah went to see Naomi because he was lonely. Negroes make fun of him and white people too. Everybody cheats him at cards and pool and penny pitching. He needed a friend, and that's why he went to see Naomi. Naomi needed a friend too, and that's why she asked him."

"That's a mature assessment, Wally."

"Are you going to put Naomi in jail?"

"What do you think should be done?"

"She wants to go to Tennessee with her mama. Naomi is a good person. I don't think she'll ever shoot anybody else."

"I'm inclined to agree."

"Is Jeremiah going to jail?"

"Not because of this he won't."

Judge Anderton walked Wally to the door. "Deputy Sheriff Posey says you are going to court in Belle Glade next Monday."

"Yes, we are."

"What do you think will happen over there, Wally?"

"If they don't split us up, we're going to live in France where people like Negroes."

The judge patted Wally's shoulder and opened the door. He announced to everyone, "Let's take a break for lunch, shall we? Be back at one o'clock, please."

Going down the corridor Jeremiah crowded Wally. "What did he ask you?"

"I can't talk about it."

"Why not?"

"The judge said don't."

"I'm going in there bald-faced and you won't warn me what to say?"

"Tell the truth, Jeremiah."

"Uh-huh, yeah, sure. Tell the white man what he needs to know so he can haul me out and make chocolate fudge."

"Where can we go for lunch?" Hattie asked Anthony.

It was still cold, the sun blindingly bright. The reporter from

Baltimore walked past as if he'd never known them.

"We can go to Morrison's Cafeteria and get a take-out to eat in the park," Anthony said.

It was either that, or eat in colored town.

On the way home to Belle Glade, a barricade blocked the road. BRIDGE OUT, the sign said. Anthony detoured north to Pahokee, then south again.

Because Wally had refused to discuss his conversations with Judge Anderton, Jeremiah reciprocated in kind. "I can't talk about what I said to the judge," he volunteered.

"That's okay," Wally said.

"The judge didn't say I couldn't, but he didn't say I could," Jeremiah offered.

Wally sat up straight in the rumble seat peering across muck fields through a row of Australian pines that bordered the road.

"Most likely the judge said the same things to me that he said to you," Jeremiah tantalized.

"Most likely," Wally agreed.

"He wanted to know could I trust you," Jeremiah said. "I said about as far as I could throw a constipated cow."

"That's what I said about you."

They laughed so hard Hattie called, "Everybody all right back there?"

Approaching town, Anthony slowed for stalled traffic. Wally heard him say, "There must be an accident ahead."

In the distance the lights of a police car winked. Flares were set down the middle of the road. Wally heard the "Stars and Stripes Forever" march blaring from loudspeakers and Hattie said, "Uh-oh."

Down at the airfield, bright lights illuminated a stage wrapped in red-white-and-blue bunting. American flags fluttered around a dais. Horns blew, voices lifted afar. Marching music gave a martial air to the setting.

They were blocked. They couldn't turn around, couldn't rush ahead. Hangars for crop dusters seemed hunkered down in the gloaming. The smell of DDT lingered from a recent spraying against mosquitoes. A crowd of men, women and children stood facing the stage. Among them walked figures in white sheets and high peaked hats, handing out pamphlets.

"Can't we drive along a shoulder of the road?" Hattie urged.

Anthony said they might end up in the canal, or stuck in soft soil. He pulled forward another few feet, then stopped again.

A policeman in full uniform and wearing white gloves directed traffic. He waved cars into the airfield with a flashlight. The line from town was longer, slower. The policeman blew a whistle, motioning them through.

The music stopped. A man's voice echoed faintly as it rebounded from hangars. "Ladies-ies-ies and gentlemen-en-en. Welcome!"

The cop whistle shrilled, cars moved; Anthony proceeded and this time he halted face-to-face with oncoming traffic. The policeman was sweating even in the cool December air. He had salt rings under his arms and a wet streak down his spine.

"We are honored-ed-ed to have with us-sus-sus . . ."

There were robed Klansmen along the highway too, distributing literature. One of them offered a paper to Jeremiah, absently, and Jeremiah took it. He crumpled the sheet and threw it at the man. The cop whistled, Anthony stepped on the gas and left the Klansmen behind.

"Why do they wear those high hats?" Jeremiah called up front.

"To look more imposing," Anthony said.

A moment later he added, "Also, they have pointed heads."

There were a lot of cars—coming out of Belle Glade, coming from the white migratory labor camp, going to the rally by the hundreds, it seemed to Wally. Even in evening light he could see they were men with hard jaws and women weathered by the sun. They were laboring people who probably stood side by side with Negroes in cane fields. There were children too, clad as if going to Sunday services.

Anthony swung off the main road, past the Belle Glade school and toward home. The sun was gone and only a fading afterlight remained. The air in Wally's face was cold.

There were so many of them, and that had surprised him. Frightened him too. Facing the Festers and a few of their friends was bad enough—but hundreds!

The coupe topped the dike and clattered across the bridge, descending into deepening shadows of twilight. When they got home, Anthony parked beneath the spreading oak, and for a few minutes nobody moved. Finally, Hattie said, "I'll build a fire."

Anthony nodded and she got out.

Several minutes later, Hattie returned. "We're out of wood and there's no ice," she said.

Then she burst into tears.

chapter twenty-two

After seeing the Klan rally, Wally dreamed of ominous men in peaked hats. He thought he was still dreaming when he awoke in the dark to the sound of breaking glass. Then came another crash, and another. He tumbled out of bed and collided with Jeremiah at the window.

In the kitchen, Hattie screamed, "Anthony! Somebody's in the yard!"

Wally saw them. In the dim light of a crescent moon, featureless figures were bashing Anthony's coupe with clubs. At the cry from Hattie they jumped into a waiting car and, with lights off, roared down the lane past the Fester house.

Anthony ran into the yard wearing nothing but underpants, a shotgun in hand. The culprits were gone but he fired his weapon anyway, and the repercussion rippled across lake and bogs. Hattie stood on the porch with a lantern. Wally climbed through the window following Jeremiah and Hattie into the yard. Wally suddenly realized Jeremiah was naked, hugging himself against the cold. "Did you see them?" Jeremiah asked.

"I couldn't tell who they were."

Anthony's anguish over his damaged car was more upsetting to Wally than the attack. The headlights were smashed, every window broken. The shattered windshield was a web of jagged prisms reflecting light of the lantern. "Damn them!" Anthony said. "I'll never find another windshield. And look. They slashed my whitewall tires."

"Be careful of broken glass," Hattie warned the boys. Then noticing Jeremiah, she said, "Go put on some clothes."

By light of day, they reexamined the car in the company of Paul Feinberg. Wally saw details he'd missed before. Every fender was bent or broken. NIGGER had been smeared on the doors with black paint.

"Last night after their rally, the Klan came to the Glades Hotel and burned me in effigy," Feinberg said to Anthony. "This morning the management asked me to move out. I refused and threatened a lawsuit if they persist. Meantime, I'm hauling all my belongings in my car because I expect the room to be ransacked while I'm gone."

Wally followed them to the front steps where everyone sat down as if too tired to go further.

"I suggest that none of you goes into town without an escort," Feinberg advised. "The ominous mood of this community promises to worsen. I've asked the sheriff to accompany you for shopping and that sort of thing. He said he'd send a car at four o'clock tomorrow afternoon, so be ready."

"Perhaps we should go to West Palm Beach," Anthony said. "We can commute from there to Belle Glade for the trial."

"Nobody would blame you if you did," Feinberg said. He held Wally by the nape of his neck and shook him playfully. "But the greatest sympathy will be gained if you stand fast in the face of adversity."

"Yeah," Jeremiah said. "We can stand it. Let's go shoot the Festers and their dogs."

"I considered asking the judge for a change of venue," Feinberg said. "Then I talked myself out of it. This morning, Pat Bryan said the New York *Times* has sent down a reporter to cover the trial, and somebody is coming from Chicago. By challenging miscegenation laws we've made this case national in scope. Bryan said United Press and Associated Press will feed the story to network radio. We're getting the attention we need, and standing firm makes us look good; therefore, stand we should."

Feinberg rose and arched his back slightly as he stretched. "I'll come back this evening," he said. "I want a photographer to shoot pictures of your car."

"Before you leave," Hattie said, "we're out of ice and groceries."

"I'll take you right now, " Feinberg said.

A photographer arrived to record the wrecked Ford, and reporter Pat Bryan came too. Paul Feinberg gave them a tour including the water tower where rainwater was stored out back. He praised self-sufficiency and spoke of the "rustic" lifestyle as if he admired it.

Wally sat on the front porch swing wrapped in a blanket as the setting sun took all warmth with it. Pat Bryan sat with him. Everybody else was inside having some of Hattie's coffee, and a bowl of butterbeans with corn bread.

"Do you like it here?" Bryan asked.

"It's all right."

"I'm a city boy," the reporter said. "I like busy streets and crowds of people. I enjoy smells of diesel fumes down at the bus station where I go to have coffee late at night. In Baltimore, people sit on their steps in the evening, visiting with their neighbors. That appeals to me."

Wally pulled his blanket nearer.

"My grandmother cooked on a wood stove like the one you people have," Bryan said. "I remember it would blister my face and hands while my backside was freezing. It didn't heat her house, which was well-insulated. I can't imagine it'll heat this place with spaces between the floorboards and shutters for windows. Am I right?"

"Yes, sir."

"But you like it here."

"It's better than a military school or foster home," Wally said.

"Yeah," Bryan said. "Purgatory is better than hell."

"Better than military school or a foster home," Wally said.

That night, Wally pulled a blanket over his head and breathed his warm breath under the bedding. He thought about purgatory, a place souls went to halfway between heaven and hell, as Mr. Bryan had explained. It was a place for people

who hadn't been all that good, or entirely bad, which was nearly everybody.

He dozed, then awoke to Jeremiah's frantic whisper. "Get up!
They're out there again!"

A gentle *whoosh* introduced flames, and yellow light flickered
on the ceiling and walls of the bedroom. Wally bounded up to
call Anthony, but Anthony was fully dressed, standing inside the
front door with a shotgun, Hattie beside him. Their faces were
crimson in the red and amber light of fire. And there in the front
yard stood a huge burning cross.

The staff of the thing was a telephone pole. How could anyone have dug a hole so quietly? Yet there it was, fifteen feet high
with a crossbar tee. The whole thing was wrapped in burlap
sacks and soaked with something that smelled like kerosene.
Wally wondered about the fuel because the fire produced flickering droplets which fell from the cross member like tiny asteroids.

He'd always thought of fire as a crackling thing—timbers hiss-
ing, sparks popping, internal gasses spewing—but there was no
sound except the sputter of burning fuel. And beyond the fire at
the edge of the yard, dozens of men stood in a row like a picket
fence. They were armed with shotguns, rifles and clubs, deadly
statues in firelight watching the incendiary they'd set.

"Put on your clothes," Hattie directed Wally and Jeremiah.

They hurried to do so, then returned to the open front door.
Heat from the burning cross rode a light breeze and warmed
their faces.

Another *whoosh,* and the battered remains of the Ford coupe
were afire. How could so many men have passed the Fester
hounds without raising a bark?

"Come out, sinners!" a voice roared. "Come out or die where
you stand!"

Anthony pushed Hattie back and stepped onto the porch with
the shotgun cradled in his arms. When he shifted it to both
hands, Wally heard the click of firearms in the dark.

"Lay it down, nigger lover! Come out while you can."

The rear of the house erupted in flames.

Anthony rushed for the kitchen to fill a bucket. Hattie raced to their bedroom but fell back with an arm across her face as fire climbed the walls and lapped at the ceiling. Jeremiah screamed, "Get out, Mama! Get out!"

Wally hurried to his wardrobe. He threw aside clothing as heat prickled his neck. He shoved garments this way and that until he found his money coat. He grabbed it, dived out the window, rolled across the porch and fell to the ground. He heard Hattie scream his name, saw Anthony run around a far side of the house.

They met out front and fell into one another's arms.

Unhurriedly, the intruders got into cars and trucks. Hattie shouted curses as their vehicles rumbled away in the dark. Tongues of flames curled leaves of the old oak tree. Behind the house, bamboo wheezed as fire heated hollow reeds. At last, the water tank toppled and cast a wave of water beneath the house where it did no good at all.

They walked to town, and when Wally looked back, even from the distant side of the dike, he could still see a glow from the fire. Surely someone had noticed the light, yet no one summoned assistance, no sirens spread the alarm.

When they reached Three Palms Funeral Home about midnight, Hattie woke her father. "They burned our house, Daddy. We lost everything. Remember the picture of you and Mama at your wedding? And the quilt she gave me?"

Mr. Willoughby hugged her. "At least you're alive," he said.

They went upstairs and Anthony called Deputy Posey. Mr. Willoughby prepared bedding for Wally and Jeremiah in a room next to Mrs. Willoughby. She was so sick she didn't notice.

Wally was sent with Jeremiah to the kitchen while Anthony met with Deputy Posey on the back porch.

"Did you recognize anyone?" Posey asked.

"It was the Klan."

Posey gazed at Wally through the kitchen window.

"I want you to call in the state troopers," Anthony said.

"To do what, Mr. McManus? You can't identify anyone."

"Are you telling me you will make no investigation?"

"What did you expect, Mr. McManus? You've rubbed your

mess in the faces of these townspeople, and they put up with it a lot longer than I expected."

"I might have shot one of them!" Anthony seethed.

"And if you had," Posey said, "I'd be investigating the slaughter of your family. Would you feel better knowing you'd shot one or two men before losing your life? You did the right thing, Mr. McManus. You saved your family."

Once again the lawman peered at Wally through the window. Still looking at him, Posey said what Mr. Willoughby had said: "At least you're alive."

Three Palms Funeral Home was an unpleasant place to Wally. The upstairs apartment smelled of pine oil disinfectants and the sickly odors of Mrs. Willoughby's illness. He and Jeremiah shared a cot in the room adjoining hers. Lying on his side, Wally could see Mrs. Willoughby's white iron hospital bed and a sack of ocher urine hanging beneath it. He watched as Minnie Lou salved Mrs. Willoughby's lips with petroleum jelly. Suddenly, Minnie Lou recoiled. "Oh, Lord, Miss Mary," she said, and Wally knew Mrs. Willoughby was dead.

Hattie and her father came to look and to weep. Eazy and Minnie Lou stayed for a while. Wally and Jeremiah remained on their cots, watching the mourning. After everybody else left the room, Mr. Willoughby got on the bed beside his wife's body and lay there a long time, crying.

With morning, Eazy disassembled the paraphernalia of illness—the roll-around rack from which bottles had dripped solutions into Mrs. Willoughby's veins, an adjustable table for eating, and a bed that could be cranked upright. By late afternoon Mrs. Willoughby lay in a wooden casket with pink silk lining, wearing a pretty dress and a corsage. A rose had been placed in hands so frail they made Wally think of a tiny bird's foot.

"You going to pine for you grandmama?" Minnie Lou asked Jeremiah, and he said, no, Mrs. Willoughby had never liked him.

"All you knowed was dregs," Minnie Lou said. "I knowed the coffee. Dregs is what was left."

Wally overheard Hattie reading an obituary she'd written for the Belle Glade newspaper: *departed this life and leaves to cherish her memory a devoted husband and obedient daughter. . . .*

Flowers arrived in such quantity that the visitation room overflowed, and Eazy arranged bouquets, sprays and potted plants in the long corridor. He removed a Christmas garland from the front door and replaced it with a black wreath. All afternoon and into evening mourners came, men and women bearing food and condolences. Little boys wore neckties and little girls flounced their taffeta skirts and frilly blouses. They filed past the open casket, peering down at the powdered, nearly white face of Mary Bethune Willoughby. Then they gathered in the foyer, around the punch bowl, and all talk was of the Klan.

"...burned two houses last night..."

"Bessie Mae Luden's boy Jo Nathon been missing since the nightriders took him away day before yesterday."

"Took him away...how come?"

"They said Jo Nathon sassed a white woman in the five-and-dime."

Sitting behind a silk screen where he could see but not be seen, Wally listened.

"Three crosses burned in colored town last night," somebody reported. "Drove by my house shooting they guns, screaming get out nigger! Where I 'posed to go?"

"Me, I ain't going nowhere. My peoples were here before any white man. My peoples and the Seminole Indians fighting skeeters, gators, moccasin snakes and the fevers. No siree, I'm not going anywhere."

"It was Jeremiah Willoughby caused this mess," they said. "Him messing with trashy white girls and shooting his own kind. He ran away to get him some sympathy, but uh-huh, he came home soon enough, his tail tucked and no worse for wear."

"Somebody down to Clewiston say the Klan hung a Negro man last evening."

"What's that you say?" Eazy challenged.

"Down by the packing houses, some said."

"You know who saw that?" Eazy snapped. "Somebody you know says he saw that?"

"I'm just saying what's been said to me, Eazy."

"And it isn't true," Eazy declared.

Nevertheless, every rumor brought renewed threats against white people. "But how we going to know which man's Klan and which man isn't?" somebody worried.

A laundress spoke of sheets she had washed and blood she'd bleached from muslin. She knew who was Klan, she said.

Mr. Willoughby could have calmed them, Eazy said, but Mr. Willoughby was busy with his grief. He could moderate hatred, he'd done it before, Eazy claimed. But Mr. Willoughby was weeping at the coffin, bending to kiss his dead wife's forehead.

Friday and into the weekend, through the wake and then the funeral, Wally heard recriminations and vows of retaliation. He didn't go to the funeral on Saturday morning, although it was in a chapel down the hall. Nor did he and Anthony attend the graveside service with Hattie and Mr. Willoughby. Jeremiah, wearing borrowed clothes too big for his spindly frame, accompanied his mother to the funeral, but he refused to see the coffin buried.

chapter twenty-three

Saturday night, still weak from grief but with the trial set to begin on Monday, Hattie and Anthony took the boys into Belle Glade to buy clothes. Since the fire, they all had been wearing borrowed, ill-fitting clothes. Accompanied by a deputy who stood a head-and-a-half taller than the throng of Christmas shoppers, Anthony led the family through crowded sidewalks. A costumed Santa rang a hand bell, pealing for donations. Children skipped and laughed and clung to the arms of their mothers.

"We should've gone to West Palm," Hattie fussed.

"How would you recommend we get there, Hattie? By bus?"

The giant deputy gently moved whispering people aside so the family could pass into a store. Their choice of merchandise was clothing rumpled from repeated examination. "Slightly damaged" or returned items were on a sale table marked "as is—50% off." Hattie held a shoe to the bottom of Jeremiah's bare foot.

"I'm not wearing those," Jeremiah balked. "They look like a horse's hoof."

"We'll take them," Hattie told the clerk.

Outside again, the street was a scene of contradictions. From the spire of a church a carillon played *Silent Night* while rowdy boys lit firecrackers below. On steps of the library a Salvation Army band played "Joy to the World" as a policeman urged Negroes, "Move along, move along."

Across the street, robed Klansmen distributed leaflets advertising the trial.

A sign suspended above the front door of the old post office stated:

SAVE THE WHITE NATION!
MERRY CHRISTMAS!

And everywhere they went, people stared at Hattie and Anthony walking side by side. Black faces turned away and white faces mirrored contempt. Clerks ignored them in the stores. Strangers murmured insults.

Anthony wheeled on one man. "What did you say?"

"I wasn't talking to you."

"But talking about me," Anthony accused.

The deputy held Anthony's arm. "Let's go," he said. "This is no time for a fracas."

Just before midnight the Klan burned a cross on the lawn of Three Palms Funeral Home. Hooded men formed a line in the street, their white robes illuminated by the fiery cross.

"Y'all go on away from here now!" Mr. Willoughby yelled above the rush of flames. "This is Christmas! Our Lord asked for peace among men of goodwill, and that's what we should have. You men go on home and let us grieve for my dear wife. There's been enough pain here this week."

They carried guns and bludgeons, their faces masked. When they didn't answer, Mr. Willoughby walked out to confront them. The burning cross wept fiery droplets, and Wally held his breath expecting the funeral home to flare at any moment, just as their house had. He tried to remember where he had put his money coat.

But then a siren pierced the night, and another. Deputy Posey's car screeched to a halt, and a second patrol car blocked the street. Carrying a billy club, Posey walked into the midst of the Klansmen. He whacked one man on the butt, struck another man on the shoulder. "Get the hell home and do it now!" he yelled. "If I see any more of this nonsense, I'll lock you in jail through the holidays. Go home to your families where you belong, and leave this man in peace."

Somebody grumbled, and Posey lifted his nightstick again but didn't strike. "You mud-sucking sonofabitch," he said. "If you ever speak to me like that again, I'll crack your skull. Now get in your car and get out of here."

Meantime, the second deputy was shielded behind his opened patrol car door, a shotgun at the ready. The Klansmen slowly broke away, got into their vehicles and drove off with horns blaring.

Posey spoke no more kindly to Mr. Willoughby. "Harold, I gave you credit for more sense than this. Out here talking to this rabble—you looking to join your wife? Go back inside and stay there. If this happens again, call me; but stay inside."

"Thank you, Deputy Posey."

Black people emerged from shadows. Wally saw that their presence surprised the lawman. The Negroes were armed.

"I don't want anybody getting in a shootout," Posey said, his voice trembling. "I want you folks to unload those weapons and go home."

Their faces were like oiled ebony in flickering light of the burning cross. A man removed his coat, wrapped it around the staff of the cross and bodily lifted it from the ground. He toppled the burden and smothered the flames. Dozens of spectators watched, and as the fire died their features submerged into darkness.

"Y'all go home now," Posey said, but nobody moved.

"Harold," Posey said uneasily. "Will you speak to these people? Tell them to go on home. There's not going to be any more of this."

Mr. Willoughby raised his voice. "Thank you for coming to our assistance," he shouted. "We're all right now, and I'm much obliged."

And then the silent posse faded into night.

The sound of male voices drew Wally from bed. He crept to the stairway, listening. Mr. Willoughby was in his office, the door open. "I appreciate what you tried to do tonight," he said. "But what would happen had somebody fired a gun?"

"There'd be a bunch of dead crackers," someone replied, and several men laughed.

"Do you imagine victory from that?" Mr. Willoughby said. "Suppose you'd killed a half dozen of those white men?"

"Would've been more than that." They laughed again.

"God was looking out for us this evening," Mr. Willoughby said. "A shootout would be front-page news tomorrow morning.

Every bigot in America would come riding in here looking for blood. We'd be under martial law. Curfew."

"What's wrong with curfew?" somebody asked. "The Klan can't march if the army is on patrol."

"Except the army would be the Klan, or their cousins, or sons and fathers. The first thing they'd do is shut down black businesses because they think that's where troublemakers meet. They'd investigate and threaten until they knew the name of every Negro man with a weapon. Your women would have to hire lawyers to defend you. You'd lose your homes. I appreciate what you meant to do for us tonight, but I thank God there was no shooting."

"Harold," a cold voice spoke. "Are you saying we should knuckle under to those rednecks?"

"I'm saying that killing white folks is not the answer. That would be the beginning of a misery we'd never forget."

"Let's get something straight, Willoughby. If those white boys in bedsheets push us, we're going to—"

Hattie tapped Wally on the shoulder, causing him to jump with fright. "Go to bed," she said. "This doesn't concern you."

But of course it did.

Sunday morning, Eazy gave them a ride back to the site of their house. Charred timbers jutted from cold ashes. Water pipes were twisted, the cookstove lying upside down in the ruins. Hattie poked through rubble, now and then picking up something she recognized only to drop it again.

Jeremiah pushed aside the ribs of bedsprings looking for anything of value. Anthony probed the remains of his files.

"When you ran back inside," Jeremiah asked Wally, "what'd you go for?"

"My coat."

"It doesn't fit," Jeremiah said.

"My mother gave it to me."

Anthony stood under the oak, an arm around Hattie, surveying the desolate scene. Eazy waited in the hearse, the front door open, listening to church services on the radio. Wally walked through the ashes, stepping over the sooty wreckage, but looking for nothing. He had his money coat; he was no poorer for the fire.

"I won't miss this place," Jeremiah confided. "I hated it the day I first saw it and I hate it still. Me, I'm going to grow a mustache and get some fancy duds and then, French womens, look out!"

Monday morning, Deputy Posey and a second patrol car came to deliver the family into court. Overnight the weather had warmed, and Wally's footsteps left prints in dew-laden grass as he walked to the car. He rode in the front seat beside Posey. Everything seemed softer. Christmas lights on doorways were wrapped in tiny halos of mist. Streets glistened. And then he saw the crowd.

Clogging the intersection in front of the old post office, Klansmen carried signs, PROTECT OUR WOMEN! WE DEMAND JUSTICE!

"We'll go to the back," Posey said and turned down an alley on the canal side of the building. In the side-view mirror, Wally saw the second patrol car follow.

Even at the rear door, a mob waited. When they recognized Hattie and Anthony, a howl rose, and people from out front came running. Men spit on Hattie, snatched her hat and tore her clothes. When Anthony shielded her, they clawed his face and struck his body. They grabbed for Jeremiah, and Posey shoved them aside.

Hands reached, fingers extended, grappling for Wally. His arms were pinned by the press of people. Posey stumbled and the crowd surged. He came up swinging his baton and drove them back. He pushed Wally inside, then Hattie and Jeremiah, followed by Anthony and the second lawman. Posey slammed the door and locked it.

Going down the corridor, Wally glanced back. Faces mashed against the windows, features twisted. They were pieces of a beast bigger than any one of them.

In the courtroom, Paul Feinberg was waiting. Judge William Watson fastened his robe. The prosecutor said, "Your Honor, three jurors are ill this morning and ask permission to be excused."

"Permission denied," Judge Watson snapped. "Go get them."

"How can we hold trial in this atmosphere?" Feinberg questioned.

"The atmosphere is your fault, Mr. Feinberg," Judge Watson said. "But this tactic won't work in my court. We are going to trial today."

"Your Honor," the prosecutor complained, "I'm missing several witnesses. They won't be able to get through the crowd downstairs."

"Deputy Posey," the judge said, "I'll give you thirty minutes to disperse the crowd and round up the jury and witnesses. Tell that mob to back off or face jail for contempt of court."

The room wasn't hot, but Wally was sweating. His buttocks itched from new clothing. He couldn't scratch with people watching, so he slid to and fro on the edge of his seat. Jeremiah picked his nose with a little finger, examined his find and wiped it under the table.

"Mr. Feinberg," Judge Watson said, "having been advised of the arson that claimed their home, and for the protection of these children, I am placing the white boy, Wally McManus, under the temporary custody of Edna Lanier and Child Welfare. She has agreed to take him—"

"No!" Wally screamed.

"The mulatto boy will remain with his grandfather so long as Mr. McManus stays off the property. No cohabitation while this case is being settled. Perhaps separating these people will cool the indignation of that crowd downstairs."

"I don't want to go with Miss Lanier," Wally cried.

"Hush, boy." The judge fixed him with a stare. "You will stay with Miss Lanier, or I'll put you in a jail cell."

"Take jail," Jeremiah said. "Play cards, tell jokes—"

Judge Watson banged a gavel. "Sit down and be quiet!"

Observers filled the pews and the noise subsided.

"Now you people, listen to me," Judge Watson said. "If anybody interrupts these proceedings with an outburst of any kind, a moan or a sigh, or any other expression of support or condemnation for either side, he will be jailed. Mr. Prosecutor, are you ready?"

"The State is ready, Your Honor."

"And you, Mr. Feinberg?"

"We are ready, Your Honor."

"Then," Judge Watson said. "Let us begin."

The prosecutor was younger than Anthony or Mr. Feinberg. Wally was fascinated by his bushy mustache which muffled words and hid his lips when he spoke. Then, like a red slug, his lower lip emerged moist and blushing.

He introduced himself to the jury. "My name is Roy Hand. I am a lawyer for the State of Florida. I represent you," he said to the jury, "and all other citizens of our state. Laws are for the protection of everybody, not just a chosen few. Law is the way civilized people maintain peace and security. We are here today because someone wants to contest our law. My job is to show you why the statute exists and why we need it; to show you what happens when this law is breached. As in this case: Mr. Anthony McManus, a Caucasian man, has been living with Hattie Willoughby, a Negro woman. Living as man and wife, they have shared bed and board. The unhappy result is here before us, this mulatto boy whose truancy is part of a community problem, and whose custody must be decided. The white child is Wally McManus, the product of a previous marriage by the father, Anthony McManus. Florida law is clear: people of different races are forbidden to have sex and get married. That law has been broken here with predictable and sad results."

A woman in the jury looked at Wally and winced as if in sympathy. *Poor thing*, her expression seemed to say. Wally didn't know how to respond, so he looked at Mr. Feinberg instead.

Feinberg stood up and introduced himself. He looked at the prosecutor and heaved a forgiving sigh. "If every law were a good and just law," Feinberg said, "we'd have no need for new legislation. But time and circumstance outdate old rules. Sometimes lawmakers make mistakes. As with Florida's miscegenation law which says that men and women of different races cannot have sex together and cannot marry. This is a useless law anyway. When in love, two people will make marriage despite the law.

However, the law itself is unlawful. It defies the Fourteenth
Amendment to the Constitution of the United States. The
Fourteenth Amendment guarantees that no state can deprive any
citizen of life, liberty or property without due process of law. The
Fourteenth Amendment also guarantees that any person born in
this nation is a citizen due all the rights of other citizens."

The lawyer picked up a tattered book. "In 1833, a writer
named Lydia Child wrote, 'The government ought not to be
invested with power to control affections any more than the con-
sciences of citizens. A man has at least as good a right to choose
his wife as he has to choose his religion. His taste may not suit
his neighbors, but so long as his deportment is correct, they have
no right to interfere with his concerns.'"

Feinberg looked into the eyes of each juror in turn. "That is
what we will argue in this court," he said. "Miscegenation is an
unjust law that has kept Anthony McManus from marrying the
woman he loves. As for custody of these boys, Jeremiah and
Wally, every mother and father knows the answer to that: a child
should remain with his parents."

Wally squirmed on his itchy bottom. Jeremiah picked his nose
until Hattie made him stop.

The first witness for the prosecution was a professor who
taught law at the University of Florida.

"Professor Reid," Roy Hand began, "what is a Negro?"

"In the United States a person is regarded as a Negro if he
possesses any Negro ancestry regardless of the number of white
or Indian ancestors he might also possess. The definition may
vary in some states, but generally a Negro is anyone with at least
one sixteenth 'Negro blood.'"

"Is the miscegenation law a recent act?" the prosecutor
inquired.

"No, it is not. Legal stricture against sexual relations between
whites and nonwhites, notably Negroes, dates back to 1622,
when it was enacted by the Colony of Virginia. The law declared
that any Christian committing fornication with a Negro man or
woman shall be forced to pay double the usual fine for the crime
of extramarital sex."

"Was Virginia the only colony with a miscegenation law?"

"Similar laws were passed by most of the thirteen colonies by the time of the American Revolution in 1776."

"Consider the case of this mulatto boy," the prosecutor said, pointing at Jeremiah. "His great-grandfather was a Negro. His great-grandmother was white. His mother is Negro. His father is white. Is he legally a Negro?"

"By law he is."

"Thank you, professor. Your witness, Mr. Feinberg."

Feinberg said, "Professor Reid, were miscegenation laws enforced upon all people with equal severity?"

"As a matter of fact, the effort to control miscegenation by law was notably unsuccessful during the slave period. Many white masters had sexual relations with their female slaves."

"How do you know that?"

"By 1860, there were 400,000 mulatto slaves born from such liaisons. At the time, there were 3.9 million slaves in the United States altogether. Importation of slaves was being banned almost everywhere. Every new birth meant valuable property for a slave owner. Abuse of the miscegenation law was so obvious and rampant that following the Civil War most northern states repealed that statute."

"Thank you, Professor."

Mr. Hand stood up again. "Professor Reid, are there any other restrictions to marriage besides racial ones?"

"The legal capacity to marry is about the same throughout the Christian world," the professor said. "The parties must be of a certain age. Persons may not intermarry if there is a close relationship by blood or by marriage. A sister may not wed a brother; in many states first cousins cannot marry."

"Why does the law forbid those marriages?"

"In most cases it has to do with preventing harm to the genetic pool from which babies would come. The word 'miscegenation' is from the Latin word *misce,* 'to mix,' and *genus,* meaning 'race, stock or species.'"

"So then," the prosecutor said, "whites are forbidden to marry Negroes because it could be damaging to the gene pool."

"Whether or not that is correct is not for me to say," the professor said.

Once more Feinberg stood up. "How many states have miscegenation laws, professor?"

"As of 1947, thirty states."

"As an expert on the U.S. Constitution, do these state laws conflict with the Fourteenth Amendment?"

"Objection!" Roy Hand cried. "That is the issue at question and the good professor can only give an opinion that has not been tested in courts of this nation."

"Sustained," the judge said.

"Very well," Feinberg said. "Professor Reid, since the prosecution has asked you to list the various prohibitions against marriage, are there others?"

"Imbecility, epilepsy in some states, tuberculosis in almost all states," the professor counted subjects on his fingers. "Forty states forbid marriage when there's evidence of a communicable venereal disease."

"Suppose the couple sneaks off and gets married anyway," Feinberg posed. "Is the marriage null and void?"

"No sir," the professor said. "In most cases, even with the presence of venereal disease, once the marriage is consummated it is considered valid."

"Other than protecting the genetic pool," Feinberg asked, "is there any other purpose to so many laws regarding marriage?"

"Laws relating to marriage invariably pertain to the contract between two people; it is an important contract because marriage is the cornerstone of society. A marriage must be healthy, mutually desired and entered into with honorable intentions. There must be some recourse for damages if one spouse breaks the terms of the marital contract. Marriage is a union specifically designed to produce children, and almost all laws are to protect those children. When a marriage dissolves, the entire community suffers."

"I notice you haven't mentioned love," Feinberg smiled.

"Love is a recent invention," Professor Reid said. "Marriage is a binding contract, with or without love."

chapter twenty-four

By late afternoon, body heat of spectators had made the courtroom hot and stifling. A bailiff opened windows, and sounds of recorded Christmas carols rose from the street below. Witnesses for the prosecution spoke of the physical differences between Negroes and Caucasians, describing cultural and historical contrasts.

But Wally heard almost none of it. His new trousers had made his bottom itch so ferociously he could think of little else. He squirmed, he half-stood, he shoved his hands into hip pockets to claw the offending rash. He excused himself. "I have to go to the bathroom," he said, and a deputy was assigned to escort him.

The courthouse was packed, the hallway filled with onlookers. The deputy held Wally's wrist and led the way. People glared with hostility, mouthing words that required no voice to decipher.

In the toilet, Wally shut the door to a booth, lowered his britches and scratched. And scratched! The more he scratched, the greater was his itch. He lined his trousers with waxy toilet tissue to keep the fabric away from flesh. Finally, he was ready to go back.

The crowd in the corridor moved toward the exits, their muttering a garbled roar. In the courtroom, Judge Watson and the attorneys had gone. Anthony and Hattie were absent, Jeremiah nowhere to be seen. Wally's heart pounded. "What happened?" he asked.

"Court has adjourned," Miss Lanier said. "It's after four o'clock, time to go home."

"I didn't get to say good-bye to anyone."

"You'll see them tomorrow."

She reached for Wally and he drew back. "Where's my dad staying?"

"At the Glades Hotel."

"Why can't I go to the hotel with my dad?"

"Because the judge thinks it wiser to do things this way."

"Miss Lanier, I don't want to go home with you."

"Nonsense. We'll talk and get to know one another."

"No ma'am, I don't want to go."

"But you are going, Wally. The judge has said you will."

The bathroom deputy accompanied them downstairs. Ike Fester sat outside on the steps with several other men. Abandoned protest signs rested against a wall. A gray pall made evening of afternoon.

Getting into her Chevrolet, Miss Lanier asked, "Do you enjoy spaghetti?"

"Not really."

The deputy stopped traffic so Miss Lanier could back out of her parking space. "If you could have anything you wanted for dinner," she said, "what would that be? Not for tonight; tonight we're having spaghetti. Another night, perhaps, what would you prefer?"

"Hot dogs."

"I'm sure that's been a staple of your diet," she said.

"We never have hot dogs," Wally replied.

He felt helpless, as if he were being drawn into a dark and sinister place. He had an urge to throw open the door and run. But where to?

Then Wally thought of his money coat.

"Miss Lanier, could we go by the Three Palms Funeral Home to get my coat?"

"If you're cold, I'll turn on the heater."

"I just want my coat."

"Perhaps tomorrow," she said. "Judge Watson doesn't want you to visit any Negroes until the town settles down."

Tomorrow would be too late if Jeremiah discovered the cash. Wally gazed out his car window, watching white children skip along a sidewalk. That's how he'd begun to think of them—

white children, with all it implied.

"Are they going to take me away from the family?" Wally asked.

"Judge Watson will do what is best."

"Does that mean he'll take me away?"

"It means he'll do whatever is best for you."

"He'll send me to a foster home," Wally said. "Like the one Mrs. Bullock grew up in."

"Did she? I didn't know that."

"She didn't like it."

"There are nice foster homes," Miss Lanier said. "I know homes where children are happier than they've ever been."

A faint mist clouded the windshield, and Miss Lanier turned on her wipers. The rubber blade squealed against glass. Wally saw a car filled with Klansmen.

"I make good spaghetti," she said.

Wally peered out his window. They rode the rest of the way in silence.

Miss Lanier's living room smelled like flowers, although there were no flowers. There were two bedrooms. One held a single bed covered with a frilly canopy. Dolls were propped against pillows. Pictures of circus clowns hung on the walls. Beside a wooden chest, toys were arranged to look as if they'd spilled from the box.

"Come into the kitchen and I'll make Ovaltine," Miss Lanier offered.

"I don't like Ovaltine."

"Then come sit with me while I drink mine."

Her stumpy high heel shoes had made dents in the kitchen linoleum. The table was already set for three.

"Is someone going to be here besides us?" Wally asked.

"Yes. Your friend, Mrs. Bullock."

"She's not my friend."

"She says she is. She thinks she is. Maybe you don't know who your friends are, Wally."

Maybe. But he knew his enemies.

Wally had never seen his mother wear slacks, but Mrs. Bullock arrived wearing sandals with socks, a blue shirt and slacks, her gray hair bound in a kerchief. She'd brought a loaf of unsliced bread and offered to help with the cooking. She stood at the stove and stirred spaghetti sauce. It looked thin.

"Wally," Mrs. Bullock suggested, "why don't you go into the living room and listen to "Jack Armstrong" or "The Shadow" on the radio?" To Miss Lanier she said, "I know what boys like."

"I think it's the wrong night for those programs," Miss Lanier responded.

"Then he can listen to something else," Mrs. Bullock said. "Go on, Wally. Miss Lanier and I have some grown-up talking to do."

Wally sat in the living room and pretended to look at a magazine. He could hear every word Mrs. Bullock said.

"There's no way to befriend that boy," she warned Miss Lanier. "He appears pliant, but he's stubborn. Antisocial. Have you met his father?"

"A couple of times."

Mrs. Bullock tasted the spaghetti sauce with the same spoon she used in stirring. "Did Mr. McManus talk about his writing? I've read everything he's written," she said. "My husband, George—he's dead now, God rest his soul—George loved that man's first novel. He could quote passages from memory."

"I haven't read his work."

"The first book was based on his own family," Mrs. Bullock said. "Wealthy, privileged, influential Midwesterners. His father made a fortune in wholesale hardware. They were killed when a train struck their car. It was a pivotal event in the writer's life."

"I should imagine," Miss Lanier said. "How's the sauce?"

"About ready," Mrs. Bullock said. "My George would have enjoyed meeting Anthony McManus. And how disappointed he would have been with this mess they're in."

"When did you lose your husband, Mrs. Bullock?"

"We'd been divorced five years when he died. George was,

well, a typical man. He wanted things his way or not at all. As it was, 'not at all' is what he got."

Wally realized that Edna Lanier knew he was listening. She winked at him.

"I have a keen understanding of what makes a solid family," Mrs. Bullock said. "I am offended when a child is hurt by negligent parents." After a moment, she added, "I know the damage negligence can do, but I survived. Wally will, too. Put him in a good institution and he'll do fine."

"You think he should go into foster care?"

"Isn't it obvious?"

"Not to me," Miss Lanier said, looking at Wally. "But why do you think so?"

"Wally is antisocial, like his father. When he finally made a friend, she was of the lowest social denominator—Naomi Noonan. Quite like his father, I think."

"Is this what you've told Judge Watson?"

"I had to be honest; what else could I say? Wally is borderline incorrigible. So, yes, an institutional setting would be good for him. Like the army helps some men. My husband, George, was a truant until the army straightened him out. Nearly straightened him out, anyway."

"I don't know," Miss Lanier said. "I believe a family of one's kin is almost always the best situation to be in."

"Even with neglect?"

"No. But if that could be changed, one's blood relatives are usually the best alternative."

Supper was terrible when they sat down to eat—tomato juice on sticky pasta. Wally pushed strands here and there, making his meal from chunks of bread spread with butter.

"It's rude not to eat what your host has prepared," Mrs. Bullock chastised.

"I think Wally would prefer hot dogs," Miss Lanier said.

They were still at the dinner table when the doorbell rang. Wally heard Miss Lanier say, "Come in, Mr. McManus." Wally started to rise, and Mrs. Bullock seized his arm. "Stay seated," she commanded.

"We're having dinner," Miss Lanier said. "Would you care to join us?"

"I brought Wally's clothes," Anthony said.

Wally yanked free of Mrs. Bullock's grasp and ran into his father's arms as he entered the kitchen. Anthony kissed him on the forehead.

When introduced, Mrs. Bullock rose and accepted Anthony's handshake. "You're Wally's counselor," Anthony confirmed.

"I'm surprised you know that, Mr. McManus."

"I read your reports to the court," he said. "I expected a woman with hard, tight lips. But here you are—" he smiled.

"Any criticism from me was an attempt to help your son," Mrs. Bullock said.

"Of course," Anthony said. "And I thank you for that."

He sat next to Wally and looked at the meal. "Ahh—spaghetti!" he said.

"Would you care for a plate?" Miss Lanier asked.

"Thank you, no. I had dinner at the hotel. Despite the marching and chanting on the street."

"How did you manage to get out of there?" Miss Lanier asked.

Anthony put a hand on Wally's knee. "My attorney, Paul Feinberg, left his car around back so I could escape."

"May I go back to the hotel with you?" Wally asked.

"That's not a good idea," Anthony said. "There's trouble coming, I'm afraid."

"What about you?" Wally asked.

"After facing the Gestapo in Paris, the Klan is merely an inconvenience."

"And Hattie and Jeremiah?" Wally said.

"They're all right, Wally. I spoke with Hattie when I went by to get your clothes."

"I thought Judge Watson forbade contact between the Negroes and you," Mrs. Bullock said.

"You won't tattle, will you, Mrs. Bullock?"

She ducked her chin. "Of course not. Unless I were asked by

the court. Under oath, I mean."

Anthony helped Miss Lanier clear the table, and he told heroic tales of war, romantic anecdotes about writers he'd known, and the trouble he'd had with his writing. Mrs. Bullock was obviously enthralled.

"My husband so admired your books," she gushed. "He made them required reading for me as well."

"I'm sorry it was a chore."

"The books were pleasant enough."

"I'd like to meet your husband."

"He died. He would've enjoyed meeting you," Mrs. Bullock said. "He spoke of you as though he already knew you. He collected magazine clippings and called you Anthony. Idolatry, I thought."

"I'm flattered," Anthony said.

"It could be vexing at times," Mrs. Bullock said. "He reported your activities as though speaking of a friend. 'Anthony was seen having coffee with F. Scott Fitzgerald and Ernest Hemingway in Paris. I wonder what they talked about.'"

"I wish I could share my reminiscences with him," Anthony said. "I've never told anyone."

The women looked at him expectantly.

"Ernest Hemingway often writes while standing up," Anthony said. "He has a Corona or L.C. Smith, I forget which. Every tap of the keys is a clack on the platen. He uses only his forefingers for typing—*clack-clack-clack*.

"His wife—I forget which wife, I've lost track—would carry on a conversation with him, and he'd walk around his flat, sometimes with people like me in the same room. Then he'd go over to the kitchen counter where his typewriter was set up and *clack-clack-clack*. He triple-spaced his work so he could edit extensively."

Anthony dropped a hand on Mrs. Bullock's hand in an easy gesture. "He tells ribald stories, but I don't want to hurt his image by repeating them. Anyway, about the conversations we had—

"Papa said—everyone calls him Papa—Papa said, 'We writers have an obligation to create the most realistic scenes possible. To capture a moment so true the reader is stunned by it.' That's what we talked about. I've never shared that with anybody until now."

"You really knew Scott Fitzgerald *and* Ernest Hemingway," Mrs. Bullock breathed.

"And dozens of other writers and artists who came to Paris."

"What kind of man was F. Scott Fitzgerald?"

"A genius. I liked him very much. I didn't know he'd died until I came here, after the war. As for Ernest, I received a wire last week."

"A telegram from Ernest Hemingway!"

Anthony lowered his voice and leaned in slightly. "He said, 'Don't let them beat you down.'"

Whether true or not, Wally didn't know. Anthony's eyes were alight with mischief, his lips curved with the promise of a smile as he related another anecdote. Miss Lanier asked about Charles de Gaulle, and Anthony took a deep breath.

"Charles André Joseph Marie de Gaulle," he said. "A man larger than life. Even his name 'of the Gauls' must have been bestowed by the gods. He is regal and unashamedly nationalistic. He aspires to the glory of Napoleon, dreams of the resurgence of France. Who knows, he may yet see it."

"Have you met the General?" Miss Lanier asked.

"Only as he pinned a medal to my tunic...."

If it was an act, it was a good one, Wally thought. When time came to depart, Anthony took Mrs. Bullock's hand again. "I appreciate your concern for Wally," he said.

"Concern is what motivates me, Mr. McManus."

He still held her hand. "But most of all I want to thank you for waking me up. Time was slipping away, precious time lost while I was preoccupied with my work."

Wally was mesmerized by the performance. Anthony *still* held her hand.

"I realize that Wally's welfare has been uppermost on your mind," he said. "I will never forget that." He released Mrs. Bullock's hand and it slowly slid across his fingers to freedom.

Wally stood with Miss Lanier on the front porch watching

him go. In the distance, lights were a soft glow over Belle Glade. Wally could hear a low rhythmic chant.

At the car, Anthony turned to wave. Miss Lanier put a hand on Wally's shoulder. He felt a tremble. "Be careful," she said, as though Anthony could hear.

After Mrs. Bullock had gone, Miss Lanier suggested that Wally take a bath. The tub was modern, sitting flush to the floor. The water was hot and there was a lot of it. The soap smelled like crushed rose petals.

He heard the telephone ring and strained to listen.

"Yes, this is Edna Lanier."

Wally stepped from the tub and stood next to the closed bathroom door.

"Yes, Hattie, how are you?"

Wally wrapped himself in a towel and went into the hall.

"Mr. McManus left some time ago," Miss Lanier said. "Is something wrong?"

Long pause.

"I can't allow you to speak to Wally, Hattie. The judge has forbidden contact between you. I'm sorry."

When Miss Lanier hung up, Wally shouted at her, "What are you doing? Why won't you let Hattie talk to me?"

"I couldn't, Wally. I'm on a party line. People were listening."

chapter twenty-five

Edna Lanier tightened her grip on Wally's hand and led him through a sullen group of idlers outside the court building. Inside, the hallways were packed with people slow to move and surly when they did so. Every pew of the courtroom was filled, and more observers stood along the walls.

Prosecutor Roy Hand stroked his walrus mustache with a thumb and forefinger. He had a witness on the stand: "Dr. Wilshire, what are your academic qualifications to speak on the subject of miscegenation?"

"I chair the Department of Social Sciences at Florida State University in Tallahassee," the professor replied. "I am author of several books on the subject of racial relations, one of which is widely accepted as the premier text on the matter."

"Which book is that, Dr. Wilshire?"

"*The Danger of Mixing Blood.*"

"*Is* there a danger, Dr. Wilshire?"

"In my opinion, there is."

"Tell us why," Mr. Hand said.

The professor turned and smiled at the jury with practiced ease. "Since this nation began, we have encouraged the mixing of nationalities. We call America the 'melting pot.' But in truth, we have restricted mixing to white people of European ancestry, excluding all other races. The United States is overwhelmingly a pure white population. Negroes are a minority. An even smaller percentage of the population is comprised of American Indians, Mexicans and people from the Orient."

Miss Lanier led Wally down the aisle and delivered him to the table where Anthony, Hattie and Jeremiah sat. Overhead fans stirred warm air. Mr. Feinberg doodled on a pad of paper while

Professor Wilshire spoke.

"The United States is almost all pure white, and that is an important point," Dr. Wilshire said. "Canada, Uruguay, Argentina and the United States have kept their different races separate. The twenty-five other nations of this hemisphere have not, and look at them. The nations which value pureblood have prospered and advanced, whereas mixed-blood societies have not."

He spoke to a hushed audience, whites seated in front and Negroes at the rear. "Nowhere else in the world has a helpless, backward people of another color been so quickly benefited by a larger and more dominant race than here in the United States," Dr. Wilshire said. "In the Deep South, segregation has always meant *set apart from the flock*. But the Negro of the American South is not isolated. He is not cast into reservations as were the native American Indians. The Negro has not been confined to barbed wire compounds. He lives alongside white people and they, by their taxes and genuine concern, educate, clothe and uplift the Negro. Whites do not intermarry with blacks, because of *preference*, not prejudice."

"What is the difference between preference and prejudice, Dr. Wilshire?"

"A huge difference," the professor said. "Prejudice is an unfavorable judgment or feeling without good reason. Preference is a natural reaction to facts and conditions observed. Living apart from those unlike themselves is what keeps a species distinct. A yellow rat snake does not breed with a gray rat snake, although they could do so. The white men and women who settled North America were mostly German, British, Dutch and Scandinavian. They colonized this nation and kept themselves separate because they had a strong race preference. Not *prejudice*, but preference! Preference keeps nature in harmony."

When it was time for Mr. Feinberg to speak, he asked, "Would you say segregation is in harmony with nature?"

"Insofar as racial relations are concerned, I would say so."

"Has mankind as a whole changed over thousands of years, Dr. Wilshire?"

"Certainly there has been an evolution of—"

"Is such evolution against the laws of nature?"

"No, of course not. But two species—"

"Is the Negro a different species from the Caucasian?"

"Well, no, but the Negro—"

"They are both *Homo sapiens*, are they not?"

"They are, Mr. Feinberg. I didn't mean they cannot breed, but that—"

"I know exactly what you meant, Dr. Wilshire. You would have this white jury believe that mixing blood would be bad for white men. That was your point, was it not?"

"It was part of my point."

"Well, Dr. Wilshire, preference and prejudice walk hand in hand, and we learn bias by example from our parents and community. Human beings are not rat snakes. You are looking for an academic way to legitimize prejudice. I think you are trying to excuse your own prejudice."

"I object, Your Honor!" Roy Hand was on his feet. "Mr. Feinberg should save his opinion for summation."

"I agree," Judge Watson said. "Mr. Feinberg, stop favoring us with your own bias during these proceedings."

Roy Hand spoke to the witness directly. "Dr. Wilshire, are you prejudiced against Negroes?"

"I am not."

"Why should we believe you?"

"I give two nights a week to teach at Florida A&M, a Negro institution of learning. I am a charter member of the National Association for the Advancement of Colored People. I sit on the board of directors of the Negro College Fund, a nonprofit foundation to which I donate time and money."

Wally heard Paul Feinberg curse under his breath. The lawyer turned to Anthony. "He walked me right into that one," Feinberg said.

Lulled by a long day and the monotony of testimony, Wally lay his head on the defendant's table and dozed. He was jarred awake by a bang of the judge's gavel.

"Mr. McManus," Judge Watson said, "I want you and your son, Wally, to remain after we dismiss." Then he hammered the gavel and declared, "Court is adjourned until eight o'clock tomorrow morning."

Feet shuffled and voices ascended. Feinberg said, "Your Honor, may we know the reason for this request?"

"It concerns custody of the boy, Mr. Feinberg."

Miss Edna Lanier sat to one side, erect and attentive, a notebook on her lap. Judge Watson rocked his chair, watching as people departed. He waved away several men who lingered. "You folks go on," he said. "This doesn't concern you."

"Regarding placement of Wally McManus," Judge Watson said. "I have received notice that his maternal grandparents intend to sue for custody."

"Sue for custody?" Anthony stood up slowly. "They are going to *sue* for custody?"

"Sit down, Mr. McManus."

"Peter and Greta Vanderberg have never even seen Wally," Anthony said. "Nor have they ever made an attempt to see him. Why do they now feel compelled to *sue* for custody?"

"A grandfather wakes up one morning," Judge Watson said, "and feeling mortal, he wants to know his heirs, Mr. McManus. Grandparents deserve an opportunity to know their daughter's child. Would you object to that?"

"I object to the manner in which they approach this," Anthony said. "It is typical of Mr. Vanderberg to first threaten, then negotiate. He has never acknowledged a letter from me, including notification that his daughter was terminally ill, or that she had died."

"They have told me the family's unhappy history," Judge Watson said. "But reconciliation must begin somewhere, Mr. McManus. Maybe this is the place. If you insist they cannot see their grandson, I will not force the issue until the trial is over and custody must be decided."

Anthony turned one way, then the other. "Wally?" he said. "Would you like to meet them? They are Kathryn's parents."

Wally faltered for so long that Anthony finally said, "Your

Honor, if I may be present during the meetings, I will agree."

"That sounds reasonable, Mr. McManus." Judge Watson spoke to Miss Lanier. "Bring them in, Edna."

Wally felt as if he'd been sucking and blowing to make himself dizzy. A moment later, the grandparents entered.

Peter Vanderberg was a tall, straight man with a mound of hair white as a cumulus cloud. His intensely blue eyes assessed people and things, coming at last to Wally. And with a hand on his forearm like a debutante being ushered to a dance, Greta Vanderberg was, to Wally, what his mother might have become. Her hair was swept back into a bun, clipped by a silver comb. Her collar and cuffs were lace. She, too, had blue eyes, and when she peered at Wally it was as though his mother gazed at him from an older woman's body.

She tried to smile and her chin dimpled, an expression Wally had seen many times when his mother was overcome with emotion. "You favor your mother," Greta Vanderberg said, touching Wally's cheek.

"Thank you, ma'am."

"Oh," she said, looking at her husband, "and polite. Peter, did you hear?"

But Mr. Vanderberg was more concerned with Anthony, the two men making no attempt to disguise animosity.

"Anthony," Mr. Vanderberg said, "I am told if you do not fight us we can take this boy home to Indianapolis."

"I can't give up my son, Mr. Vanderberg."

"We are reading about this spectacle in newspapers. If you genuinely care for him, let us give him the life Kathryn would have wanted."

"Kathryn wanted him with me," Anthony said. "She sent him here because she did not want Wally to grow up under the same unyielding, straight-laced, puritanical upbringing she had suffered."

"She did not suffer until you came along, McManus."

Wally heard Judge Watson say to Edna Lanier, "I don't know about this, Edna. All right, gentlemen! You have until this trial ends to resolve your differences."

They all left by a rear staircase, Wally and his grandmother following the men, Edna Lanier trailing.

"Kathryn would certainly not be happy to know her son was living in the home of an alcoholic," Mr. Vanderberg said.

"She knew," Anthony said, "but it was better than sending him to you. And as for drinking, I've been drunk and may yet be again, but I haven't touched a drop since Wally arrived. I am not the man I was."

They stopped and Mr. Vanderberg said, "Nor am I, Anthony."

Wally realized his grandmother was watching him, not the men. She looked deeply into his eyes. "I see Kathryn in there," she crooned. "I see my baby."

From court they walked to the Glades Hotel down the street and around the corner. Unfriendly evening shoppers paused to glare, and ugly whispers twisted their lips. Even the bell-ringing by imploring Santas seemed more urgent than festive.

The Glades Hotel was a balcony-bound building, decorated with potted palms and trimmed with Yuletide lights. Furniture in the lobby was woven white wicker with overstuffed cushions that smelled of mildew. Waiting for a table in the dining room, Wally's grandmother held his hand. It was the first time since his mother's death that anyone had held his hand lovingly. He had to resist clinging.

He saw his mother in unexpected gestures: the way Greta Vanderberg tilted her head listening to him speak; the loving way her eyes traveled his features as she gave him her undivided attention. When his voice rose, her eyebrows lifted as if riding the wave of his inflections. Upon completing a statement, she bathed him with an approving smile.

She smelled like his mother, too. Not the cinnamon and vanilla spice of Mrs. Bullock, or the powdered talcum scent of Edna Lanier, but a fresh, natural smell like newly laundered fabrics. Waiting for the maitre d', Greta Vanderberg hugged Wally in a spontaneous burst of affection, and his heart almost stopped. These were the arms of his mother. His grandmother's laughter was an echo from the past.

In unexpected moments he caught breathtaking glimpses of his mother in a flourish of Greta's hand, or the manner of her stride, or the way she seemed to lift herself above the scarcely veiled insults of strangers around them. Talking to Wally about his interests at school, her voice was that of his mother.

Anthony saw it happening, and Wally saw that Anthony saw it. He was astounded to see, also, that Anthony was jealous! Not only did Anthony detect the natural bond between Wally and his grandmother, so did Mr. Vanderberg and, at a nearby table, Miss Edna Lanier. But Wally didn't care. He sat closer to his grandmother than he had to, connived to touch her arm like a puppy begging favor.

"What do you want to be when you grow up?" Greta asked.

"A writer," Wally said, and the spontaneous statement shocked him as much as anyone. He'd never verbalized that thought before.

"There are many kinds of writers," Peter Vanderberg growled, "and most tend to starve."

"I think Wally could be a very fine writer," Greta said. "He's had such rich experiences. Even sad moments are good for a writer."

"That's what Mama said," Wally replied. "Mama said a writer reflects things people feel. She said that's why my dad is such a good writer, because he reflects other people so well. Have you read his books, Mrs. Vanderberg?"

"I am your grandmother," she said. "*Please*. Call me grandmother."

"Yes, ma'am."

She glanced at her husband, then said, "We have read all of Anthony's books. You are right. He's a talented author."

Then she reached for Anthony and squeezed his wrist. "I often saw Kathryn in those passages, and I saw the passing of love to—what is her name?"

"Hattie," Anthony said.

The waiter appeared impatient, and Peter Vanderberg allowed his wife to order for both of them. Mostly to please her, Wally selected exactly what she'd chosen: meat loaf, green beans, mashed potatoes and creamed corn. It was not his first choice, but he knew what his mother would've recommended.

A man stopped at the table, legs spread, fists at his sides. "Lemme ask you one question, McManus," he challenged. "Why did you come live in Belle Glade anyway?"

"This is where my son, Jeremiah, was living during the war," Anthony said. "I came here because he was here."

"The nigger boy."

Anthony started to rise and Greta said, "Sir, did you mean to be unkind?"

"I'd like to know, lady. Why did he stay here?"

"I didn't intend to," Anthony said evenly. "I was drinking and not thinking. It happened without conscious planning."

"Well, look what you've done to us," the stranger said. "Belle Glade is the mock of the nation. Folks up north think we hate niggers and the truth is, no such of a kind. But we don't live with them."

"Love is a fickle fancy," Anthony said. "I doubt many men could say why they chose their wives."

The man pondered that, rocking back on his heels. "I reckon I understand that," he said. "I married my Lucille because I liked the way she put beer on the table."

After the intruder moved away, Peter Vanderberg said, "The important question is, where do you go from here, Anthony?"

"Paris."

"What about Wally? What of baseball games and Labor Day picnics? Going to France destroyed what was American in Kathryn. Greta and I shook off European influence to become citizens of this nation, then Kathryn threw it away to go back. I didn't understand that. Anthony, we can do things for this boy. I'd like to teach him who we are and what we stand for."

"We made mistakes with Kathryn—" Greta began.

"We did the best we could!" Peter snapped. "Kathryn bears some responsibility for her actions."

"Mostly what I want," Greta said, "is a chance to be better than the mother I was."

"Living with us, the boy will have opportunities he'll miss

otherwise," Mr. Vanderberg insisted. "We will guide his way. The friends he chooses today will be his business associates tomorrow. Selecting the right caste of companions is critical at this age."

"I have a brother," Wally blurted. "His name is Jeremiah."

His statement stopped conversation. At a far table, Edna Lanier met Wally's eyes, then she looked away again.

After dinner, from the hotel, Wally walked with Miss Lanier back to where her car was parked. A misty drizzle left pearly droplets on their clothing. Around the post office lay signs discarded by the Ku Klux Klan.

"Weather like this would soon turn to snow in Indianapolis," Miss Lanier said. "Children up there have sleds as children here have wagons."

Kathryn's childhood sled was still good as new, Greta Vanderberg had reported during dinner. "I have scrapbooks with photographs of your mother from the day she was born," Greta said to Wally. "I will show you crayon drawings Kathryn made when she was in kindergarten."

Wally had been warmed by the thought.

Miss Lanier interrupted his recall. "Have you ever been ice skating, Wally?"

"No ma'am."

Because the streets were clogged by slow-moving Christmas traffic, Miss Lanier detoured through colored town to avoid the gridlock. Up ahead, Wally saw men wearing hooded robes and carrying torches. He heard sirens and a blaring Klaxon. Figures dashed back and forth across the street like fleeing deer in a forest.

"The Vanderbergs want you to live with them, Wally."

But their invitation did not include Jeremiah, Wally thought.

"Indianapolis would be a good place to grow up," the social worker suggested. "They own a nice home, and you would attend the best schools."

"Jeremiah wants to go to Paris," Wally said.

"Which is well and good for Jeremiah," Miss Lanier said. "But, Wally, what in the world do you know of France?"

"My mother lived there."

"And didn't like it!"

"That's true," he said softly.

"French people don't think as Americans do," Miss Lanier noted.

But that was good, Wally thought. It would be a shame if Jeremiah got there and Paris didn't meet his expectations.

Even with the car windows closed, he smelled burning wood. He heard cries in the distance and people cursing. Men were fighting in a vacant lot.

"Would you like to try living with the Vanderbergs?" Miss Lanier pressured.

But Wally couldn't bring himself to say it. It was almost cowardly to take the selfish choice—exactly what Jeremiah would expect of him. Who would blame him if he abandoned them for a more comfortable life?

"If I went to Paris," Wally said, "I'd have to learn to speak French."

"That would be the least of your worries," Miss Lanier stated. "You'd have to adapt to a completely different culture."

"Yes," Wally agreed. "But I did that when I came here."

chapter
twenty-six

M iss Lanier woke Wally by shaking his leg. "Time to get up," she said. "You're having breakfast with your grandmother this morning."

While he dressed, the telephone rang. He heard Miss Lanier answer, "Yes, Deputy Posey, we're going to the hotel. Mrs. Vanderberg wants to see Wally."

He moved to the bedroom door, listening.

"What kind of disturbance?" she asked. "Very well, we'll go in the back way. Don't worry about us, we'll be all right, Leon."

When she hung up, Miss Lanier came to his door. "Hurry and dress, Wally."

She drove through mist too heavy to be fog and too light to be rain. Avoiding main thoroughfares, Miss Lanier followed a circuitous route to the Glades Hotel. Wally saw cars from out of state with signs taped to the doors: JUSTICE OR DEATH! SAVE AMERICA!

Miss Lanier approached their destination by way of an alley. A man from the hotel kitchen dumped garbage into a bin, and a wave of rats poured over the rim. The air smelled wet, with a musky stench of rotting vegetables. From the street came a chant like the singsong cadence of men chopping sugar cane. Miss Lanier held his wrist, going through the hotel pantry past sacks of flour and large cans of food. Out of a steamy, noisy kitchen they emerged into a quiet dining room. News photographers sat at a table with cameras on chairs beside them. Wally saw Mr. Bryan at a table with other men, all eating with their hats on. A Negro busboy worked nervously, setting up tables.

"Over here, Wally," his grandmother called from a front table near the window. She dismissed Miss Lanier with a pleasant smile, "Thank you, my dear."

Outside, despite rain, robed men in peaked hats filled the street. The smoldering remains of a cross lay on the tiny, neatly trimmed hotel lawn. At the front door, two policemen stood guard, stoically watching angry demonstrators wave signs and shake their fists.

"What would you enjoy for breakfast?" Greta Vanderberg inquired.

"I'm not hungry."

"You must eat, though." She summoned a waiter. "Scrambled eggs, bacon, orange juice and milk."

"Where's my dad?" Wally questioned.

"He won't be joining us, Wally. I asked for a chance to be with you by myself, so we could talk."

Men in the street undulated rhythmically, chanting, "Nigger lover go . . . nigger lover go. . . ."

"Those men are fools," his grandmother said. "Someday their children will be ashamed of what they're doing here."

She looked at him and Wally said, "Yes, ma'am."

Her hand fell on his and she squeezed his fingers. "Everybody is telling everybody what should be done with you," she said. "I haven't heard what you think."

Before he could form an answer, she said, "I told your father I would take you home gladly only if you wanted to be with us. One thing I learned from raising Kathryn, you cannot force happiness on anyone. First, find what other people want, then try to accommodate them. Would you like to live with us, Wally?"

"Could my brother come too?"

She peered out at the Klansmen. The chanting had stopped; the rain fell harder. Then she looked at Wally again. "I won't lie," she said. "Jeremiah would not be welcome."

She put a cube of sugar in a cup of hot tea and stirred. "We aren't racists, Wally, but we do believe people should be with their own kind. When they stray, sooner or later, there's trouble. Like now, with those men in the street, your father in court, the family divided—trouble, trouble."

A waiter brought Wally's breakfast. There was a slice of melon on the plate, which he pushed into a saucer.

"When Kathryn was a child," Greta said, "your grandfather was a loving father and constant chaperone. He was too doting, I think. He had to approve every dress to make sure it was modest. He inspected her boyfriends and found them lacking. Kathryn once accused him of holding her prisoner in our home. She said she was going to marry the first man who would have her. That was Anthony."

Wally choked down food and chased it with orange juice. Men in the street had surged onto the hotel porch to get out of the rain.

"Jeremiah cannot come with you," Greta said. "I won't apologize for that. You are the son of our daughter, and we are related. Jeremiah is the son of a man who was once married to our daughter, and we are not related. Jeremiah wouldn't be happy with us. However, Wally, we want to be with you."

"If I have to go to France, will you come visit me?"

"If you live with us, that won't be necessary."

"Jeremiah already thinks I'm selfish because I won't share my money," Wally said. "He'll believe I only wanted out of the family. I don't think Hattie cares if I go. I'm not sure about my dad. He was thinking about sending me away to a military boarding school. You wouldn't do that, would you?"

"No, I wouldn't."

"You look like mama," he said. "The way you stirred your tea, that's how mama did it, with a little finger sticking out from the spoon."

His grandmother sighed. "The judge is going to make a decision about this," she said. "Whatever he says will be final. I want to know, if you are told to live with us, is there any chance for contentment?"

"I would like to live with you," Wally said, "but I worry a little bit about Jeremiah. He doesn't have friends except me."

While Wally wrestled with his feelings, Pat Bryan and a photographer came to the table. They wanted a picture of Greta Vanderberg with Wally.

"I think not," she said curtly, and excused herself. "We'll continue our conversation later," she said to Wally. "Miss Lanier will be by for you in a moment."

After she left, Pat Bryan straddled a chair backward and sat down. He helped himself to a biscuit off Greta's plate.

"I have some good news, pal," Bryan confided. "I spoke to Judge Anderton in West Palm Beach yesterday. Your friend, Naomi, is going to Tennessee with her mother."

Wally nodded.

"That's what she wanted, wasn't it?" the reporter asked.

Wally thought so. He thought Naomi thought so. But maybe Naomi was like him now; he *thought* he wanted to go with his grandmother, but he didn't want to reject Jeremiah either.

The photographer caught him off guard and took a picture of Wally worrying. So far, every published picture had shown him without a smile.

Another reporter yelled through the door. "Hey, you guys! Have you seen what's happening around the corner? Black on one side, white on the other."

Pat Bryan and the photographer ran out the front door with other reporters.

Wally was still there watching Klansmen through the window when Anthony arrived. His father sat down and ordered coffee.

"How will we get past those people?" Wally asked.

"Don't be afraid, Wally. Men who wear masks are cowards."

"I have to go to the bathroom."

"I'll wait here for you," Anthony said.

But when Wally returned, Miss Lanier was there and Anthony had gone. "Deputy Posey came to get your father," Miss Lanier said. "You and I will go over together."

"He said he'd wait for me."

"It's safer to go with me, Wally."

Once more they passed through the kitchen and pantry, out into the back alley. Puddles the color of mercury dotted the lane. Empty cardboard boxes littered the ground. Shredded paper was strewn like wet confetti.

At the far end of the alley half a block away, Hattie and Jeremiah stood under an umbrella beside Mr. Willoughby's hearse. Eazy and Minnie Lou were there with two deputies to escort them.

"Hey, Jeremiah!" Wally hollered.

"Get in the car, Wally," Miss Lanier said sharply. "Don't draw attention."

"Nigger lover go . . . nigger lover go. . . ." echoed through the alley.

Again, Miss Lanier took a winding route, finally ending behind the old post office building where half a dozen lawmen waited to see them inside. The chanting had disintegrated to random shouts. Wally saw Hattie standing tall, Jeremiah holding her hand as two deputies ushered them into the same passageway.

When Jeremiah reached Wally, his green eyes were wild. "Man," he said, "I was scared. Mama said, 'Hold your head up, walk slow.' But I was scared, Precious. I've never been so scared."

There were no spectators in court nor was the jury in place. The prosecutor, Roy Hand, stood at a window looking down at the mob. Paul Feinberg was talking to Deputy Posey and Judge Watson. "Has anyone called for state troopers?"

"Two men were sent from nearby stations," Posey said. "Most personnel are on overtime because of Christmas holidays."

"Have you appealed to the governor?" Feinberg asked.

"His office says he cannot act unless civil disobedience warrants martial law."

Jeremiah leaned nearer Wally. "Last night a bunch of crackers came by blowing horns and screaming the rebel yell. I hate that sound. Granddaddy and Eazy stayed up most of the night. Did you see the colored people across the street?"

"We came in a back way," Wally said.

"Go to the window and look."

"How bad does it have to get?" Feinberg continued. "Homes have been burned. Men are being assaulted by marauding hooligans. Every hour the mood becomes uglier."

"Deputy Posey," Judge Watson asked, "can you handle the crowd?"

"We've managed so far, Your Honor."

Wally stood at the window with Jeremiah and the prosecutor. The scene below was somber. The sky was gray, as were the buildings and faces of white men, and uniforms of deputies barricading the street. On the near sidewalk, robed Klansmen directed a crowd of white people in various chants: "Nigger lover go . . . We want justice . . . Save white America. . . ."

Facing them from the opposite curb, a wall of black men stood shoulder to shoulder, wearing hats with rain dripping from the brims. "They got guns under those long coats," Jeremiah said. "Shotguns, rifles, pistols, knives, lighterknots. First cracker to cross the street will be dead."

Aghast, the prosecutor said, "What did you say, little boy?"

"I didn't say nothing."

"You said those Negroes have guns?"

"No sir, I said, this is no *fun*."

A bailiff came into court. "Your Honor, you want an audience this morning?"

"Can't keep them out," the judge said. "Fill the seats and no more." He shifted his black robe to make it fit more comfortably. "All right, gentlemen, let's get this done and go home. Let in the spectators, bailiff. Then bring in the jury."

The moment they were seated, a juryman stood up to speak. "Your Honor, most of us have children at home and families to think about. Tomorrow is Christmas Eve, and some of us haven't had time for shopping. Besides, that crowd is worrying us. We request a recess until after the holidays."

"That won't be necessary," Judge Watson responded. "I have no intention of spoiling your Christmas, despite our Jewish lawyer from West Palm Beach."

"What does that mean?" Feinberg snapped.

"It means you don't give a thought to Christmas, Mr. Feinberg."

"I want that prejudicial remark on the record," Feinberg said. "Or I want an apology."

"Mr. Feinberg," Judge Watson growled, "come to the bench."

Wally watched them exchange angry remarks, and the lawyer

returned with cheeks flushed. Judge Watson said, "I should point out that Jews have holidays, and I have made no mention of them."

People laughed and the judge tapped his gavel lightly. "Now then," he said, "can we get started? Mr. Feinberg, call your first witness."

Mr. Feinberg's witness was Dr. Sherman Hawkins, a Negro who taught law at Howard University in Washington, D.C. He didn't sound like any Negro Wally had ever heard. He spoke with what a teacher would call how-now-brown-cow round sounds, every word carefully pronounced and with no southern accent. At Feinberg's request, he explained amendments to the Constitution:

"The Thirteenth Amendment put a legal end to slavery, completing what the Emancipation Proclamation had failed to do."

His voice was deep and strong like an actor's on stage. But his message did not interest the audience. People squirmed and whispered.

"The Fourteenth Amendment conferred citizenship upon the Negro," Dr. Hawkins said. "All persons born or naturalized in the United States are citizens of the nation and the states wherein they reside. No state can deprive any person of life, liberty or property without due process of law, nor deny any person equal protection of the laws."

"Would you say that miscegenation laws offer equal protection?" Feinberg questioned.

"They do not. They are laws created to exclude, not include."

Mr. Feinberg gave the floor to Mr. Hand. The prosecutor stood up to cross-examine. "There are three amendments which specifically deal with Negroes, is that correct?"

"Yes, the Thirteenth Amendment put an end to slavery," Dr. Hawkins said. "The Fourteenth conferred citizenship upon the Negro; the Fifteenth Amendment says citizens of the United States shall not be denied the right to vote on account of race, color or previous condition of servitude."

"Three amendments aimed at the Negro specifically," Roy Hand confirmed. "The Thirteenth and Fourteenth are called

Civil War Amendments, are they not?"

"That's right."

"The Thirteenth was ratified eight months after the Confederacy surrendered at Appomattox, and the Fourteenth Amendment was a precondition to readmission to the Union for the rebel states. Am I right?"

"You are right, Mr. Hand."

"At the point of a bayonet," Hand said, "the utterly defeated South was being punished for going to war. And the best way to punish them was by beating them with the Negro."

"I object!" Feinberg said. "Your Honor, may we skip editorial comments?"

Judge Watson waggled a finger at Roy Hand. "Don't do that," he said.

"Dr. Hawkins," the prosecutor said, "a contract signed under coercion is invalid."

"But I assure you the amendments are legal," Dr. Hawkins said.

"Even at the point of a bayonet?"

"I object!" Feinberg cried.

The prosecutor yielded. "Thank you, Dr. Hawkins. You may go back north now."

"Objection!"

"Or wherever you live," Roy Hand said.

Next came depositions, which Feinberg described as "sworn testimony from people who cannot be here."

The ceiling light glinted on his spectacles as he read the words of a Harvard biologist. "There is neither a biological nor psychological justification for claims that the Negro race is in any way inferior to the white race. . . ."

Feinberg's tones were not round. He tended to mumble. One of the jurors dozed, and Feinberg stamped his foot to wake the man.

On and on he droned. . . .

Those brave enough to walk the street had gone out for lunch. A clerk brought in sandwiches for Judge Watson, the jurors, attorneys and defendants.

The clerk recited his inventory: "Pimento cheese, tuna fish, chicken salad."

"Don't look inside a sandwich if you aren't going to eat it," Hattie rebuked Jeremiah.

"How do I know I'm not going to eat it without looking?"

Sitting next to the judge's office door, Wally heard a local businessman demand an end to the trial. "These are the last two Christmas shopping days, and we can't open our doors," the man said to Judge Watson. "People are scared to come downtown."

"What do you expect me to do?" Judge Watson countered.

"End this trial! Let everybody go home and cool off."

Another store owner arrived. "There's a rumor you've sent for federal troops; is that true?"

"We're trying to get them," the judge said.

"Well, don't! You have managed to ruin the best selling season we've got, damn you! The town put up with McManus and his Negro woman all this time, and suddenly you decide to have a trial in the middle of Christmas shopping."

Wally slipped his chair nearer the door.

Deputy Posey came and listed his manpower: the Florida state police, members of the fire department and several law officers from nearby towns. But they were not enough, Posey said; he needed more men.

When court resumed, Judge Watson called Mr. Feinberg to the bench. "How much longer to finish this?"

"I have one more witness."

The yells of the crowd below had intensified. Wally thought they sounded nearer.

"Deputy Posey," Judge Watson said, "can you silence that rabble?"

"We've blocked off the street, Your Honor, and that contains them. But I wouldn't want to break them up. They'll spread out all over town if we do."

"Nigger lover go . . . nigger lover go. . . ."

"Well, go down there and tell that loudmouth with the megaphone to knock it off, or I'm going to put him in jail. Bailiff,"

Judge Watson said, "bring in the jury and shut the doors."

When everyone was settled again, Mr. Feinberg called his witness, Carlton Edward Maddox.

"Mr. Maddox," Feinberg began, "are you a member of the Ku Klux Klan?"

"I used to be."

"What was your position in that organization?"

"I held various offices in the Palm Beach County chapter of the Klan. I was Grand Dragon of the Invisible Empire of the South for two years, and a board member of the Knights of the White Camellia for a year."

This was the enemy? Carlton Edward Maddox wore a neatly-pressed, double-breasted herringbone suit. To Wally he looked like a kindly grandfather with eyes that crinkled when he smiled, and he smiled easily.

"Do you and I know one another?" Feinberg asked.

"Grew up together back when West Palm was a wide spot on the way to Miami."

"Are we friends?"

"I like to think so."

"You belonged to the Ku Klux Klan, and they hate Jews. How could we become friends?"

"By the time we knew that, it was too late, we were already friends."

"Mr. Maddox," Feinberg said, "there's been a lot of talk in this courtroom about Negro blood and Caucasian blood, and the mixing of blood. What is your opinion of interracial marriages?"

"I've fought to keep the races separated my entire life," Maddox said.

"The jury has heard that there is no difference between Negro and Caucasian races," Feinberg said. "You had an experience I'd like you to share with the jury. Do you mind?"

The courtroom was so quiet Wally could hear breathing behind him.

"Three of my sons went to war for this country," Maddox said. "One to the Pacific, two to fight in Europe. I lost my boy in the Pacific at Tarawa. My youngest son died at Bastogne. My oldest son was wounded at the Rhine River. Shrapnel took off his ear and severed an artery in his neck. He was commanding officer of a truck convoy delivering supplies. His first sergeant was a Negro from Demopolis, Alabama. He clamped my son's gushing artery but couldn't hold it because blood made the skin slippery. So he bit it. Took hold of my son's neck and clamped that artery with his teeth until they got him into surgery."

Mr. Maddox swallowed and Wally saw his Adam's apple bob.

"My son lost so much blood he had no pulse," Maddox said. "That Negro rounded up drivers from every convoy, every driver being a colored man. Those with the right blood type had to donate twice what they should to save my son. He was transfused with so much Negro blood it replaced his own blood completely."

Feinberg said. "There are men who would die rather than allow Negro blood into their bodies."

"I was one of them," Maddox said.

"So what happened, Mr. Maddox?"

"My boy came home alive. He didn't agree with the way I felt about colored people, he said. But it didn't stop there at home. He went out and made speeches about what the Negroes had done for him. He invited that colored sergeant to our house, to sit at my table and eat from my plates. The sergeant was a blue-gum nigger, black as Kentucky coal. He walked like a nigger and talked like a nigger, but his blood ran in my son's veins and my son wanted the world to know it."

"Your Honor," Mr. Hand interrupted. "I object to hearsay—"

"Overruled, Mr. Hand."

"At first I argued with my son," Maddox said. "I told him somebody lied about him getting colored blood. If he had it in him, he'd be different. He'd be colored too. He wrote off for information and brought folks to the house who worked with blood. They said any man of any race can give blood to any other man of any race, so long as they have the same blood type. We had some long, bitter fights over that."

His cheek quivered. "The Klan turned on my son for making those speeches. He couldn't get a job and couldn't hold one when he did. He lost his family and everything he owned. Then, eight months ago he hanged himself in my garage. His note—God . . . damn . . . me—his note said he'd rather be the son of any Negro than my son. He said he had never known such shame as bore my name."

"Did Negro blood make your son a Negro, Mr. Maddox?"

"No sir, Mr. Feinberg, and that's the truth. There is no difference between a white man and a black, except the skin you see."

"Thank you, Mr. Maddox. The defense rests, Your Honor."

chapter twenty-seven

When the prosecutor, Roy Hand, stood up to begin his summation, the courtroom hushed and the air felt heavy to Wally.

"The law is the law," Roy Hand said. "In their wisdom, the Virginia Colony passed a miscegenation law in 1622, and other states quickly did the same. They knew, as we know, that mixing Negro and Caucasian blood is not good for either race."

He looked pointedly at Jeremiah sitting with Anthony and Hattie at the defendant's table. "Who can believe that mulatto boy will ever be equal to the white child? He is neither black nor white, condemned by the accident of his birth to live in a shadowy world between the two races from which he comes."

The prosecutor faced the jury. "But whether or not we agree with the idea, Anthony McManus and Hattie Willoughby have broken the law. Negroes and Caucasians are *forbidden* to have sexual relations. They cannot marry. They are banned from making a family in our society. It is the *law*! You must bring in a verdict of guilty, for there can be no other." He bobbed his head and returned to his chair. Members of the jury looked at Judge Watson, then at Feinberg.

After a full minute of waiting, Judge Watson said, "Mr. Feinberg?"

Another minute passed.

"Mr. Feinberg, are you ready for summation?"

"I am, Your Honor."

"Then be about it, please."

Still seated, Feinberg said, "I was wondering if the jury knows the power they wield when they go into that room to deliberate. I wonder if they know how unimportant we are, Your Honor, you and the prosecutor and me."

"Mr. Feinberg, you are out of order," Judge Watson said.

The attorney stood up. "Because, you see," he said, "in this nation, law is *of* the people, *by* the people and *for* the people. The jury can say 'guilty' and reaffirm a bad law, or they can say 'not guilty' and prove they won't tolerate a statute so immoral as the one we're here to decide."

"Mr. Feinberg," Judge Watson said, "I'm not going to warn you again. I'll charge the jury. You do the summation."

Feinberg leaned over the railing which fenced the jury. "All you have to do is what your conscience says to do. Laws are made by the majority to perpetuate their own power. The miscegenation law is wrong. To say a man cannot marry the woman he loves, to say that love cannot legally produce children, to legislate against the natural affections of mankind—is wrong."

He paced and reasoned and stood behind the family, holding Wally's shoulders with both hands. "The members of this family love one another," Feinberg said. "Yes, it would be better if Anthony McManus and Hattie Willoughby were married. If the law permitted, they *would* be married."

He pointed at Mr. Hand in the same way the prosecutor had pointed at Wally and Jeremiah. "Mr. Hand is wrong," Feinberg declared. "In America, the individual is greater than the government we individuals have set up to govern us. The only valid laws are the ones we accept. It may be written as law, but in this country we can challenge and change any law, especially when it is wrong. All it takes is for you ladies and gentlemen of the jury to say 'Not guilty.' Not guilty of anything immoral or unnatural. They fell in love! They were overseas fighting for the right of all men to live free, and they fell in love. Then they came home to face the prejudiced rule of a former slaveholding state that doesn't know when to cease shackling darker members of its society."

Wally heard Eazy cry out, "Say so say right, sir!"

"Amen," Negroes chorused.

Judge Watson hammered his gavel.

"Amen, Mister!" somebody yelled.

"Uh-huh," Minnie Lou said. "Yessir. Amen."

Finally the room was quiet again. Outside and below, voices began to rise and the vile word "nigger" floated in the air.

"Listen to your hearts and your minds," Feinberg said. "And then let this family live in peace. That's all they've asked for."

Feinberg sat down and Judge Watson spoke to the jury. "We are a nation of laws," the judge said. "We as individuals do not make the laws; our elected representatives do that. If we don't agree with a law, the place to change it is in the legislature. Until then, law is the rule we live by, and you are charged with determining whether this man and woman have broken the miscegenation law of the State of Florida. Everything else is an emotional appeal to override your good judgment."

Then he sent them to another room to deliberate.

Wally went to a window and gazed out over the crowded street. Negroes stood as before, along the far sidewalk. Spectators left the courtroom to smoke cigarettes in the hallway. Judge Watson retired to his chambers. Mr. Feinberg sat with Anthony and Hattie, speaking in whispers.

An hour ticked away, then two. Day gave way to twilight.

Judge Watson finally returned to the bench. "The jury is ready," he announced.

Reporters rushed for their seats. People in the hall pushed through the door but remained standing in the rear. Wally knew the verdict before the jury spoke. They entered the room with eyes averted, looking at no one—not the judge or the prosecutor, not Feinberg or the family. Wally's stomach cramped from tension, and he bent over his arms.

"Mr. Foreman," Judge Watson said, "have you reached a verdict?"

"We have, Your Honor."

"What say you?"

"We, the jury, find the defendants, Anthony McManus and Hattie Willoughby, guilty of miscegenation."

The audience whooped. Flashbulbs popped. Anthony put his arm around Hattie. Paul Feinberg shouted, "Your Honor, I wish to serve notice of appeal."

Women were screaming, people clapping and whistling. Judge Watson banged his gavel and shouted for order, but the cheering and jeering reverberated into the hall and spilled downstairs to the street.

"Nigger lover go . . . nigger lover go. . . ."

"Bailiff!" Judge Watson called. "Clear the courtroom except for those involved in the matter of child custody."

It took time to empty the room. Judge Watson dismissed the jury with thanks and compliments for their judgment. Anthony held Hattie in a hug. "We'll beat this," he said. "Don't worry."

Finally, the noise subsided.

"I will not wait until after the holidays to finish this case," Judge Watson said. "That would leave everybody in limbo, and there's no need for it."

Feinberg placed several papers before the judge. "Intent to appeal," he said.

"Sit down, Mr. Feinberg."

The judge heaved a sigh. "I have several difficult decisions to make," he said. "Whether these boys should become wards of the state; whether custody of young Wally McManus should be given to his maternal grandparents who have asked for him."

A window shattered and glass showered the floor. Judge Watson yelled at Deputy Posey, "Get those people away from the building!"

Hattie sobbed, and Anthony stroked her back.

"Years from now," Judge Watson said, "I will think of these boys and wonder how they're doing. I will ask myself if I made the best choice for them. Unfortunately, I won't know the answer until it is too late for change."

The judge looked at Anthony and shook his head. "This didn't have to happen, Mr. McManus. You need not have come to Belle Glade, Florida. You have the means to live anywhere, and yet you showed blatant disregard for everyone around you."

"Your Honor, may I speak?"

"To say what?" Judge Watson snapped. "That you are sorry? That you will change your life and be a better parent?"

"But it's true."

"I doubt it, Mr. McManus."

"Your Honor," Hattie said, "we want to go back to France. I'll be a better mother, I swear it."

"I doubt that, too," Judge Watson said.

"I've been overwhelmed," Hattie pleaded. "My mother was dying. We were grieving the loss of friends in the war, coping with so many changes."

"You divided this town along racial lines," Judge Watson accused, "and the town deserves better than that. Tomorrow, newspapers will speak of us as bigots and rednecks. But never mind that for the moment. You did not care enough for your son, Jeremiah, to make him attend school. Your lack of supervision is directly responsible for his involvement in assault, and a young girl's murder of her father. The town is ready to riot. Now, where should this end? It didn't have to happen."

The judge took a deep breath and exhaled. "Anthony McManus, I am going to allow you and Hattie Willoughby and your son Jeremiah to leave the jurisdiction of this court—and I hope you will go to France, if that is your pleasure."

"Thank God," Hattie said.

"And as for Wally McManus," Judge Watson said, "I have worried long and hard about this lad. It is obvious to me his natural mother was an intelligent and loving woman. She endowed this youngster with social skills, a good beginning education, and maturity beyond his years. I cannot believe she would want her son to degenerate into the truant he is becoming. Therefore, this court awards legal custody to his maternal grandparents, Peter and Greta Vanderberg. Bailiff, please see that this order is carried out. Case closed." And he pounded his gavel for dramatic closure.

Dumbstruck, Wally looked to Jeremiah for his reaction.

"Hey, Precious," Jeremiah said. "I'm sorry."

Anthony pulled away from Hattie's exuberant hug. He grasped Wally by the shoulders. "Your mother was angry with her parents," Anthony said. "But actually, they're good people, Wally."

"Yessir."

"I don't honestly believe you'd be happy with us in France," Anthony said. "But I think you'll be happy with the Vanderbergs."

"Just don't get to be a tight ass," Jeremiah counseled. "And if they let loose any of that money, send some to me. I'll send you a picture of me with my mustache and French womens."

"Deputy Posey," Judge Watson called, "can you escort these people out of town safely?"

"We're ready when they are, Your Honor."

There, for the first time in his life, Wally was hugged by his father in an embrace more eloquent than his best writing. "Good luck, son," Anthony said. "I'll write to you."

Guarded by a circle of deputies, Hattie, Jeremiah and Anthony left the courtroom. Wally watched from the window, his grandmother at his side.

Under misting clouds in the darkening of evening, Christmas lights made a radiant screen behind the crowd. White people spit at Anthony and Hattie. Jeremiah made a vulgar sign at the crowd around him. Wally saw Paul Feinberg pass unnoticed, going toward the Glades Hotel.

Judge Watson came to shake Wally's hand. "Make me proud of you, Wally," the judge said. "Be a good grandson and do good things."

Greta said, "Thank you, Judge Watson."

Down below, patrol cars eased away from the curb, one leading and another following the car which transported Jeremiah, Anthony and Hattie. Across the street, Negroes moved down side alleys, soon absorbed by structures around them. Signs littered wet pavement. Christmas music played.

"Come along, Wally," Greta Vanderberg said. "Let's go home...."

twenty-eight

Several weeks later, Jeremiah wrote to say that it had snowed the day they arrived in Paris. He said the streets were glazed and treacherous. That was the word he used, *treacherous*.

In his letter, Jeremiah told Wally they had trouble finding an apartment and couldn't keep it warm when they did. They bundled up in layers of clothing even going to bed, he said. His most treasured possession was a goose down quilt.

In the year that followed, subsequent letters told of too many people living in Paris without enough of anything to satisfy their needs. The only available fuel was coal, and the sulfur smell of it gave Jeremiah a headache that lasted until spring. Two and a half million Parisians created so much winter smoke, Jeremiah said, the sky turned gray and stayed that way until the weather warmed and rains came.

His letters changed with passing months, becoming more mature. Jeremiah said that Hattie tried singing in nightclubs again, but the postwar crowds were in no mood for her style of songs. He mentioned that Anthony continued to write his book, and two years later he mentioned it again, saying Anthony couldn't find a publisher. Anthony never wrote to Wally.

They moved from Paris to Avon, southeast of the capital. Jeremiah's letters spoke of Fontainbleau, a "chateau in the forest" since the days of Francis I, in 1528. Hattie taught English to French children at the same school Jeremiah attended.

"I'm going to school whether I like it or not," Jeremiah wrote.

He spoke of sports in which he excelled, and he reported that he was making good grades. In a strange turn of events, he began to write of America in the same way he once yearned for Paris. He had decided he wanted to be a lawyer, "like Mr. Feinberg," and to live in Washington, D.C., where laws were made, he said.

It took Wally a while to adapt to Indianapolis, but his grandparents loved him, and he loved them. He had his own bedroom upstairs, with a dormer that overlooked the two-acre lawn surrounded by a high brick wall. His grandmother set up a desk and a file cabinet, making his bedroom an office where he could study and write. Peter and Greta read every word he composed, and although his grandfather was very difficult to please, he was increasingly proud of Wally's abilities. Wally's grandmother helped edit his first short story, which sold to a magazine published for young people.

Wally's grandmother died while he was a senior at Notre Dame. His grandfather died a year later. Wally spent six months settling their financial and legal affairs. He inherited everything. There was no reason he could not pursue a writing career.

He went to Washington to visit Jeremiah, who had married his French sweetheart and had passed the bar to become a lawyer, but there was little of the boy left in the man.

"We had some times, didn't we?" Jeremiah the man inquired.

"We sure did," Wally said.

"Your having come to live with us changed my life," Jeremiah said. "I don't know what would have happened to me without your influence."

"It changed my life too, Jeremiah."

Taking Wally to the airport, Jeremiah said his law firm was suing the State of Virginia to overturn the miscegenation laws, and that he had been assigned to the team working on the case.

"Good for you," Wally said.

"Where are you going, Wally?"

"Atlanta."

"Why Atlanta?"

"I don't know. That's where I began, I guess."

The truth was, he'd been waiting months for a telegram he'd only recently received: APT AVAILABLE APRIL 1. He had detoured by Washington, D.C., only to see Jeremiah and his wife, Antoinette. He might return to Indianapolis someday. He might, but not likely.

At age twenty-four, he still kept his money coat, and except for the few dollars he'd removed in Florida, the same currency was sewn into the seams—his last tangible connection to his mother, her final effort to shelter him.

He was going to Atlanta, irresistibly drawn and yet fearful. As his airplane flew over the city, he looked down at broken highways under construction and at skyscrapers new since his departure at age eleven just after his mother died. He relished the warmth and humidity of the South. He took a taxi and told the driver not to hurry. "Follow Peachtree Street north," he directed.

The dogwoods were in bloom. Wally rode with his window down and breathed deeply the fragrance of southern foliage. Electric buses coursed the streets, and everything was so clean. He recognized the Varsity Drive-in where he and his mother ate pimento cheeseburgers, and the Fox theater where they'd gone to see movies. They'd sat in the highest balcony, eating popcorn, watching the film *Bambi*, and cried their eyes dry.

Even automobile fumes were sweeter, downtown sidewalks graced with trees, lawns newly mown and redolent of crushed grass. Entering the neighborhood of his youth, his heart ached with a mix of anticipation and dread. But there was the red and yellow brick three-story apartment building, and little was outwardly different. He paused to touch the head of a marble lion which guarded the front steps. Down the street, uniformed students marched from the military academy, young martinets homeward bound.

The landlady was a woman of Irish extraction, her complexion burnished by sun and dappled with freckles, her southern drawl music to Wally's ears. "I never had anybody apply for a special apartment," she said. "Especially a full year before they wanted it. You say you lived here?"

"Yes ma'am, I did." Wally carried a suitcase and a portable typewriter. He had no furniture, but he wanted to sleep here tonight anyway.

"It'll most likely seem smaller than you remember," the landlady cautioned. "You know how our minds play tricks with childhood memories."

"I do know."

Walking up steps to the second floor, Wally remembered the wisteria flowering outside opened windows. The woman unlocked the door and pushed it open. Wally paused. "If you don't mind," he said, "I'd like to go in alone."

"I don't mind." She gave him the keys.

Wally latched the door behind him, leaving his bag in the foyer. He walked into the living room. The balcony overlooked the shady street outside.

He was not at all surprised to see his mother standing there.

"Hello, Mama. I've missed you."

He moved toward her and she floated like a feather before a breeze.

She kissed her fingertips and blew a kiss.

Then slowly faded away. . . .

On June 12, 1967, the Supreme Court of the United States ruled in the case of *Loving v. Commonwealth of Virginia* that a statutory scheme adopted by the State of Virginia to prevent marriage between persons solely on the basis of racial classification violated the Equal Protection and Due Process Clauses of the Fourteenth Amendment to the Constitution. Thereby, miscegenation statutes in all states became invalid.